BURN

BABY

BURN

BURN BABY BURN

Meg Medina

CANDLEWICK PRESS

Excerpts from *"Cops to .44 Killer: Sons of Sam . . .
We Wish to Help You"* (04/29/77) and
"Breslin to .44 Killer: Give Up Now!" (06/20/77)
© Daily News, L.P. (New York). Used with permission.

First paperback edition 2018

Library of Congress Catalog Card Number 2015954454
ISBN 978-0-7636-7467-0 (hardcover)
ISBN 978-1-5362-0027-0 (paperback)

18 19 20 21 22 LSC 10 9 8 7 6 5 4 3 2 1

Printed in Crawfordsville, IN, U.S.A.

This book was typeset in Fairfield LH.

Candlewick Press
99 Dover Street
Somerville, Massachusetts 02144

visit us at www.candlewick.com

For Alice,
a true and lifelong friend

Chapter 1

Mr. MacInerney drives way too slow, which is weird for a man who spends his life running into burning buildings. It could be that being a fireman has made Kathleen's dad a safety freak, but I think it's really that he likes to show off his Impala. He calls it his baby, after all. It's gold with a convertible roof and whitewall tires. The chrome is sometimes so shiny that Kathleen and I can put on lipstick in its reflection. If you ask us, though, its best feature is the backseat. It's wide and springy, a nice option should the right guy ever happen along. Not that Mr. Mac needs to know—or that we've ever had the chance to test out our theory.

Kathleen fidgets. She just got off work, and we're running out of time before the matinee starts at the Prospect. She leans over the cream-colored seat and rests her chin near his ear. "Dad, step on it. Aren't you supposed to be at the station by now? *Hurry.*"

I see his blue eyes in the rearview mirror. They're clear and smart, just like hers.

"All in good time," he says, smiling.

That's Mr. Mac. Calm, easy. You'd never guess that he's a fireman. He's skinny, with boyish red hair and a quiet voice, not exactly a testosterone specimen, if you know what I mean. Still, he's tougher than he looks, which comes in handy. When the Chiclet gum factory in Sunnyside blew to smithereens in a chemical explosion last fall, Mr. Mac had to dodge chunks of concrete and melted gum that rained down on him as he saved workers whose skin had burned off. He smelled of cinnamon and ash for days.

We've had a lot of fires in the city lately, actually—and not just because old ladies forgot their stoves. Arson fires are smoldering all over the place.

He points at the theater when it finally comes into view up ahead. The line of people snakes all the way down the block. "Looks like you'll have a wait."

"Ugh." Kathleen rolls her eyes. "Drop us off here," she says, pointing at the corner bus stop. "We'll walk the rest of the way."

She grabs my hand and pulls me out to the curb.

Mr. Mac powers down his window before we get too far.

"Be home by dark," he tells us.

Kathleen turns and gives him a look. "Oh, come on. We're nearly eighteen."

"You're *seventeen,* and you promised your mother. She worries."

"Yes. About everything. Don't be crazy."

"By dark," he says again, suddenly looking serious.

I shift on my feet in the pause that follows. I know what the fuss is about, even though no one will say it. It's

2

that shooting that happened not too far from Kathleen's job. Back in January, somebody shot and killed a secretary while she was kissing her fiancé in his car. Nobody knows who did it. Kathleen and I actually know the exact block in Forest Hills where it happened, since we go there all the time. Sometimes when I meet her after work, we hop off the train at Continental Avenue and walk around that neighborhood, fantasizing about life there. The Tudor houses are huge and sit back on wide lawns that don't have a single kid playing on them. That's nothing like where we live, of course. I live in an apartment, with Mima and my brother, Hector. The MacInerneys have a small yellow house around the corner from our building. It's the one nearest the tracks. Their windows rattle like loose marbles every time the Port Washington train passes through.

Anyway, I step in to save Kathleen.

"We'll be home right after the movie, Mr. Mac. Promise," I say. "Now, be careful out there."

Mr. Mac smiles at me and shakes his head. I've been saying good-bye to him that way since I was in second grade. It always gets him.

He kisses his fingertip and taps the figurine of St. Florian he keeps on his dashboard. "I have your word, then, Nora. Have fun."

He pulls out nice and slow, so everyone can see.

"This is depressing," Kathleen says, looking around at the line. It's a mob of cuddling couples. The pair behind us is even making hamster noises as they kiss.

"Relax. Didn't we already agree that dating is a pain in the horns?"

She makes a face, but she knows I'm right. One way or another, guys always complicate things for us. When she starting going out with a guy named Lou last year, she got so swept up by his weight-lifting pecs and green eyes that I practically became invisible. Turns out, he was cheating on her the whole time with a girl from the Mary Louis Academy. When it all went down, I was secretly relieved. It sucked to see her cry, but I'd been missing my best friend for a while.

Besides, it's not as if there aren't lots of guys waiting to fill his spot. Kathleen has legs like one of those Nair commercial girls. Her boss at Macy's took one look at her gams and *begged* her to model in the mall's fashion show last year. She agreed—despite being "objectified"—because she got to keep the clothes. Me? I'm not that lucky. The only thing I model is pastrami when I'm working the slicer at Sal's Deli.

"Uh-oh," Kathleen says, pulling me close. "Idiot alert."

I follow her gaze.

Who's coming toward us? My own ex, Angel—yet another poster child for crappy boyfriends everywhere. He's holding hands with a curly-haired girl in a tight T-shirt.

Why, God, *why*?

"Hey, look. It's Betty and Veronica!" Angel stops at our spot and grins. He's always found it funny to compare us to the blonde and brunette in the Archie comics, since we're always together. He likes to add that we have the same tits. This pretty much sums up his brains and reading powers.

4

"No cutting, pal," says a guy behind us.

"Take it easy," Angel says. "We're all together. I was just parking the car, right, Nora?" He flashes a smile and steps closer to me.

"Do I know you?" I ask.

Kathleen gives him her frostiest glare. "He doesn't look familiar at all." She hates Angel almost more than I do, never forgiving him for what she calls "his inexcusably dickish ways." Angel was my first experience with a guy, a fact that I try to forget daily. I blame it on the fact that he has the same puppy eyes as Freddie Prinze, may he rest in peace. But Angel is nothing like the character I fell in love with on *Chico and the Man,* all kindhearted and sexy. Nope. One minute we were kissing in Angel's room, and a little while later he was driving me home, my shirt buttoned wrong and a wad of toilet paper in my underwear to catch the blood. I cried to Kathleen that whole night, worried about babies and all the scabby diseases Miss Sousa covered with great gore during Health and Hygiene. But mostly, I already knew in my gut that Angel had used me, and sure enough, he spread the word to anybody who would listen. I was easy.

"Good-bye, Angel," I say.

His smile fades. "Dykes."

He slings his arm over his girl's shoulder and moves toward the back of the line.

"Smart and classy as always," I say sweetly.

I look up at the marquee and try to shake him off. We've got slim pickings: *Carrie* or *Rocky.* I already sat through *Rocky* twice with Hector when it first came out in November. (It was his birthday, and I felt bad.) Since then, he has sneaked in and seen it four more times. Now he can quote you every little scene in annoying detail. His favorite part is when they take razor blades to Rocky's swollen eyelids.

"Not *Rocky* again," I say. "I beg you."

Kathleen frowns. "But that leaves *Carrie*." Her voice sounds doomed.

We haven't been much for horror ever since we read that Stephen King book during freshman year. I spent months having nightmares about being burned to death in our school gym. Kathleen was no better. She hates anything about the occult. I think it's all the church her parents make her attend.

"Show?" the ticket guy asks through the window.

"Adriana saw *Carrie*," Kathleen warns me. "She told me the eyes on the statue of Jesus at St. Andrew's glow just like the ones in the movie."

"She's a nutcase," I point out. Adriana Francesca wears black and believes she has been reincarnated from the sixteenth century. She is also, inexplicably, the smartest girl in our English class.

"Come *on!*" somebody yells from the back of the line.

I glare at the guy who said it and turn back to the ticket man. "Two for *Carrie*."

"I don't know about this," Kathleen says as we take our change from under the glass.

"We'll be *fine*," I say.

•   •   •

Well. I stand corrected.

Kathleen's screams were ice picks to my eardrums, especially when Carrie's blue eyes got wide and she unleashed her telepathy.

"Oh, God! Oh, God! Oh, God!" Kathleen screamed as Carrie, dripping in pig's blood, slammed the gym doors shut and set off electrocutions and fires.

"I will never forgive you," Kathleen says when we finally reach the lobby again. Her hands are still shaking; her face is pale.

I put a finger in my ear and wiggle it. Her voice sounds muffled, the way it does after we've been to a concert. I don't pay much mind to her threat, though. She said the same thing to me after we saw *The Omen*. The cameraman's decapitation scene nearly did her in. She wore a rosary as a necklace and slept with her parents for a week.

"Some prom, huh?" I say.

"You girls piss yourselves?" Angel's voice makes us turn. His date must be in the john because he's outside the ladies' room, waiting. "Christ, Kathleen, you were loud in there," he says. "'*Oh, God! Oh, God!*'" he mimics. "It was like you were getting banged."

What I wouldn't give to unleash some telepathic powers myself right now. His private parts would be my first target.

"Really?" I ask him. "I couldn't really hear her over *your* prissy screams, Angel. Did Curly have to hold your hand? Or were you busy pawing her?"

Just then, his date comes out, waving her hands to dry

7

them. She gives me a cool look and pushes out her chest. She'll learn soon enough, I guess.

"Let's go," I say as I pull Kathleen away.

Kathleen keeps glancing at her watch as we eat at Gloria Pizza next door. It's only five thirty, but she's antsy.

"You realize that we haven't had a home-by-dark cur-few since the summers of junior high," I say. "It's like we're twelve-year-olds instead of high-school seniors. You're lucky I like you."

"I know. I'm sorry. It's ridiculous," she says. "I don't know what the hell is up with them."

"The dead girl."

Kathleen gives me a look. "Please. This is New York. It's not like she's been the only person killed this winter."

I bite into my pizza. True enough. People are getting offed all over the city; I heard it's the worst crime year on record already.

"Maybe we should look on the bright side," I tell her. "We could have truly psycho mothers like Carrie's."

Kathleen looks stricken. "God, she *was* scary." She shakes red-pepper flakes onto her slice of Sicilian. "What kind of mother tries to plunge a knife into your chest?"

I chew on that for a second. There are other ways to kill your kid, a little bit every day. I think of the days Mima loses her cool. *"Son unos demonios,"* Mima says about me and Hector, just loud enough for us to hear. We're devils. "There are little knives," I say.

"Huh?"

"'You look fat today. That tight dress makes you look like a *cualquiera.*'"

She nods slowly and mimics Mrs. MacInerney's voice perfectly. "'Oh, sweetie, you broke out again. . . .'"

"Exactly." I yank on a long string of melted cheese until Kathleen breaks it with her finger. "And your mom is one of the *nice* ones."

We finish up as soon as we can, but by the time we step outside, the sky is deep purple, and the neon signs for the shops are bright. We hurry along, but my guess is that we'll have fifteen minutes, tops, before it's officially dark. Mrs. MacInerney will turn up their police scanner and start pacing. I hate that thing. It makes it an all-day crime show at their place: four channels, one for the firehouse where Kathleen's dad works, and the other three for police stations nearby. No wonder they get worked up.

"We're going to miss it," Kathleen says, pointing at the bus ahead. We run full speed, but just as we reach the stop, the doors snap shut and the driver pulls away.

"Hey, wait!" I pound on the door, still jogging alongside. But in a great display of MTA customer service, he just plays deaf and keeps going.

"Crap," Kathleen says, waving off the cloud of diesel smoke left behind. We're both out of breath. "Now I'm going to hear crime statistics all night."

"Let's take the 28 instead," I say, looking down the street. Another bus is idling at the corner, and the driver is still reading his newspaper by dome light. The 28's route has a stop a little farther from home, but at least we won't have to waste twenty minutes waiting. "We'll get off by St. Andrew's and walk."

The only other passengers with us are three Indian women wearing bright saris the color of spring flowers. They're clustered near the driver, where they are looking unsure of where to get off. Kathleen and I have the backseat to ourselves.

We pass Murray Hill Bowling Lanes, its gigantic bowling pin reflecting in the window. You'd never know it, but Small's Adhesives, where Mima works, is directly under that place. Twenty women packing tape all day long, or at least as long as their boss, Mr. Small, will pay them. When I was little, I thought it was the best place to work. I loved the neon pin and how the bowling balls rumbled like thunder overhead.

"We should have gone bowling instead of going to that dumb movie," Kathleen says as the bus drives by. "How am I going to be able to sleep?"

"You want a real nightmare? How about picking up athlete's foot again from those shoes? *No, gracias.*"

"You just hate to lose."

Not true. I hate everything about bowling. The dim lights of the alley, the nubby little pencils, the boozy men who check us out when we reach down for the ball. I don't even keep the score straight: all those x's and slashes for spares and strikes. Most of the time, I just draw smiley faces and give Kathleen all the points she wants.

Personally, I can't wait for summer, when there will be a

lot more to do. High school will finally be behind us, hallelu-
jah. And to kick things off, we can celebrate our eighteenth
birthdays. Kathleen and I were born only one day apart,
although people always think I look older than the twenty-
four hours I have on her.

The bell tower of St. Andrew's finally comes into view
as we round the bend. You can see its relief sculpture of the
crucifixion against the sky for blocks.

"This is us." I yank the signal cord. "Come on."

Kathleen is quiet as we hop out the back exit and start
for home, but her eyes keep drifting upward the closer
we get to the church. Suddenly she stops and reaches for
my hand.

"What?" I say.

"His eyes . . ." she begins. Her face starts to twist into
panic mode.

"Stop it," I tell her. "You're imagining things."

"I am not," she whispers. "I've been dragged to this
church every Sunday my whole life. I know what the damn
statue is supposed to look like." She squeezes my hand tight.
"Adriana was right. Jesus's eyes are turning bloodred right
now. Look."

I don't wait for more.

Suddenly we're running like horses startled by a pistol.
We race for the corner, round 158th Street, and head down
the hill toward home. I haven't moved this fast since ele-
mentary school, though, and I guess I'm out of practice. In
no time, a stitch in my side stabs at me, and pizza sauce
starts to rise from my stomach. I'm going to puke.

"Wait," I say, gasping.

We bend over and strain for breath. When my heart finally slows enough for me to speak, I straighten.

St. Andrew's is far behind us, but no one is out, as far as I can tell. It's completely dark now. In the daytime, this is a quiet stretch, lined on either side by a few old houses with tiny front yards. We'll have to walk beneath the train trestle, after which comes the block of buildings where I live.

I think sheepishly of Mima, who always tells me not to walk this way alone, especially not at night. A thousand times she's warned me, and I always sneer at her dramatic lectures about this patch of weeds and broken glass, about the dark corners where a girl could be pushed, dragged off to the dead end, and then God Knows What. It has always seemed so stupid, so *Mima*.

But now . . .

I stare ahead at the gaping shadows we'll have to walk through and wish we had just waited for the next bus. I think of the graffiti and the broken bottles in there, the smell of urine that sometimes chokes you when you walk by. Suddenly I think of the murder in Forest Hills.

"We just need to get past the underpass. We'll get close and run," I whisper as Kathleen and I link arms.

I practice our sprint in my mind the way athletes do. We'll race through that patch and break through to the other side, victorious. It will take only a few seconds, no more.

But as we get closer, my feet slow down, and it feels as though I'm trying to walk through molasses. Kathleen slows down, too. Each tree trunk we pass makes us skittish. Anyone could be hiding behind there in the shadows.

I hear a man's voice in my head.

Hey, girls.

Click, click, click, like a gun cocking over and over.

It's just our boots, I tell myself, closing my eyes. *Move faster.*

But behind my eyelids, an ugly picture waits. Kathleen's pretty white coat is soaked with blood as she lies on the ground.

"I don't want to," Kathleen whispers suddenly. "Let's go back. We can call my mom from a pay phone. She'll be pissed, but she'll get us."

I pause, unsure. Northern Boulevard seems so far behind us, and the shops are all closed and dark. We're already at the trestle. We'll only have to run twenty, maybe thirty steps. We're practically adults, aren't we? Nearly eighteen, as Kathleen always says. Not scared little girls.

"We're almost there," I say stubbornly. "We're just psyched out from the stupid movie."

And with that, I pull us into the darkness.

The temperature has dipped again for the night, and the spring chill makes me shudder. "We're fine," I say.

"We're fine," Kathleen repeats.

Click, click, click.

But Kathleen stops again. This time, she raises her finger and points ahead without a sound. A parked car has come into view. It's up on the sidewalk, headlights off. Why didn't we see it before?

13

Someone is definitely inside.

The door opens, and I suck in my breath as a tall man slips out of the driver's side and faces us.

Everything happens quickly after that. A bright light shines in our faces, blinding us. In that fraction of a second, I see a gun at his waist, one of his arms outstretched. I don't even have time to scream. Instinctively I yank Kathleen to the ground and cover my head, waiting for the blast.

But a second later, instead of gunshots, I hear footsteps running in our direction. And another person—a woman— stands over us. She's young, with long dark hair, and she flashes a silver badge from inside her jacket.

"Police," she says.

I stare at her from the ground, confused. My mouth is completely dry, but I'm soaked in a chilly sweat.

I struggle to my feet, trying to make sense of things. Police? These two cops staring down at us look barely older than we are. They're in jeans and boots, like us. If it weren't for their NYPD badges, it could be a joke.

"You looked like you were running from something. Anything wrong?" she says as she helps Kathleen to her feet.

I'm too stunned to answer. Sure, I've watched plenty of *Charlie's Angels,* but I've never had a live encounter with a female cop. This one is nothing like Farrah Fawcett Majors with her big hair and lip gloss.

Kathleen is the first to speak. "We were just . . . running, I guess." She taps her cheek and winces at the blood on her fingertip. There's a scrape. She must have hit the ground hard.

"Just running?" the cop asks. "Not drinking or tipsy, right?" She pauses as Kathleen and I exchange looks. "You girls have ID?"

My heart is pounding now. It's no big deal for Kathleen — her dad's a firefighter. But you can't always trust a cop, especially not if you have the wrong skin color or a last name like López. Look at that kid in Brooklyn. A cop shot him in the head on Thanksgiving Day for the big crime of being black and standing in front of his building around the time somebody else reported a robbery. Randolph Evans was fifteen.

Kathleen fumbles in her purse for her license as the blood starts to drip down her face.

"We're not drunk," she says. "You scared us, that's all."

I hand over my school bus pass, which is all I've got to prove who I am.

"MacInerney." The cop holds her flashlight to read the cards. "López."

I try not to look nervous. Cops brought Hector home last summer. They picked him up at Kissena Park for carving graffiti of a penis into the park benches. He told them the benches were so old and broken down, his artwork made them look better.

Would they remember that, or make the connection?

Kathleen puffs up a little. "That's right. My dad is Patrick MacInerney, with the fire department. He's with Engine Company 258 in Sunnyside. We live right around the block."

I hold my breath. *Good thinking, Kathleen.* I once watched Mr. Mac get out of a speeding ticket by mentioning he was a firefighter. Apparently there's a network of civil servants giving one another a free pass when they break laws.

The cop hands back our IDs.

I look from her to her partner, waiting.

"You're going to have a nice lump," she finally says to Kathleen. "You need a ride home? I can explain to your parents."

My stomach seizes up. Very bad idea. What would Mima say if she finds out the cops stopped me under the trestle in the dark? Not to mention Manny, our super, and the neighbors, who gawk and gossip about anybody they can.

"I live in that building right over there." I point at the next corner. "We can walk. I'll get Kathleen cleaned up at my place."

"Yeah, I'm totally fine," Kathleen adds quickly.

Silence.

I try not to stare at their guns. "Can we go?" I ask. "It's kind of cold out here, and her parents are expecting us."

The cops look at each other, a secret message passing between them. "Go right home," the guy finally says.

We hurry off, too shaken to look back at them or ask any of the million questions running through our minds.

"Holy crap," Kathleen whispers when we finally step into the lobby of my building. The bump on her cheekbone is bright red. "What are they doing hiding like that? There's nobody to arrest around here, is there?"

We look at each other, but neither one of us mentions the girl in Forest Hills aloud.

I take a look at her scrape. Sure enough, a lump is rising fast. "Wait here."

I run upstairs, pop a few cubes out of the ice tray, and am back out the door before Mima can even ask what I'm doing.

Kathleen presses the compress against her face for a few minutes, as we think of a good explanation for her parents. It's never easy with underdeveloped lying skills like hers, but I coach her as best I can.

"Just say you fell, and leave out the part about missing the bus," I tell her. "It's easy. You could have fallen getting off the Q12, see? Those stork legs of yours could have tripped you up, right? Tell them you're late because I was patching you up."

I stand behind the glass doors and watch her race around the corner for home. When she's gone, I climb the stairs slowly. I don't stop on my landing, though. Instead, I go all the way up to the roof and prop open the door.

It's blustery up here, but I can still see the cops' darkened car under the trestle. The sight of them leaves me uneasy. I've watched enough episodes of *Baretta* to add things up. They're decoys, I'm sure of it, and they're here to lure somebody in.

Two cops dressed to look like teens are being used as bait?

I cross back over the roof and head for our apartment, thinking. I won't sleep tonight, but it's not because of *Carrie* or the eyes of some statue turning red.

It's because I know plenty about bait, thanks to all those times I've been fishing with Kathleen and Mr. Mac.

Fake lures don't fool the prize fish you're trying to catch.

It's always the real worm, hopelessly writhing on the hook, that draws what you want from the dark.

Chapter 2

"Nora!"

Ms. Friedmor, our head guidance counselor, is on bus duty when she spots me leaving school on Monday. I've got no cover. Kathleen hitched a ride home with a guy named Eddie. She said she didn't want to ride the bus with the bruise on her cheek. I tried to tell her it didn't look too bad, but she knew I was lying. She wore sunglasses on the ride in, but people still stared.

"Leaving already?" Ms. Friedmor checks her watch as she catches up to me.

The bus pulls away from the stop, stranding me until the next one. "Senior privileges, remember?" I say.

My schedule is amazing, at last. I have exactly two classes left in my high-school career. Wood shop is first thing in the morning, which is actually okay, followed by English IV with Mr. Darius, a flat-out coma inducer. I'm home every day by noon.

Ms. Friedmor nods and pulls her jacket around her. "Making any progress on your college application?"

She is such a pain. She's always bugging us about filling out our postgraduate action plan. She's big on *being intentional*. "Knowing what you want is ninety percent of the battle," she always says, as if we're warriors.

Well, I wish to defect, madam.

I've already tried to explain to her that what I really want to do is get a job and an apartment instead. Plenty of people do that, but you'd think I was explaining that I was going to throw myself in front of a train.

Last month she dragged me to her office. She pretended to listen to me, but she was really just scowling at my FOXY LADY T-shirt. When I was done, she leaned across her desk and pointed at my lapel button. It's from Mrs. MacInerney's endless collection of women's-lib pins. A WOMAN'S PLACE IS IN THE WORLD. Kathleen and I have a pretty good spread on our jean jackets. You'd be surprised how they come in handy. When we need extra bus fare, we can hock a few buttons at lunch, easy.

"So, are these just fashion slogans or what?"

"What do you mean?"

Ms. Friedmor shook her head. "You're a smart young woman. Life is more than disco dancing with your friends. Get your education first. *That's* where you'll find power and independence."

"I'm not much for books, Ms. Friedmor. You know that."

"So? You love working with your hands, don't you? I saw Mr. Melvin's display of his students' work. Maybe woodwork or construction is your passion. If it is, follow it," she told me.

20

"No way am I going to Apex Tech. Have you seen the commercials? Pure cheese!" Apex is a tech school in Long Island City that's always begging for students. *Call and get started on your new career right away.*

"Think bigger for yourself, Nora," she said, sighing. "Thanks to Title IX, a lot of women are moving into non-traditional jobs. That's where the money is." She reached for a folder and handed it to me. "Apex is *not* the only option for you. How about New York City Community College, in Brooklyn? You can get a degree in construction technology and even go on to a bachelor's degree from there. Who knows? You might run a business yourself someday."

I stared at her. Me? Have a job where I could call the shots and make goons like Angel fetch me coffee? Not a bad idea, even for Ms. Friedmor.

"Life gets hard and more complicated later, Nora. Get your education while life is still fairly easy. Otherwise, you might not go back."

More complicated? The thought plagued me all day.

Right now she's eyeballing me, so I know she hasn't forgotten. I shift on my feet. The application to NYCCC is still in my bag. "I'm having trouble finding a typewriter," I tell her.

She crosses her arms and gives me a pained look. "There are plenty of machines available for use in the typing lab, and you know it. You just have to schedule with Mrs. Pratt."

Will this woman never let up? Can she not see the signs of senioritis? I've explained several times now that it is an established condition.

"Oh, good," I say. But in my mind, I'm typing her a little message.

[Shift. Cap lock.]

I AM OVER THIS. [Return.]

"Deadlines, Nora," she warns. "And one thing more, please."

I take a deep breath and turn around. After four years, I am actually starting to hate her. If she says one word about aspirations, I will scream.

"Your brother," she says.

Oh, even better.

Now what? Hector hasn't exactly made many fans among his teachers over the years. Luckily only a few of them still care enough to call home to tell Mima about his late assignments, his absences, his general attitude problem — or, to be more accurate, to tell *me* so I can explain it to Mima in Spanish. But now I can see they've called in the big guns. He's a guidance case.

"Did Hector do something?" I ask innocently.

"No. That's the trouble," Ms. Friedmor says. "He's not here. Again."

"He's been sick," I say. That's not technically a lie. He's been coughing, though what can you expect if you smoke a pack a day?

"Please ask your mother to call me," she says. "There are a few matters we have to discuss about his course work."

"Sure, I'll let her know." Poor Ms. Friedmor. She has no idea that it will mean nothing.

"And you'll speak with Mrs. Pratt, too?"

I give her an exasperated look. "Yes, Ms. Friedmor."

She pats my cheek. "Have the application on my desk in a week and I'll add my recommendation."

The following afternoon, I climb the stairs to our apartment. As soon as I turn the key and step inside, I can tell that I've landed smack in the middle of one of Mima and Hector's showdowns.

Crap.

If only I'd put my ear to the door first, I would have heard the muffled voices and waited out their argument. It's a pretty day; I might have been able to ride the city bus all the way to the island and back to kill time.

I try to back out quietly, but it's too late. Mima spots me. *"Aqui está tu hermana,"* she says, announcing me.

She's at the sink, elbow-deep in soapy water. Hector stands in the kitchen doorway, a lit cigarette dangling from his lips while he does hand tricks with one of his Zippo lighters. He can close it with a sharp flick of the wrist alone. Sure, it's impressive, but how many lighters does a person need? The answer is infinite, if you're a pyro like he is, and matches just aren't enough. I find Zippos rattling in the dryer after I do the laundry every week.

The truth is I feel a little guilty watching him smoke. It wasn't so long ago that Hector and I sucked on peeled Crayola crayons, pretending to be a movie star and a cowboy, all my idea. But now it's not a game. He smokes like a fiend. At first, Mima nagged him about his lungs and all that. Eventually she stopped because it pissed him off. Now,

23

along with smoking, he's acquired a new habit of overturning kitchen chairs to let you know when you're on his nerves. I had to swipe a tube of Mr. Melvin's best wood glue to keep on hand for the busted legs.

I hang up my coat in the hall closet and notice that the orange light from my turntable is on. Haven't I been perfectly clear? No touching my stuff unless I'm home. Hector's Led Zeppelin LP is still sitting there, too. I have a good mind to scratch it up for him.

"No lo tengo," Mima says. I don't have it.

"You do have it." Hector flicks his wrist and snaps the lighter. "You just don't want to give it to me. That's different."

Mima digs for the rubber stopper under the murky water. "I didn't get all my hours this week. You know that."

Her boss, the aptly named Mr. Small, has started closing his tape factory in the middle of the afternoon. He claims that business is bad because the City of New York, his biggest client, is nearly broke. Okay, everybody knows that's true. Even the teacher in 3D rushes to cash her paycheck on Fridays in case it doesn't clear at the bank. But how bad can it *really* be for Mr. Small if that little Napoleon still drives around in a new car every year? I think he's full of it. Still, Mima worries constantly about losing her job in *"un la-yuff."*

"And the rent was due last week, in case you don't know," she adds.

"So? You don't pay that." *Snap! Click!*

True. In theory, Papi's child-support check more or less covers the rent. Plus, Mima makes me pay her fifty dollars every month from my earnings at the deli to "teach me responsibility." I have mentioned that Kathleen still gets an *allowance,* but Mima says it's another way Americans raise unappreciative children.

"Well, he hasn't sent it," she says. "He's late. As usual." She shakes her head and sprinkles Ajax into the sink.

"Then call him."

Mima sighs and stares at the ceiling. Then she turns to me with a pleading look.

I see where this is going. My parents haven't spoken directly since the day they signed their divorce papers. Guess who's their messenger pigeon?

"*I* don't want to call him," I say, squeezing past Hector to get to the refrigerator. Slim pickings, as usual. I reach for the cheese and fan away the cloud of cigarette smoke that has filled the room. "Jesus, Hector. Have a heart. It's not like we can open a window in this cold."

"I need ten bucks," he says.

"Yeah. Ha — me, too."

He doesn't know about my stash, thank God. I keep a little wad of bills hidden inside my old boots at the back of the closet. I've been socking away what I can so I can avoid asking Mima for anything. This month, seniors had to buy their cap and gown for graduation, plus, sue me, I splurged on a pair of Sasson jeans. So now I'm running low, considering that I should also be saving my money to move out. Mima would never understand, so she doesn't know. She thinks girls should live at home in the *calor de su familia* until they get married, no matter what. I say family warmth isn't all it's cracked up to be, at least not in this family.

Hector inhales deeply. "Seriously. Ten measly bucks."

"For what?"

"The Ramones are at CBGB's in a couple of weeks. I want to go."

I wrinkle my nose. The Ramones are nothing I'd spend ten hard-earned bucks on. They're punk, best known for giving their audience the finger. I don't know what he sees in them except attitude. Personally I like dance music, or what Hector refers to coolly as "disco shit." Kathleen and I have worn out the needle on her turntable listening to Vicki Sue Robinson's "Turn the Beat Around," the best song on the radio. The violins mixed against a heavy dance beat make us hustle across the room until we're dizzy. It's a known fact that we're good dancers, too. We've been getting in at the Arena for at least a year. Hector, on the other hand, says disco makes him puke. He likes to groan like Donna Summer singing "Love to Love You Baby" and grab at his crotch. Gross, but somehow it always makes me laugh.

Mima has no idea who the Ramones are, of course, or even who Donna Summer is. Her understanding of American music pretty much ends at Lawrence Welk. But she smells trouble. She starts muttering in Spanish, not looking at either one of us. *The subways are a death trap at that hour. Murders are the order of the day.* Her mind is swirling in ugly waters. And maybe she's right. The club is on Bleecker Street, in the Bowery. If the pimps and junkies don't jump him, he'll still have to ride the subway home at midnight. Then again, maybe it's the other riders who should worry. I wonder if Mima has ever stopped to think that Hector isn't exactly defenseless. Has she forgotten last summer? He bought nunchucks from who-knows-where and practiced on the sidewalk scaring kids until their parents complained to Manny. Mima had to throw his little toy down the dumb-waiter chute when he wasn't looking. "Sometimes boys like to show off like they're big men," she whispered to me as it clattered down four stories. *Really?* I wondered. *By threatening to bust little kids' brains out?*

I try an evasive maneuver. "You have to be eighteen for that place."

"Idiot. It's sixteen plus two IDs. Besides, Sergio knows the guy at the door."

I take a bite of my cheese and fall silent. Sergio lives in the basement apartment of the building behind ours. He's technically Manny's "assistant," but that's only because Sergio's uncle owns the building. He's always checking me out with his mole eyes and talking shit. A sleazeball through and through.

"Sergio?" I ask. "Since when are you two buds?"

Hector doesn't answer. "Gimme the ten bucks," he says, turning back to Mima.

The flatness in his voice makes the hair on my arms bristle. We're sliding into a hole, and I have to figure out how to hold on to the edges. It's one of my few gifts: trouble radar, like one of those dogs that can sniff explosives before the big *ka-boom.*

"*Niño,* I told you, I don't have it." Mima turns to me. "Talk some sense into him. *Háblale.*"

But I don't get the chance. Hector snaps like one of his

lighters. His cheeks go blotchy, and he shoves past me into the entry hall, where Mima's purse hangs in the coat closet. He grabs it and digs inside, tossing out her eyeglass case, her pens, her citizenship card, used tissues.

"*¡Pero hijo!*" Mima stands helplessly at the doorway as he empties her purse. Soapy water drips from her hands onto the floor. "*¡No lo tengo!*"

My stomach squeezes into a familiar knot as I try to figure out the puzzle, fast. I could give him the ten bucks to cool things off, or I could hide in our bedroom and let them combust. The neighbors will complain, though, and I'll still have to deal with it all week. Last time we had a "family discussion," people stared at me in the hall for days.

I go on instinct.

"Shhh!" I hiss at Mima. "Hector, what do you want her to do? She doesn't have it." My voice is even as I try to pull him back to calm.

He gives me the finger and keeps searching.

I'd love to slap him. Or better, I'd like to see Mima walk over to him for once, yank her purse back, show him who's boss. She's supposed to be in charge, isn't she? But I know better. Mima's never been able to stand up to him. Not when he bit the kids at the playground when he was four and not when he told his principal to fuck off in middle school. Not even when she had to take me out of school last year so I could translate with the security staff at Alexander's department store. Hector had been picked up for shoplifting, of all things, cuff links. It was the start, the cops warned him, of his yellow sheet.

28

I try again in an even softer voice. "Buy the album next week when she gets paid," I offer. "It's better, anyway. You can listen to them whenever you want."

But it's too late. Hector has slipped into that strange place where he can't hear anyone. Finally he yanks out her wallet and flips it open. There are only three singles inside. He stares at the bills, mute with rage. For a second, his expression reminds me of that Christmas when he was six and he found a pack of socks from Woolworth's beneath our tree instead of the Matchbox track he really wanted.

He hurls the wallet across the room. When it hits the wall, pennies explode into a supernova.

"This is bullshit!" he shouts, the veins in his neck thick. The door slams, and his army boots echo down the stairs.

Mima stands in the sudsy puddle that has formed around her feet. She looks about a hundred years old.

I don't meet her eye as we bend to pick up the coins. I dig out dimes from around the stove and force myself to think of the bright side, the glass half full and all that shit the MacInerneys and other happy people say.

Nobody screamed loud enough to get Manny to call the cops. Mima still has her three bucks. We didn't do the Chair Fandango, so the furniture is still in one piece.

So, really, all things considered, it went pretty well.

Chapter 3

Sometimes after school, Hector balls up pages from the newspaper and lights them. He holds the edges until I'm sure the flames will catch his sleeves, and then he drops them out the window. The first time I caught him, I ran over, yelling at him to stop. All these years listening to Mr. Mac's fire stories made me worried. But standing there next to him, I could see what he liked. The flame balls spun in the air like fiery birds being consumed. They turned to harmless ash before they ever hit anything below.

I don't know if Mima knows about Hector's flame birds. Probably not. But would she mind? It's hard to know. Mima is tough to read sometimes, but she says the same about us. She complains that she can't understand what we say if we speak English too fast, and she can't tell whether David Bowie is a man or a woman. Last year when she sat me down in the kitchen for what I thought was going to be the long-overdue sex talk, she told me that drug use would lead to a life of prostitution on Times Square. That very specific information might have been helpful to know, if I actually ever bothered to get high. It's Hector who partakes, not me. I'm too cheap to waste money on weed.

But how Mima sees Hector is what is strangest of all. She lives here, doesn't she? She has eyes and ears. She deals with Hector's foul mouth, his bratty fits, and yet she actually gushes to her friend Edna all the time about him. How clever he is, how handsome, how adventurous and unusual.

¡Mi madre! Okay, fine, he's *guapo*—even with cystic zits—but she's leaving out a few important things that might dampen the glowing review, if you ask me.

Like his habit of treating her like crap.

"Men are reckless, Nora," she likes to tell me. "They're born that way, impulsive, but eventually they find a good woman and outgrow it. You'll see."

It's a nice fantasy, I suppose, although why she's so charitable to men I'll never know. It's not like Papi did her any favors. I was almost four the day Papi's silver razor just went missing from the toothbrush rack and his big shoes weren't crowding the door. I remember that night because Hector pitched an epic fit and tore the linoleum from the floor with his fingers. We still have the holes near the bathroom. Mima stayed in bed for a long time after that, too.

It's no use talking to her about real life, though. She just doesn't participate in it. Take her stories about her life back in Cuba before *el desgraciado* Fidel. She says it was about *familia*, about freedoms, about beautiful palm trees and a simple life. I don't argue, but I can't help but notice that she never mentions that they nearly starved during the

Depression, that her father shot himself in a field, that all they ate was corn-mush *harina*.

That was perfection?

I'm thinking all of this when I flip on the TV news, hoping Hector will come through the door on his own before Mima starts in on me, the way she always does when he's roaming.

A yearbook picture of a pretty brunette flashes before us. The news anchor fills us in:

> "The university coed was gunned down early this evening in Forest Hills. . . . She has been identified as nineteen-year-old Virginia Voskerichian, who was discovered near Dartmouth Street, her purse untouched. Witnesses report hearing screams . . ."

I listen uneasily as the camera pans the crime scene, and it's like déjà vu. This is only a couple of blocks from where the other girl got murdered in January. Cops are lingering around, smoking. A pair of boots sticks out from the bottom of a sheet on the ground.

I look over my shoulder at Mima, who's staring at the screen, trying to cobble the story together from across the room.

"*¡Señor ampáranos!*" She crosses herself and starts to sweep again. "There are devils all over this city." The bristles sound like someone sharpening knives. She's been cleaning for hours, her favorite task when she's nervous. So far,

32

she's cleaned the baseboards, wiped down the plastic slip-covers on the sofa, and scrubbed the bathroom. Our whole place stinks of Clorox. "Filth, not poverty, is the sign of low people," she always says. As chilly as the apartment is getting, streaks of perspiration still run down her neck. Finally she leans the broom against the wall and peers out the window.

"The whole city is going crazy! And your *hermanito* is out there." Her jaw quivers. "Did he take a coat?"

"I don't remember."

"What if something has happened and he's cold? What if he doesn't have spare change to call home?"

I ignore her.

"And what is his fascination with this screaming music? Why are a bunch of grown men yelling and jumping like that, anyway?"

Pass.

I turn up the TV and pretend to concentrate as the news drones on. I can't stop thinking about this girl's rag-doll body, the police standing over her, the strange angle of those stylish boots. I'm thinking of the decoy cops who might be sitting down the block right now.

Maybe I *should* be worried.

Mima sits down. For a second I think she's calming down, but just then a fire truck goes by. The spinning lights fill our kitchen as the siren wails. She crosses herself and crumbles again. Mima believes in omens, after all.

"*Ave Maria purisima*, what if he's dead? There's a murderer out there!"

I give up. She will not quit until he's home. I flip off the TV, pull on a sweatshirt over my pajamas, and stick my bare feet into my sneakers. Does anybody care that *I* am going out to find my brother with said murderer on the prowl? *No, señores,* apparently not.

"Try the roof first," she says as I slip out the door.

A hunter looks for tracks. Hector has left clues on the roof — old cigarette butts, an *X-Men* comic, beer cans — but nothing's fresh and there's no sign of him.

Damn.

I cross the rooftop and peer over the ledge to the street below. The moon is half full tonight, so I can see pretty well. Unfortunately, Hector is not walking home from either direction. At least the unmarked car is under the trestle again. The cops are nearby.

I head back inside, dejected. This leaves only one logical place to look.

Sergio's Den of Darkness.

I have to run all the way around to the back of our building and down a flight of concrete steps to reach it. It makes sense that Sergio lives underground like a rodent. He's got the beady eyes, the yellow teeth.

I knock and wait, hopping from one foot to the other to keep warm. Sergio's car is parked right across the street, so I know he's home. These days, he thinks he's big shit driving that Monte Carlo, which I'm pretty sure he funds with his side business of selling nickel bags outside the Satin Lady Lounge. He's always peeling out so people will turn around and ogle. I try my best to avoid him, but I still run into him on the block every once in a while when he's lugging his toolbox to somebody's apartment to make a repair. He always tries to chat me up. *"Noooora! Can't you say hello?"*

I knock again.

That's when I hear a whine. From down here, I can see only the legs of anyone who might walk by on the street above me. But there's a dog sniffing at me from the sidewalk. It's the wiry stray we all call Tripod, on account of his having only three legs. We all sort of feed him, but no one knows who owns him. When it's bitter cold, he hangs near the dryer vents, which is how he survived the bitch of a winter we just had. But the rest of the time, he likes to wander.

"Hey, buddy," I tell him. "What's the matter?"

He perks his ears and looks off into the distance, growling. Then he hops off, spooked by something or other. Is somebody coming along the street? It suddenly occurs to me that I'm boxed in down here at the bottom of Sergio's stairwell.

"Excuse me, miss," a stranger might say, and then — *pow* — my brains will be splattered all over this door.

"Sergio!" I bang with my fists. "Open up!"

The door finally flies open. Sergio is barefoot and in jeans. He's got a pigeon chest and hairy nipples, I notice. Yuck. It takes a second for him to recognize me. Then he breaks into his oily grin.

"Noooora!" He leans an arm on the doorframe. *How can anyone have this much pit hair?* I wonder. He lowers his voice and coos, "What brings you to me?"

"Is my brother here?" I'm too shaken to be polite, especially since he's also ogling my boobs. I wrap my arms around myself tighter. "It's late, and my mother wants him home."

His grin doesn't change as he puts an unfiltered Camel to his lips and lights up. "You always look so uptight, Nora, you know that? You never relax, but you'd be really pretty if you smiled." He picks at his tongue absently and spits a thread of tobacco near my feet. "There's stuff to help with that, if you want some."

I glare at him and call into the apartment. "Hector?" I have no plan B, of course. If Hector isn't here, I'll have to go back home empty-handed. Then what? Mima will end up in the loony bin once and for all, like she's always threatening. *"Hector!"*

"Take it easy, Nora." Sergio motions for me to come inside. "He's in my room."

The place smells like a bag of Fritos. A brown velour couch with a big burn mark on one cushion is pushed up against the wall. Sergio holds up his ringed fingers and points toward his bedroom in the back.

For a second, I stay put. What if he's lying?

Luckily, the buildings on this block are all the same. The layout of this apartment is almost exactly like ours, except that the bathroom is on the opposite wall. I walk backward and keep my eye on him. When I reach the bedroom door, I push it open with my foot.

36

"Hector?"

There's no answer, but I spot him. He's lying right beside the unmade bed, headphones on, drumming with imaginary sticks against his knees. His eyes are closed. Relief floods through me, but honestly I don't know whether to hug him or kick him in the gut. I stand over him and lift the ear pads to get his attention.

"Time to go."

Hector blinks. His eyes are glassy. Shit; he's stoned. His expression reminds me of the day I taught him how to float at Rockaway Beach. I held my arms under his back, promising that he wouldn't sink if he put his head back and breathed. It took all afternoon for him to believe me, but finally he lay back and looked almost peaceful.

I can feel Sergio watching us from the doorway. Hector isn't budging, like maybe his pride is still pressing him to the floor. "Please," I add quietly.

He grins up at the magic word and tosses the headphones on the bed.

"This song sucks, anyway." He hops to his feet and grabs his jacket from the mess of sheets. "Later," he says to Sergio as he heads out the door.

I try to squeeze past Sergio, too, but he steps out. "Nooora," he whispers, reaching for my hand. I pull it away, watching as my brother dashes up the steps.

"Stay away from him," I say.

Sergio grins. "He came to visit me, remember?"

"Leave him alone, Sergio." Then I run to catch up to Hector.

We don't say a word as we step inside the lobby. I let Tripod in behind us, hoping Manny won't kick him out of his hiding spot near the mailboxes until morning.

Our place is on the top floor, so it's a steep climb with lots of time to think. There are a million things I could say to Hector as we go from landing to landing, our footsteps echoing against all those closed doors.

That it's dicey to get wasted with the likes of Sergio.

That he shouldn't treat Mima like shit.

That a killer just shot a nineteen-year-old girl on her way home.

That I'm sorry about not giving him the money for the Ramones.

But neither one of us says a word.

Instead, we step back inside our apartment. Mima is in the kitchen, frying an egg, although it's past midnight. Hector doesn't say a thing to her. He just pulls open the sparkling refrigerator and starts to root inside. Mima turns off the flame and slides a chipped plate onto the table.

"Eat something. You're still growing, *hijo*," she says. And then, without a word to me, she heads off to bed.

Chapter 4

Kathleen grabs me at the bus stop the next morning. I'm barely awake. It took me a while to go to sleep after finding Hector. Every time I dozed, I kept seeing that girl's rag-doll feet on the ground.

Kathleen looks wide-awake, though. If I didn't know better, I'd say she dipped into the Café Bustelo I taught her how to brew at exam time.

"I almost called you last night, but it was late, and I thought your mother might freak," she blurts out. "I can't believe I've had to wait eight hours with this."

I stifle a yawn and try to focus. "With what?"

"Dad called from work last night."

"What burned now?" Mr. Mac works two twenty-four-hour shifts in a row, and then he's off.

She waves me off impatiently. "Did you see the news about the Forest Hills murder?" she asks.

I check down the street for the next bus. "Yep. I'm not going to wander around Continental for a while, that's for sure."

She pulls me close.

"It's worse than that." Her eyes have that look she gets when she's hoarding a secret.

"What are you talking about?"

She looks over her shoulder at the other people waiting at the stop and pulls me off to the side. "You know how my parents have been acting overprotective and weird for weeks? There's a reason. And it's big."

I spot the bus in the distance. It's pulled over at the stop a couple of blocks down, so I fish in my bag for my bus pass. "Bigger than a shooter?"

She takes a breath. "The news said the cops found no connection between the two murders in Forest Hills, right?"

"Yeah . . ."

"That's bullshit. The cops just told the papers that because they don't want people to panic."

I feel a flutter in my stomach that I don't like. Around us, people start to line up as the bus idles at the light. "Panic about what?"

She lowers her voice even more. "Dad said they've suspected for a couple of months now that we might have a serial killer."

"Kathleen," I say uneasily. It wouldn't be the first time her imagination went wild. "A *serial killer*?"

She gives me an exasperated look. "Think back," she says. "Not just the girl in January. Remember the couple that got shot at Halloween? The ones in the VW?"

I'd almost forgotten. One of Mr. Mac's friends is a detective at the 109th Precinct, on Union Place. Around

40

Halloween, his daughter and her date were shot on Depot Road, not far from here.

"And how about the girls in Bellerose?"

Again my mind goes back. A man came up and asked for directions while they were sitting on their stoop. He opened fire, and now one of them is in a wheelchair.

"Holy shit."

"And there's probably more," Kathleen says. "They're checking for bullet matches."

The bus pulls over and throws open the door to let people board. For a second, neither one of us moves.

"Well?" the bus driver says. "You getting on or what?"

We climb up without another word, but I suddenly feel wary around all these strangers. The whole ride, I look around at the bored faces, wondering if one of them might have something to hide.

I just can't shake what Kathleen shared. Even climbing the stairs after school feels scary. I reach each landing and look around to make sure nobody is lurking in any dark corners. Then I run for the next set of stairs.

"Nora."

Mima nearly gives me a heart attack.

She's sitting on the sofa, still wearing her work clothes. Her hands are folded in her lap, like she's waiting for a bus or something. What's she doing home?

"*¿Qué te pasa?*" I ask. What's wrong? I can feel something buzzing in the air, even though Hector isn't home. "Are you sick?"

Mima swallows and looks over at me with that expression that tells me she'll be taking to her bed with one of her daylong headaches.

"My hours were cut again," she says. "I'm down to half time. Edna is going to try to put in a word for me, but it doesn't look good." She shrugs and stares into her lap. "Nobody is hiring," she mutters.

Then she points at the table, where the bigger trouble is waiting. I see the pink paper and know what it is right away. Manny has left us an overdue notice.

> *Rent in the amount of $275 was due on March 1, 1977, for the period of: February 1–28, 1977 for unit 4E, which you are currently occupying.*
>
> *Please deliver your rent promptly to Mr. Emmanuel Barros, building superintendent. You may disregard this notice if payment has already been made.*

By the time I finish reading it, Mima is already heading to her room. She's got dark circles under her eyes and a run in the back of her hose.

"I'm going to lie down," she mumbles.

The last time I talked to Papi was Valentine's Day. It's easy to remember because Papi only calls on official holidays. He has a lousy memory for dates, which is why he almost never remembers our birthdays, and probably why he's always confused about exactly how old we are or what grade we're in. He makes up for it by calling on holidays that have big symbols on his calendar: Halloween, Thanksgiving, Christmas, Valentine's Day, Memorial Day, and the Fourth of July.

"What do you expect from a man who can't even remember his own name?" Mima always says. What she means is that Papi's given name was Federico. Everybody in the whole world once knew him as Fico, but all that changed when he married Linda. He goes by "Rick" now.

Apart from our holiday chats, we don't see each other much. He lives in the city with Linda and their kid, Pierre, who's five. I wonder if the kids at school make fun of *that* stupid name. Anyway, the last time Hector and I visited them, Pierre was still in a stroller and wearing Cookie Monster slippers. It wasn't exactly a great day, either. Hector fed Pierre all the plastic pieces from an Evel Knievel Colorforms set until the kid nearly choked. Linda rolled up the welcome mat after that.

I take a deep breath and try to sound calm and pleasant. I was kind of grumpy last time we talked. I had my reasons, though. Valentine's Day is tough for a loveless girl like me. I had just lived through the annual carnation sale at school that raises money for the prom, which I have no intention of attending. At least Kathleen got a carnation from Eddie and some from mystery admirers, plus the one I sent her. The only flower I got was from her. She wrote, *From the foxy ghost of Freddie Prinze. I'll always love you.* Ricky, the Student Council president, delivered it to my homeroom. The smart-ass just looked at me with pity. "Sad," he said.

Anyway, Papi sounds a little surprised to hear from me when he picks up.

"Hi, Papi," I say. "It's me. Nora."

"Nora! What a surprise," Papi says. "I was just thinking about you. I was telling Linda that maybe you could come spend a Saturday with us. We could take you shopping at Bloomingdale's. Buy you something nice."

"Sure," I say, but I don't let myself imagine all those pretty clothes or those shiny black counters. Papi has big ideas all the time, but that doesn't mean anything. Disney, Great Adventure, a baseball game at Shea Stadium, he's offered all of them at one time or another, but we've never actually gone on those trips, as Mima likes to point out. Something always wrecks the plan. Pierre gets sick. Papi gets called into work. Linda heard people are getting jumped at the Central Park Zoo. One way or another, the trip gets canned.

I twirl the phone cord and zone out as Papi tells me about all the things Pierre has been learning in kindergarten this week.

"Your little brother is so smart," Papi says. "Especially at numbers."

At first I think he's talking about Hector, but then I realize he still means Pierre. Could Little Pepé Le Pew really be smarter than Hector? Probably not. Hector is hard to beat, especially if you factor in the criminal-mastermind angle.

I glance at Mima's door, which isn't closed all the way. She's still napping, or maybe she's just eavesdropping as I do her dirty work, as usual.

"School is fine," I tell Papi when he finally asks. I pile it on thick, like I'm somebody on *The Partridge Family* or something. Yes, spring semester of senior year is really fun. I *love* it. Yes, I've already put in my application to college. I should hear any day now.

It's all a lie. I am counting down the days to be done with high school so I can move out. No matter what Ms. Friedmor says, it will be easier than going to college. I'm just not into it, and why should I be? I'm not like Kathleen, who's going to escape to a dorm decorated with a comforter and matching pillows. Even if I get in, come September, the only change in my life will be getting a bus to Brooklyn. Being a commuter student isn't the same. I'll still be stuck with Mima and Hector. And that's if I even figure out how to pay for it all. It used to be free to go to any of the colleges that were part of City University, but broke as the city is, now you have to pay to be tortured. Four hundred bucks a semester! I looked at the financial-aid papers a while back and nearly threw up. It will be a bitch trying to translate it all for Mima, so I'll have to answer most of the questions myself. I'm not even sure whose name goes under "Head of Household." Isn't that supposed to be the person who calls the shots? That position is more or less empty around here.

Still, if I don't apply for aid, where am I going to get $800 a year, plus books? *Papi?* Ha! He's busy paying Pierre's private kindergarten for geniuses.

Papi pauses on his end of the line, and I can tell he's running out of things to say. "So, everybody's good?" He always asks about this mysterious everybody. It's everyone and no one at the same time. Neat trick.

"Yep." I close the door to Mima's bedroom just in case she's faking it and listening in. I don't like an audience when I grovel. "Mima's at work, and Hector is staying after school with track." (What a whopper!) I take a deep breath and try to sound casual. "So, Papi, I think something might have happened to the mail again, because Mima didn't get your check."

There's a rustling on his end and a long pause that I hate.

"Really?" He sounds genuinely surprised, which is kind of impressive, considering how often this happens. "I'm almost positive I sent it. Are you sure?"

"You know how the mail is," I say vaguely.

We actually have excellent mail. Our carrier is a lady named Sheila. She pushes her overloaded postal cart up and down the block at four p.m. like clockwork, and she always says hello.

I think about Papi and Linda's fancy digs in the city. They've got good mail in their building, too. It was Linda's place before they lived together, up on First Avenue. The doorman is a Dominican guy who holds the door open for the tenants and accepts mail deliveries all day long. He calls Papi *Mr. López,* although I'll bet he secretly wants to call him Fico, too.

"Well, I'll send it again," Papi says. "No problem. Be watching for it."

I stand in the window staring up the block for the unmarked cop car, but it's not there. Maybe they found who they're looking for, or have decided that there's a better place to look. That's a good sign, right?

Just then, I spot Hector coming up the block toward our stoop. He's wearing his sweatshirt, hood up against the chill. It's too short in the sleeves on him, and his shoulders are shrugged up against the wind. I almost forget how mad I was at him this morning for keeping me up late looking for him.

Papi's voice is loud in the receiver. "Well, I've got to get back to work. But I'll call you next week about Bloomingdale's," he says.

My throat squeezes tighter. He'll call me on Easter, not a day sooner, but why point out his lie? It will make us both feel weird, and I don't want him to hang up.

"Hey . . ." Words swirl in my head, but I can't pull them to my lips in the right order. *I need . . . We need . . .* I want to tell him that I'm a little scared of the shootings, that we still need him, but it gets jumbled inside.

Papi waits. "Nora? Hello?"

"I'm here." I send him the rest of the message in my mind. *Mima's hours got cut and she needs your help with Hector, who's jacked up worse than usual. Maybe you could talk to him? Yes, I know the arrangement. You pay rent and Mima covers everything else. But could you help, this once, maybe not tell Linda?*

But my mental connection doesn't work.

"Look, *mija*, I've got to go," Papi says cheerfully. "Spring break is coming. Maybe I can get away and we'll go to Florida. I'll check into it when I get a minute."

The lobby buzzer sounds. Hector's key, I notice, still hangs on the hook by the closet.

"Nora? Are you still there?"

Pierre's high voice sounds in the background at Papi's place. I'm remembering long ago, when Papi was still here, how he swung Hector high above his head, laughing. And then those later days when Hector was Pierre's age, big brown eyes, no front teeth, kicking too hard or pinching when we played.

"Listen, Nora," Papi says, "I have to go. I'll put the check in the mail as soon as I get off the phone. You watch that mailman, okay?"

"Okay." I wait to hear the click before slamming down the phone.

Then, bracing myself, I let Hector in.

Chapter 5

There's been drama in the building.

Mrs. Murga's apartment, 1A, was burglarized last night while we all slept. What a week. If it's not scary enough to think about a killer lurking around, now we have this. It figures that those stupid undercover cops were gone when we really needed them.

From the looks of the splintered frame, the crooks pried open a window and climbed in from the street. According to Stiller, the head of the tenant association—who already came by with a petition for security cameras and upgraded windows—they made off with Mrs. Murga's color TV, a transistor radio, and the Social Security check she hadn't taken to the bank yet. It doesn't sound like much, but that's pretty much everything that was worth anything in Mrs. Murga's place. I've fed her cat a couple of times when she's gone to visit relatives, so I know. The place is a museum of old-lady crapola: crocheted doilies on her sofa's armrests, crystal bowls filled with stale candy, plastic roses.

"*¡Qué horrór!*" Mima says. "They could have slashed *la viejita's* throat if she woke up. They could have violated her! They could have killed any one of us in the hall, too!"

Bad is never enough for Mima. We must go to gruesome. But now that we might have a serial killer roaming around, maybe her worries aren't so crazy.

Mima's words worm inside me all night. What makes someone a burglar and someone else a killer? I wonder. Where's the switch that lets someone look you in the eye and pull the trigger anyway?

I toss and turn as I try to fall asleep, but I keep imagining sounds outside my window. Is it the wind, or is someone climbing the rusted rungs of the fire escape? The blinds move, but it could be a draft. I don't dare get up to check. Instead, I back against the wall and stare at the blinds, waiting for the sound of a crowbar splintering wood. When I finally drift to sleep, a stranger follows me into my dreams.

He's not a burglar. It's the serial killer.

Click! Bang! Blood splatters the wall like it did in *Carrie*. I try to scream, but no one hears me at all.

The very next day, Mrs. Murga is gone. Just like that, her son has packed up her museum and moved her out to Levittown. When I get home at noon, the U-Haul is pulling away.

Manny has wasted no time, of course, in making plans to rent the place again. The painters are already sitting in their van, parked out front, eating lunch while they wait for the coast to be clear. Vultures.

The men stop eating and watch me go by in that way

that always makes me want to gouge out their eyes. What is it with horny men? Are there no women their own age? And why are they everywhere in this city? Construction sites, the schoolyard, even dressed up in business suits at the bus stop (but only if they think no one else is listening). *Hey, Mami. What's up, beautiful?* When I complain to Mima, she tells me to ignore them. "Besides, you'll miss the attention one day when you're old and shriveled."

Sometimes I want to send some of Mima's advice straight to the No Comment column at *Ms.* magazine. It would fit right in with the other sexist ads readers spot and submit each month. The reigning champ so far is a bowling ad: BEAT YOUR WIFE TONIGHT.

"Good day at school?" one of them calls. He's practically Papi's age and has the bloated face of a boozer, clearly not the type of man with a healthy interest in the quality of my academic experience. Normally, I pretend to go deaf and ignore guys like this, but this time I pause at the lobby doors. What if the serial killer is a sleazy painter who gets back at girls who ignore him? I could be an eyewitness that helps lock him up.

I turn around and study his face for a second. He licks his fat lips and waves hopefully as I register his features. Then, to his obvious disappointment, I let myself into the lobby to get the mail.

I scan the envelopes for Papi's handwriting. Nothing yet. If Manny knocks on our door, I'll have to pretend no one is home, watch TV with no sound.

I take the first flight of stairs but stop at Mrs. Murga's

51

open door. It's kind of sad to see how fast nothing of her remains except a few rumpled tissues and dust bunnies on the floor.

"Hello?" I walk all the way in to get a better look.

It's a studio, so the kitchen, living room, and bedroom are all in one. This wouldn't be a bad place to live if I fixed it up nice. Small, sure, but I'd buy shag carpet and beaded curtains to make a bedroom. I'd burn incense, too, and leave a big space in the middle to practice dancing.

It's all a dream, though, unless I can get the cash together to make it happen, which means, unfortunately, that I have to get to work, pronto. I'm scheduled today from 1:30 p.m. until closing.

Thumping music sounds through the walls. At first I think it might be coming from a car driving by, but no. I recognize the Ramones. Hector is upstairs blaring "I Don't Wanna Go Down to the Basement" through my stereo. Any minute, somebody will complain. I turn to go, but I don't get far. Someone has followed me inside.

"Nooooora!" Sergio is holding a toolbox in one hand and a new toilet seat in the other. He checks me out from the doorway, lingering at my chest, and grins. "You looking for me, babe?"

"Absolutely not."

Even from here, I can smell him. His blue work jumpsuit reeks of cigarettes and BO, same as always.

"Come on, don't be like that."

"Like what? I'm late for work, Sergio." I head for the door, but he puts his arm out to block me. "Move," I say.

He doesn't budge. Instead, he leans toward me and croons along with the Ramones.

His smile reveals a piece of tobacco lodged near his gums. "Great song, right? But maybe you and me could go down to the basement instead, huh?"

I'm planning a well-executed shot to Sergio's nuts when Manny appears in the hall. For once, I am happy to see that man.

"You're not finished with the john yet?" he barks at Sergio. "I sent you over here half an hour ago."

Sergio plucks the thread of tobacco off his tongue. "Going." He winks at me and disappears inside.

Manny sighs. I'm pretty sure he can't stand Sergio either, but he's stuck with the boss's kid, I guess. Anyway, I try to slip away, but he stops me before I get too far.

"I've been looking for you," he says.

"I've been looking for you, too," I lie. "Mima has a check for you. I'll bring it by later."

He gives me a doubtful look. He's about to say something when the music seems to get even louder. The little veins in Manny's temple start to get pronounced, and I can see the familiar look of irritation forming. We have a permanent spot on Manny's shit list, after all. I've known it since we were really little. Nobody fools a kid's barometer when it comes to how adults really feel about them. He's one of those fussy supers. He barks at you for stupid stuff like stepping on his newly seeded grass or feeding burnt toast to the squirrels from the window. But Hector's antics get him completely undone, and I can't really say I'm surprised. Hector

53

once threw one of my metal roller skates off the fire escape. It missed Manny by mere inches, and, boy, was he mad.

I was too scared to tell Mima what happened. But that night, Manny rang our bell and gave it to her from the hall.

"Your son could have killed someone!" He held up the offending roller skate, now dented.

Mima slid her eyes to me in an accusation. I knew what she was thinking. It was my skate, so somehow it was partly my fault. I'd left it out, a temptation, maybe, the reason Hector had gotten the idea.

Naturally Mima didn't argue with Manny. To her, Manny, like every man in the world, is the boss.

"¡Ay qué vergüenza!" She told him how sorry she was, how ashamed. She pleaded her case. Boys were always getting into mischief, weren't they? She'd try to get him under control, but it was hard with no father around.

Hector and I were playing Clue on the floor. He pored over his cards and made a wild guess about Colonel Mustard in the library with the lead pipe. I scowled at him, angry that he'd gotten me in trouble. But then he crossed his eyes at me and farted—the long, pealing kind that you could hear all the way out in the hall. I couldn't help it; I started to laugh.

Anyway, since then, we've been marked.

Like right now.

"He's going to have to turn down that racket," he says. "It's disturbing the peace."

"No problem."

"And another thing, Nora. Remind your mother that the

54

first of the month will be here again in three weeks. I can't keep making allowances for people. I've been a nice guy long enough."

Nice guy? Really?

He walks past me in a huff and disappears into the apartment.

I hope Sergio and my other neighbors haven't been listening in, but who am I kidding? There aren't many things you can keep secret in a building, thanks to heat pipes, peepholes, and thin walls.

Sure enough, I don't go three steps when I hear a lock click open in the hall.

It's Stiller, Manny's archnemesis. Sometimes I swear she waits behind her peephole, itching to make an ambush.

"Hey, Nora." She's wearing a tie-dye shirt with a huge peace sign.

Mima has given me strict instructions not to talk to Stiller even though she is the head of the tenant association.

"How are you doing, Stiller?"

I don't know why Mima is so scared of her, but every time Stiller comes to our door, she makes me keep the chain on. Stiller always has to hand me her tenant petitions through the chain.

"I know that look," Mima whispers, as if we're surrounded by spies, a leftover from her last days in Cuba. "Communist, through and through." She points to what she considers irrefutable evidence: Stiller is black and nearly six feet tall. She supports feminism and wears a big 'fro. Mima informs me that women like Stiller "infiltrate" society, foment unrest, and before you know it—*wham-o!*—you're wearing gray and living as part of the evil Soviet empire.

Really, Stiller's just an activism junkie with a capital A, as in Anti-War, Anti-Imperialism, Anti-Misogyny, and so on. There's not a cause she won't defend if it means giving it to the establishment. And there's no cause she likes more than housing. Before she started demanding better windows this week, she was on a kick about "clandestine eviction tactics." She claims that building owners want to boot out tenants like us and turn these old places into luxury condos. "Only rich white cats will be able to live here one day; you'll see!"

I always think of the drafty halls, the roaches in the cellar, and the old glass doorknobs that break off in my hand if I turn them too hard. This place? A luxury condo? You'd have to be a miracle worker.

"A shame about Mrs. Murga, right?" she says. "But I know what's going on here. If we're not careful, Manny will jack up the rent in her unit. Don't worry, though. I'm doing some research on the limits."

"Oh."

Hector's music fills the hallway.

"I'm sorry," I tell Stiller, following her glance at the ceiling. "He likes this song, I guess."

Stiller waves her hand like the music doesn't matter. Then she steps into the hallway and makes sure Manny is out of earshot. She's no fan of Hector—no one in the building is—but she likes Manny even less.

"He can't harass tenants, you know," she says, towering over me. "Renters have rights in this city. Officially, it has to

56

be past nine p.m. to make a noise complaint." She checks her watch. "It is now one p.m., so you are well within your rights, honey." She leans even closer to me and glances over her shoulder again. "And in case you don't know, all tenants have until the tenth of the month to pay rent. After that, there's a whole *process* involved in collecting it, not just bullying teenagers in the hall. It pays to know your rights, Nora. I can help your mother fight if she needs me. I know some people."

Oh, boy. I don't have the heart to tell her that her pinko reputation has doomed that plan forever. Plus I'm a little embarrassed that she knows we were late on rent again and that she's talking about it, even though she means well.

Still, it *is* kind of comforting to hear someone offer to stand up for us. I wonder what would happen if Manny ever showed up at Stiller's door to complain about something. I'll bet he'd lose some teeth; Stiller takes absolutely no shit. Even funnier to imagine: What if Mima could be turned into a badass like Stiller? What if she grew her hair and told Manny to stop harassing her kids or she'd feed him his balls for dinner, the way he deserves?

It's the stuff of dreams.

Just then, Sergio comes back into the hall, whistling and checking me out again. Stiller whips around and impales him with one of her cold stares. She couldn't care less who his father is. In fact, it might make her loathe him more.

"Is there a problem with your eyes, son?" she snaps. "Because I *know* you would not be disrespecting a woman and objectifying her in my presence."

Sergio slinks out the lobby doors without a word. I grin and turn on my heel.

"You might want to have a word with those painters, too, Stiller." I point to the van outside at the curb.

She smiles brightly as I dash up the stairs.

"I might just say hello," she says.

Chapter 6

"Turn it down!" I shout, but Hector doesn't even look up. The music is practically rattling the walls, but he's hunched over the Cyclo-Teacher, deaf to the world around him.

Strangely, this contraption has become one of my brother's inner-weirdo passions, along with Hulk Hogan Marvel Comics and Bruce Lee movies, all the remaining shreds of himself as a boy.

It never fails to surprise me. It's one of those self-test learning kits that came as a bonus gift with the set of *World Book* encyclopedias that Mima bought on installments from Edna's niece.

Don't ask me how, but Hector is a whiz at the Cyclo-Teacher and all its questions. He opens the circular lid on the machine and loads the question sheets inside just like an LP on a turntable. Then he closes it and advances through each question that appears in the window when he slides the lever. He almost never gets anything wrong, which makes me think he actually reads the encyclopedia while we're sleeping. Who does that—and why? He can name the African countries and every abbreviation for elements. He knows about Pompeii and the history of the Incas, the difference between mollusks and crustaceans. You name it; if you can find it in the encyclopedia, he knows it. All that meaningless information should make school a breeze. But no. Hector hates school even more than I do. He says it's for idiots.

What's worse, though, is that Hector likes to wield what he knows like a weapon. He's always quizzing Mima and me on random facts and pronouncing us morons when we don't know the name of a tsarina—or if we don't care.

"How could you be so dumb?" he asked me last week when—imagine it!—I couldn't name all the moons of Jupiter. I got as far as Io, Europa, Ganymede, and Callisto, just to shut him up. I thought I was doing pretty good, since I haven't taken Earth Science since the ninth grade. "There are more than four?" I asked.

"They're discovering more by the day, idiot," he told me, a satisfied grin on his face. "It's called space exploration, moron."

Anyway, he's still deep in concentration when I walk over and pull the needle off the LP.

"Manny complained about the music," I tell him when he glowers at me. "You can hear this shit down the block."

No reply.

"What are you doing home again?" I ask him in the sudden quiet. "Friedmor is looking for you, by the way."

He moves the lever and smiles at his answer. "Dying of

consumption." Then he looks up. "Do you even know what that is, Nora?"

"You don't have TB, Hector." Ha. Got him.

He hacks up phlegm on a rattling cough. Mima's probably right when she says he needs medicine, but there's no use trying to get Hector to the doctor. He hates them, especially our pediatrician. He calls Dr. De Los Santos "the fucking Chilean quack."

I toss my jacket on the chair and head to the kitchen, starved. But when I open the refrigerator, I see that we still have limited options: one egg, grape jelly, and two individually wrapped slices of cheese that are hard and orange at the corners. Mima never goes grocery shopping if she hasn't paid the rent. She'd rather us starve, I guess. Papi's check better come soon.

Music starts up again. This time it's Pink Floyd. A heartbeat, followed by voices, clangs, and evil laughter starts up on the track. Perfect for a drug trip, I suppose. I grab a cheese slice, break off the hard part, and head back to the living room.

"Hands off," Hector warns, his eyes still glued to the Cyclo-Teacher.

That's when I notice the ashtray near the speakers. Six of Hector's Marlboro butts are in there, but there's also a different kind. Unfiltered Camels.

Well, well. He's had company.

I turn back to Hector. "What did Sergio want?" I ask.

No reply. Just the trippy sounds of Pink Floyd's guitars floating from the speakers. I turn down the volume.

"What did he want?" I say again.

Hector looks up and cocks his head. "You a frickin' reporter or what? Turn the music back up."

"Why was he up here, Hector?"

He tosses away the Cyclo-Teacher and comes close. Hector has gotten bearlike and hairy, and my heart starts to race a little. I've been taller than him most of my life, but now I only reach his nose. I try my best to look bored, unworried, but the truth is, all this new size is kind of imposing.

"I borrowed some albums," he says. "He came to get them back. Not that it's any of your business." Then he walks down the hall to the bathroom.

Fact: I haven't noticed any new albums in the small piles we keep lying around. And I would know: I'm always stuck picking them up.

Sergio in our apartment. That might be worse than the time we had a rat roaming inside the walls last year. All night long, I'd listen to the scratching. In the morning, there were droppings inside my shoes, and the edge of the linoleum was gnawed down. No matter how many times I took a shower, I could feel rodent germs all over me. At night, I could feel beady eyes staring at me from the corner.

My stomach rumbles loudly. I have to do something about food. I turn up the stereo and sneak past the bathroom door so Hector won't hear me go to our room. Then I crawl into the back of our closet, where I keep my money boot. A tight roll of bills is jammed inside the toe. It's smaller than I'd like, but what can I do? Stuff like this comes up all the time. I'm starved and there's nothing to eat. I stick a few bills into my pocket and start to crawl back over the old shoes and coats.

My knee hits something hard, though. I dig around in the dim light and pull something free.

Even in this bad light, I can see it's an old transistor radio. We don't own one like this, but it looks kind of familiar. Whose is it?

Then I think of Mrs. Murga, and my mind starts to race. She kept a radio on her kitchen window, and it looked an awful lot like this one. Please, God, don't let this be her radio. If it is, I can't think of a single innocent scenario that could have gotten this here.

Just then, the closet door clicks closed, and I'm in complete blackness. I push against the door, but I already know that I've fallen into a snare. Hector is on the other side.

I try my best not to sound freaked out, even though it's already feeling stuffy in here.

"Let me out, Hector. I have to get to work."

"Please?" he says.

"Please." I push again, but he's still against the door.

"What's in there, Nora?"

Does he mean my money boot? Or is he worried I've found the radio?

Either way is bad.

"Clothes, what else?" I say, playing dumb. "Open the door and see for yourself." I wait for a few seconds, trying to stay calm, but the door stays closed. Then I hear the *flick* and *click* of his lighter on the other side. I get very still.

"Is it dark in there?" he finally asks.

"Open up the damn door." I push with all my might now, beads of sweat on my lip, but he' leaning up against it tight.

"You keep secrets in there, Nora?"

I keep my eye on the line of light coming in under the door.

"You can't keep secrets in a four-room apartment, Hector," I say. "Don't be stupid."

"Who's stupid?" His voice has an edge I don't like.

Stupid was too strong. I can practically hear Mima's whispers. "Stay on his good side," she always says. "Don't start trouble. Don't provoke him."

I close my eyes, thinking. After a few minutes of stand-off, I shove the radio back where I found it and cover it with clothes. *I've never seen this,* I tell myself, trying not to imagine him prying open Mrs. Murga's window, creeping around her as she slept. "Let me out," I say. "I'm on at Sal's today. I'll get us some food. Pop-Tarts, if you want."

What do you know? The way to a man's heart— especially if it's tiny and vicious—is still through his stomach after all. Just like that, the door flies open and I tumble out, blinking into the brightness. Hector takes one look at me, and he starts laughing.

I grab my jacket and head out the door, fuming.

Hector follows me down the stairs, though I'm trying to outpace him.

"What are you running from?" he asks, grinning.

I turn and stab him in the chest with my finger. "I'm not running from anything." I can see the pustules near his hairline, the stubble rising on his chin. "But do us both a favor. Keep your mouth shut at Sal's. And *don't* steal anything."

Chapter 7

Salerno's Delicatessen is on 162nd Street, just a few blocks away. I've been a cashier there since I got my working papers the summer I was fourteen. It's not a bad gig, if you can make change in your head and don't mind small talk with customers. Besides, Sal has a soft spot for me, always giving me extra hours if I ask for them and sending a little food my way—the end of a hard salami, an "over-order" of Vienna sausage. He even cut Hector slack on my account once. He caught him swiping candy bars, but he didn't chase him out or threaten to break his fingers the way you'd expect.

Hector and I walk up the street together, but I'm ignoring him, still mad. I wave at the bakery lady as she slides a new tray of cookies in the window and then at Mr. Farina, who owns the corner drugstore. He's filled people's prescriptions around here for as long as anyone can remember, and he can pretty much save you a trip to the doctor if you're sick. Farina's is the old-timey kind of drugstore, too, the kind that used to have a soda fountain. He's even got a picture of the place in 1939 when he bought it, at the start of the war. Anyway, since he's Sal's favorite Mets sparring partner, Mr. Farina comes by every afternoon while his delivery boy, Matt, cleans up. He likes the coffee and good arguments, he says. He'll be due any minute.

Just as I'm about to dart into Sal's, I notice Sergio's car outside the Satin Lady Lounge, as usual. I already know there are a few losers nursing beers inside and waiting for Sergio or somebody else to make the rounds with their wares.

I throw open Sal's door and step inside.

"Uh-oh. Double trouble," Sal says when he sees us.

"Hello to you, too."

Sal's laugh fills the room. He's a giant guy with bushy eyebrows and anchor tattoos on his forearms from his days in the navy. He's got a bum leg and blown-out hearing from the Korean War, but *nobody* messes with Sal. He's got a bit of a rep, built with the help of an old golf driver he keeps behind the counter. Even Sergio knows not to park anywhere near the deli's front door. Not ever.

"Finally warming up out there?" He's at the slicer, a Mets sweatshirt under his bloodstained apron.

"Thinner, please." A lady at the counter frowns at the turkey slice Sal holds up for inspection.

He purses his lips. "Any thinner and it's gonna break apart, lady, but if you wanna be stingy, what can I say? I'm glad it's not my sandwich." He hands the fat slice across the counter to me and readjusts the blade. *"Mangia."*

Hector settles himself on the edge of the produce bins to watch the delivery guys. They're wheeling hand trucks loaded with merchandise to the sidewalk vault below. When he was little, Hector used to say that dragons lived down there and they were going to burn all of Queens with their fiery breath. Ever the sweet growing boy, he just got darker with his fascination. He read all he could about sidewalk vaults and told me about a 1902 murder. Cops investigating a terrible smell had crawled into the sidewalk vault at the Empire Garden Cafe on 29th Street and found what? A human head roasting in the furnace.

Obviously I don't go down there if I can help it.

I walk to the back of the store to get my work apron off the old meat hooks Sal recycled into a coatrack. On my way back, I pull a half gallon of milk from the refrigerated case and a box of strawberry Pop-Tarts. There are lots of other things I'd like to grab, but I'm out of hands — and money. Twinkies would be nice, some Oreos maybe. All the stuff Mima almost never splurges for. It's not that she's on a high horse about junk food or sugar. She's from Cuba, after all, so sugar is practically its own essential food group. It's more that she just can't seem to get the hang of American food in general. We eat strange approximations of everything. Our hamburgers have olives in the patties. Instead of pancakes and syrup, she makes us cornmeal *buñuelitos* with honey. Even if we could convince her to make a cake from a Betty Crocker mix like Mrs. MacInerney, she'd probably frost it with that egg-white merengue that hardens to plaster. Jeez. You could chip a tooth. Is it too much to dream of a bologna sandwich on Wonder bread?

When I get to the register, I find Hector reaching into the pickle jar that Sal keeps on the counter.

"Use the tongs," I tell him.

The register is still locked and unmanned, so I dump my stuff and lift the hinged door in the counter to step behind it. "Where's Annemarie?" That's Sal's wife. She works the register when I'm not around.

"Working the dungeon," he says. That's what they call the sidewalk vault. He holds up sliced Muenster for the customer's review. "The new guy started today."

"Not a moment too soon," I say. The only other employee they have is a part-time stock guy, but the last one recently quit for a job pumping gas. The floor has gotten filthy with sawdust and mud. Unpacked fruit crates crowd aisle one, and the cans on the shelves are looking furry with dust. I don't mind standing for hours at the register, but I hate cleaning. Absolutely none of Mima's need for scrubbing has rubbed off on me. I don't see the point, really. This is an old brick building, like all the others on the block. No matter how much we scrub, the deli always looks dingy. Sal agrees, but he insists that a little dirt gives the place charm.

I total my bill. When the cash door springs open, Hector wiggles his eyebrows at the sight of the money inside. He also opens his jacket quickly to show me two apples he just swiped. I put in the money I owe—plus another buck for the fruit—and slam the drawer shut.

"Go home," I whisper, and then signal to the lady behind him. "You're next?"

Hector starts to light a cigarette on his way out.

"No smoking, pal," Sal says. "But hold on a minute." He wraps the end of the cheese in white paper and ties it with string. "It's too skinny to push through the blade with my big mitts," he says without looking up. "Stupid to waste food."

Or so he says.

"You staying outta trouble?" he asks.

My brother shrugs and grins. "Define 'trouble.'"

Sal leans across the top of the meat case and hands over the cheese. "Oh, a *fannullone*. What you need is a job, Mr. Wonderful. Work makes the man. Remember that."

I finish ringing up my customer. Hector? A job? Ha! He'd have to follow directions, do what he's told.

"Look at me," Sal continues. "I've been working since I was ten. Delivered papers all over the place. Now look at me!" He rubs his fingers together to mean money. "*Il dinaro.* A good honest living will make you irresistible to the ladies."

Hector snorts and tucks the cheese under his arm like a football. He blows out without so much as a thank-you.

"Who's irresistible to the ladies?" Annemarie comes through the door out of breath. She's a round lady with a head of red hair and two gold teeth. The new stock guy trails her with two soggy cartons of produce stacked in his arms. Only the top of his head shows over the load he's carrying.

"The lettuce bins are on the left," Annemarie tells him. "Cut off any brown leaves first. Rot spreads fast. Wait: You'll need the knife." She pats my cheeks and points at the bucket of tools we keep under the register. "How are you, Nora, sweetie? Hand us that blade, would you?"

I don't have a chance. All at once, the bottom of one of the cartons breaks open, and a dozen heads of iceberg lettuce go rolling across the floor in every direction. Just as the

70

stock boy tries to catch them, the second carton spills from his arms, too.

"Oh, man," he says, scrambling to pick them up. "Sorry!"

I stare stupidly—and not just at the mess.

Is this a mirage? Our old stock guy, Norman, had warts. This guy is about my age, a little older. Olive skin, a perfect DA haircut.

"*Fuori di testa!*" Sal thunders. "Anybody around here ever hear of a hand truck?"

"Well, if we could *find* one in that mess down there, we would have used it! When are you going to throw out all that scrap wood?" Annemarie quips.

"Yeah, in all my spare time!"

I step from behind the counter and start gathering lettuces while Sal and Annemarie argue.

"Thanks," the new guy says. "I don't know how I did that."

"Those boxes are pretty flimsy when they're wet." I try not to gawk at him, but my heart is already thumping.

"I'm Paulie," he says.

"Nora." I hand over a muddy lettuce. "Leonora, actually, but Nora is fine. It's like the last part of my name and not so ugly. It's Spanish." My God, why is my mouth firing off on its own?

He grins. "That's funny."

My cheeks feel hot; my tongue is suddenly thick in my mouth. "Leonora. I know. I hate it. Ha. What a name." *Stop talking!*

"No, no. I mean, I'm not really Paulie," he says. "It's actually Pablo."

71

I stop and look at him. The same way Papi went from Fico to Rick?

"Where are you from?" I ask.

"I live over in Hollis, but we're from Colombia, if that's what you mean." He says *Colombia* in knee-buckling, perfect *español*. Right there, I know I'll never call him Paulie.

My mind races. What do I know about Colombia? Nothing, except that it's at the top of South America. Oh, Cyclo-Teacher, where are you?

"How about you?" he asks.

"Soy cubana," I finally say. And then because we both stand there with nothing else to say, I point to the ground. "There's more under there."

We stoop under the counter to reach for the last of the spill. It's close quarters in here, which is kind of awkward, but holy *God*, I can feel the electricity. He smells so nice, like Irish Spring, I think. And when he reaches for an escaped lettuce, I stare at his biceps, too. They're on full display inside a green T-shirt that reads ELÉPHAS across the chest.

"You dance there?" I manage to ask. Eléphas is a new disco in Bayside. Everybody talks about it, but I haven't gone. It gets crowded, so they're picky some nights and check IDs.

He looks down and shrugs. "Sometimes. My buddy Ralph picks up hours as one of the bouncers. Thursday is free T-shirt night, so I have one of these in every color. It's a cheap way to get a wardrobe, I guess."

My head is a spinning disco ball. *He's a dancer.*

"I haven't seen you there," he says.

My stomach plunges. "Oh, it's been on my list," I say, trying not to sound like the pathetic high-school kid that I am.

"Come when Jimmy Yu is deejaying," he says. "He mixes Latin in. I'll find out when he's coming next if you want." He smiles and stares right at me.

Oh. Oh. Oh.

Suddenly Sal peers under the counter. He looks from Pablo to me with that knowing look of his.

"You're not going make me regret hiring you, are you, Paulie?"

"Absolutely not, sir." Pablo climbs out in a hurry and brushes the sawdust from his pants. The counter is crowded with the lettuces we rescued.

"Go rinse those in the back sink and tear off the dirty leaves," Sal says. "Dry them good when you're done."

Pablo turns to me before he goes. "Um, do you mind, Nora?" he says.

That's when I realize that I'm clutching two heads of lettuce to my chest like veggie boobs. I hand them over and hold my breath as he makes his way down the aisle. Thelma Houston is singing "Don't Leave Me This Way" in my head again. I see Pablo and me spinning in a hustle.

Sal clears his throat and crosses his arms.

"What?" I step behind the register, trying not to look at him. "I was just helping."

Chapter 8

As much as I'd like to go out with Pablo, I might have to give it a second thought.

The ballistics tests for the Forest Hills shooting are finally back, and our fine friends at the NYPD have no choice but to publicly admit the worst.

The same gun killed both girls in Forest Hills, but it's also the same one that paralyzed the girl in Bellerose, too. They've linked it to the bullets sprayed into the car with the detective's daughter and even to a girl who got shot through the neck and killed in the Bronx last summer.

I can't stop reading the gory articles in the paper, my stomach squeezing nervously. Murders are nothing new in New York, but a serial killer is scary, even by our standards. The cops are asking for witnesses. Teary neighbors remember the girls, and even psychics are giving theories. Worse, there's a psychiatrist who pointed out that the victims are "romantically active girls with long dark hair," as though something about brunettes in love draws murder.

I stare at the picture of a Bulldog .44 revolver in the paper for a long time. It has muzzle flash, they say, and huge recoil. Only someone who has been trained to shoot can really handle it well.

I put down the paper, wondering. The shooter could be a veteran, or even a cop, somebody you'd never suspect. He could just wander up my street, looking ordinary.

"Scared?"

I jump at Hector's voice. He leans over the newspaper I'm reading.

"No."

"Liar," he says slyly. "You could be next, you know. All that silky hair." He rakes his fingers through my hair, snagging on a tangle.

"Ow!" I shoot him an ugly look. "Stop."

He laughs and goes off to rifle through the refrigerator for breakfast.

"There's no fucking food," he says.

I put my dishes in the sink and run the water. I have to be at Kathleen's in five minutes. "It's your own fault for eating all the Pop-Tarts in one sitting," I say. "Guess you're out of luck."

I'm soaping the sponge when something whizzes right by my head. There's a loud smack against the wall to my left, and I feel something wet on the back of my shirt. I turn to see an egg dripping down the wall. Bits of yolk and shell have splashed all over me.

"What the hell, Hector!" I hiss, trying not to wake Mima. "What was that for?"

He grins at me. "Better pay attention, Nora," he says. "You never know when someone might be taking aim at you."

Kathleen, her mom, and Stiller are already waiting for me when I come jogging up to their stoop. Boxes, rolled banners, and clipboards are piled around them.

Kathleen takes one look at me. "I see you read the paper this morning, too." She gives me a knowing glance. "Not a bad idea to cover up your dark hair."

I adjust my bandanna, but I don't tell her I'm mostly just covering the egg splash.

"No gruesome talk today," Mrs. MacInerney tells her. "Today isn't about murderers. It's about empowerment."

We're heading to the Women's Day march in the city. Mrs. MacInerney is on the planning committee, so naturally we got roped in. It's a nice day, so I don't mind the idea of trekking from Herald Square to Union Square. Besides, it's much better than our last volunteer assignment: a phone-a-thon in support of the Equal Rights Amendment. *God.* I'm all for liberation, but it sucks to spend four hours having people hang up on you.

Stiller stands up and leans the banner over her shoulder like a bayonet. She's got blue glitter in her hair, and her entire shirt is covered in slogan buttons. LIBERTY, EQUALITY, SISTERHOOD. THERE CAN BE NO FREE MEN UNTIL THERE ARE FREE WOMEN. BLACK POWER. ERA WON'T GO AWAY. REPRODUCTIVE RIGHTS!

She and Mrs. MacInerney have been pals since they met

76

at Hunter College when Mrs. MacInerney was working as a secretary. Stiller helped organize a sit-in to demand a Black and Puerto Rican Studies department. "I would have liked to hate her," Stiller always says. "But Mary kept bringing us coffee and doughnuts to keep up our spirits."

Mrs. MacInerney hands me a box of flyers. "Let's get moving, or we'll be late."

I wonder what Mima would say if she could see me here with all these "agitators." She thinks I'm working on an English paper with Kathleen all day, but here I am about to be part of one of those demonstrations she hates. Mima doesn't get feminists at all. In fact, she says they're lunatics. Who wouldn't want a good man to take care of them, she wants to know.

Interestingly, none of the volunteers that are already gathered look particularly insane to me—except maybe the weird kid who is actually wearing a costume for the occasion. Her hair is pinned up, and she's wearing a high-collared blouse and a long skirt with a bustle made out of crumpled newspaper. She's trying to look like one of the girls who burned to death at the Triangle Shirtwaist Factory in 1911. It's a little over-the-top, if you ask me, but I'll give her points for morbid creativity. We're marching to the spot where 146 women and girls died in a fire thanks to crappy work conditions, after all.

I'm not the only one who notices her, of course. A reporter wanders among the crowd and zeroes in on her right away.

"Why did you come today?" the reporter asks her.

Kathleen and I are standing close enough to eavesdrop on their conversation.

"The girls at my school are only interested in boys and makeup," the kid says. "They'll be women one day, and then they'll understand why they should have been here."

Kathleen rolls her eyes.

"What's wrong?" I ask.

"She looks like she's twelve. You think she really knows what she's doing here? Can she really know what reproductive rights are?"

I glance over at the girl. "Well, do we know much more?"

Kathleen loses steam and gives me a guilty look. "You think we suck as feminists?" she whispers to me. "We *do* argue about Wella Balsam versus Prell."

"That doesn't make us Mrs. Shoo-Flies," I point out. Phyllis Schlafly is public enemy number one at Kathleen's house. She's always on TV making speeches about God's true plan for women as homemakers.

"True," Kathleen says.

We wander to the display tables, where they're taking sign-ups for the first *national* women's conference being planned in Houston this summer. All the former first ladies will be there, and Battling Bella Abzug is going to preside. I've already heard Stiller and Mrs. MacInerney arguing about it. Kathleen's mom is sure it will be the Big Feminist Kahuna to end oppression. Stiller says she wants to see the needs of black women included or she won't go. "Being oppressed as a woman is just one way of being held down, Mary," she said.

I jot down my name on the sign-up sheet and then thumb through a women's "herstory" calendar while I wait for Kathleen to sign up, too. I check tomorrow's celebration. March 13 is the day Susan B. Anthony died. Sixty years of fighting for it, and she never saw women get the right to vote. I'll be thinking of you when I pull the voting lever in November, Sue.

"All right, girls. Time to get busy." Mrs. MacInerney appears with our volunteer badges and the agendas. She points across the street. "I need you to give these out at the entrance to the subway and point people in this direction," she says.

I glance at the flyer to see what's in store. The president of the National Organization for Women. Someone named Carmen Vivian Rivera talking about forced sterilizations of women. Somebody else on women's literacy in the Third World.

My brain hurts, and no one has even said a word yet. Not that I can say so. Kathleen is smart, but Mrs. MacInerney reads the *New York Times* from the first page to the last and finds it relaxing to pick apart stuff like President Carter's crappy gas policy and whether it's the labor unions or the banks that are killing New York City. Kathleen sometimes resorts to a silent recitation of the names of her nail-polish colors to counterbalance the heft. *Optimistic, BoingBoing, FlowerPower* . . .

"No window shopping," Mrs. MacInerney warns Kathleen. She knows we'll be standing dangerously close to

79

Macy's front-window display. "This is more important, you hear me?"

"Roger, captain." Kathleen salutes and turns on her heel.

At first, we have only a few stragglers, so Kathleen and I have a chance to talk about less pressing matters than the state of the world for women.

"There's a new guy at work," I tell her.

She gives me a sly grin. "Details . . . ?"

"His name is Pablo. Adorable."

"Are you going to make a move?"

"I just met him yesterday."

"So? We're liberated, remember?"

"We're also good targets for a psycho who hates girls and their boyfriends. At least *I* am, remember?" I rub my hand along my bandanna.

She purses her lips. "Why don't we dye your hair? You'd be a *va-voom* redhead."

I give her a pained look. "Or I can just lie low until the cops catch the shooter. How long can it take? The whole city is looking for him."

"I don't know, Nora. They never caught Jack the Ripper, you know," she says.

"Oh, thank you very much."

A train pulls into the station beneath us, and a large group of women climbs the steps in our direction.

"More on this matter later," Kathleen tells me. Then we get to work.

Before I know it, an hour has flown by and we're out of

handouts. Across the street, a surprisingly huge crowd has gathered, some with handmade ERA NOW signs. There are hippies and business-looking types, women who look kind of like guys, others who could be models, and still more who look ordinary, even like Mima. My favorite is a group of older ladies in sneakers and visors, sporting T-shirts over their jackets that read THE GRAY PANTHERS.

It's a thousand people at least. Normally, I hate crowds. Even walking in the hall at school makes me feel uncomfortable. But this feels exciting somehow, like a party.

Kathleen checks her watch and signals to me. "It's starting," she says. We link arms and dart back across the street.

We're jostled around as we try to find a spot. At this rate, we'll be at the very back.

Suddenly a hand reaches out for me, and I'm yanked inside the throng.

"Whoa!"

Stiller has dragged us into her row. She's holding a banner with a few other women.

"Make room," she orders, and I swear, it's like the parting of the Red Sea. Kathleen and I take our spots.

A chant rises from somewhere behind me.

A woman's place is everyplace! A woman's place is everyplace!

It will be an hour's walk, but the energy in the crowd is contagious. Kathleen and I chant at the top of our voices and pump our fists in the air. There's a power and an energy that feels like we're giving the man's world the finger. I like it.

And then, as one, the mass starts to move.

Chapter 9

"Well, look at you!" Annemarie steps away from the cash register and gives me the once-over when I get to work. "What's the occasion?"

I blush. Okay, so I'm wearing my Sasson jeans and my favorite Huckapoo shirt, the brown and orange one with the good collar. Kathleen coached me this week. She says polyester "accentuates the positive." I took a risk of attracting the killer and wore my hair down. I know it's stupid, but Pablo is on today. I checked the schedule.

"I just felt like looking nice," I say. "It's the first day of spring."

She purses her lips and gives me a knowing look. "I see," she says, glancing across at Sal. "I remember looking nice for spring once, too. Right, old man?"

Sal starts whistling, and his cheeks go bright red.

I step behind the register. Old people are weird.

Pablo works with a feather duster tucked into the back pocket of his Calvin Kleins. When he walks, it looks like a delicious rooster tail. I have to force myself to look away when he lifts the bags of cat litter onto the shelves, too. All I can think about is how nice it would feel to be wrapped inside those arms, dancing at Eléphas, hot and sweaty.

Not that Pablo notices my outfit or anything else. He doesn't have time, for one thing. Sal is working him to death. He made Pablo reshelve the pantry in the dungeon, mop all the floors, clear out the loading dock, and stack oranges, which is harder than it looks. And all that was in the morning. It's two o'clock before Pablo comes to the front of the store.

"Is it break time, sir?"

"Break?" Sal roars. "Whaddaya think this is?" He turns to me and winks. "Right, Nora?"

I think I'm going to faint. Pablo is sweaty around the collar of his blue T-shirt, and it's glorious. "Give him a break. He should eat," I say.

Sal smiles wide and pops open a couple of Cokes. Then he hands each of us a soda and half a ham-and-cheese hero over the counter. "Here you go, kids. You've earned it."

Pablo grabs a stool and pulls it up to my register counter.

"How's it going?" he asks me before taking a long sip.

I stare at his Adam's apple as he swallows. Every word I know goes flying from my mind. "Same old," I say. Pathetic.

"Those your wheels out there, Paulie?" Sal asks. He motions to a blue Camaro parked at the curb.

"Yeah."

Sal steps from behind the counter to get a better look. "A 'seventy-five?"

"'Seventy-three."

Sal whistles. "She's a beauty, but it's a bumpy ride for my taste. You want *real* luxury, try a Caddy. A Coupe de Ville!"

"I'll need a raise, then, sir."

Sal gives him a withering look. "You're dreaming."

"Actually, my friend Ralph has one," Pablo adds, smiling. "Girls like it. They always want to ride in it, anyway."

"A lovemobile!" Sal says, wiggling his eyebrows.

Pablo grins and takes a swig. "Pretty much."

Mercy. Don't let me swoon.

But soon they forget all about me.

I pretend to read the paper as they blab on and on about muscle cars until my ears bleed. I decide to use the time for reconnaissance. Careful eavesdropping reveals the following juicy tidbit: Pablo is a sophomore at St. John's. A college man.

Before I can glean much else, Pablo's break time is up.

"See you later." He leaves his empty soda can on my counter and goes to the back of the store to check the mousetraps.

Who am I kidding? I think as I watch his feather duster wiggle away. He's too old, or else he's got a girlfriend. He's definitely not interested.

It may be spring, but it's still dark at closing time.

My feet hurt from standing in nice shoes all day, so I decide to ride the bus one stop and get off at my corner.

Nobody else is at the stop when I get there, and I'm wary

of standing out here alone. On a scale of one to ten, how tempting to a serial killer is a girl with long dark hair all alone at a bus stop? Crap. An eleven. I rummage in my purse for a ponytail holder or even a stray rubber band to pull up my hair. Every pair of headlights that goes by makes my heart race a little as I search inside every pocket and still come up empty. Finally, I tuck my hair into the back of my shirt as best I can. Maybe I should just run home and be done with it.

I'm about to make a break for it when a car turns the corner and pulls close to me. I flinch and take a step back before I realize it's Pablo's Camaro.

"I thought that was you," he says, leaning over to talk to me through the window. "Need a ride home? I don't mind."

Look calm, I tell myself, but my hands are still shaking.

Mima's voice is stuck in my head. *Muchachas decentes* never get into cars with boys, unless they're engaged. *La gente* will talk, she always says, although what "people" she means, I will never know. Who would be sitting in a window watching my romantic moves except a perv?

Sorry, Mima.

I open the door and slide in beside him. "Thanks."

He checks his mirrors and pulls out. "Well, *that* was a beating." Pablo laughs. His fingers are still pruny from handling the mop. "Did he work the last guy like this?"

I shake my head. "He's trying to break you. Sal has weird navy ideas."

For once, I wish I lived really far from work. In fact, it

might be nice to have a small car wreck or something, just to keep us here. Otherwise, the four-block ride is going to be over in exactly three minutes.

I notice textbooks tossed at my feet. *The Tools for Good Business, Intermediate Accounting.*

"You can move those if they're in the way," he says.

"I'm fine," I say. "Accounting, huh? You like it?"

He laughs. "Not really. But I can't think of anything else. What's your major?"

I don't know what to say for a second. Why didn't I anticipate this? I'm so grateful to be in a dark car because it absolutely kills me to tell him. "I'm not in college. I go to Francis Lewis High, but I'm a senior. Only fifty school days left, minus weekends. Not that I'm counting."

He looks a little surprised, but nods anyway. "I got sick of high school at the end, too."

"Where did you go?" I ask.

"The Hirsch School. My dad is the Spanish teacher there. *Señorrr* Ruiz." He says the name with a fake American accent and smiles.

I know the place. It's over in Little Neck. The girls wear blazers with embroidered lions on their breast pockets and plaid skirts that they hike up short as soon as they get on the bus.

"Fancy place," I say.

Pablo shrugs. "I was a teacher's kid, so I got a deal on tuition," he says. "Where will you go in the fall?"

"Not sure." I'm glad he can't see me blushing. I point at the corner. "It's here on the right."

86

Pablo pulls over. "Wow. Look at that dog!"

I turn to see my favorite mutt sniffing around for a place to dump. I'm so used to seeing his three legs that I forget it's unusual.

"That's Tripod," I say.

"He's yours?"

I shake my head. "He's just a stray, but he's been around forever. We all feed him. He's everybody's dog, more or less."

Suddenly the door to my building opens, and Tripod makes a bunny-hop dash for the walkway, probably trying to sneak in for the night.

Oh, no.

Hector.

Pausing on the stoop, he cups his hands over his cigarette to light up.

My hand is frozen on the door. Do I get out?

"You okay?" Pablo asks.

"Oh, fine." I've dropped my hands in my lap and turned back to face him. Maybe Hector won't notice me in here. The last thing I need is to have him mention to Mima that I was in a car with a member of the penis-carrying gender. In fact, I have a strict policy never to let Mima find out *any-thing* about my love life. Who has the energy to deal with all it would mean? I'd have to answer questions about my possible smuttiness. Who is this boy? Where were we going? Do I remember the girl down the street, the one who got pregnant a few years ago? Do I know you can eventually go blind from syphilis?

No, señor, I cannot have it.

"Why don't we drive around the block?" I suggest.

Pablo gives me a funny look. "I'm meeting friends in a while . . ."

Of course he is. Friends who are in college and hang out at Eléphas and other cool places. Not friends who are high-school cashiers.

I swallow hard and grab the handle again. Tripod is at Hector's feet now, barking in excitement. Maybe he's expecting Cheetos or some other crap we feed him occasionally. But in all his frenzy, Tripod tangles himself in my brother's feet instead.

In a flash, Hector kicks him hard in the ribs and sends him flying through the air. I hold my breath as the terrier's back curls awkwardly. Tripod yelps and lands with a thud before dashing into the bushes for cover.

"Did you see that? What an asshole," Pablo mutters.

Just then, Hector looks up and spots me in the car.

"Thanks for the ride." I jump out and hurry for the lobby, ignoring Hector completely as we pass each other. I don't look back, praying that Hector doesn't speak to me, that Pablo doesn't make the connection at all.

And it works. Pablo watches for a second and then pulls away into the dark.

All night, I'm thinking about Pablo with his friends. But Hector crowds my thinking, too. Did Tripod bite him without my noticing? Otherwise, there's no reason for Hector to have slammed that old dog in the ribs. Why else would someone do that?

I tuck Mima's transistor radio under my pillow so I can listen without waking her. I hum along to "Love Rollercoaster" by the Ohio Players, my stomach pitching at the thought of Pablo at Eléphas, dancing with some college girl, having fun.

It's really late when I hear Hector's keys in the door. The springs on his bed squeak as he drops. I mean to ask him something about Tripod, but I don't have the energy, or maybe I just don't want to know.

"Don't tell Mima," I mumble, but he doesn't reply.

And then I'm fast asleep.

Chapter 10

"A stone-cold Latin fox," Kathleen concludes. She drops the needle on her new Parliament album. "Give Up the Funk" starts to play. "I can't believe I'm going to say this: He might even be better than Freddie Prinze, God rest his soul."

"Sacrilege, but you may be right."

We're in her room practicing the bump. Anybody can touch hips in time to the music, but to spin and backbend like a *Soul Train* line dancer, you've gotta have funk.

She turns up the volume and starts moving to the beat.

I've told Kathleen about Pablo, but she's been too busy with work and getting to know Eddie to come see him. Today she finally stopped by Sal's after school. I was off, so I waited down the block at Farina's while she bought a gallon of milk and checked out Pablo for herself.

"The question is"—she spins and bumps her hip to my shoulder as I move in time—"is he interested in *you*?"

The train rumbles by outside, and the vibrations make the needle skip, ruining our groove.

I throw myself on the bed in a sweaty heap as Kathleen turns off the music.

"Like I said: He gave me a ride home last night, but I think he was just being nice. He said he had to go meet friends, blah-blah."

Kathleen lies down beside me and stares at the ceiling. "What you need to do, then, is snag his imagination," she says. "Get him to notice what is right under his nose."

"Okaaaay . . ." She's dangerous when she's plotting.

"Right now, Pablo thinks of you as Cashier Nora. High-School Nora. Little-Kid Nora. He needs to think of you as I-Really-Want-to-Date-Her Nora. *La-Chica-Mucho-Sexy* Nora."

I blink. "*Muy. Muy* sexy." Three years of high-school Spanish have meant nothing to this girl.

She ignores me. "He has a Camaro," she says.

"Yes."

"So, he likes cars."

"Looks that way."

She turns on her belly and gives me a wicked grin. "Then I have the perfect idea."

When we were little, Kathleen and I liked to go to Adventurers Inn over by the Whitestone Parkway. It was nice then, not the shell of rusted arcade games and homeless guys that it is now. Her dad would drive us over and sit on the bench eating ice cream while we stood in line for the Flight to Mars. Our favorite ride was always the bumper cars, though. We loved nothing more than to ram everyone in our path.

I'm thinking about all those head-on collisions as we

unlock the MacInerneys' Chevy Impala. I slide behind the wheel nervously and take a deep breath. Kathleen is the one who took drivers' ed and has her license, not me. I don't have any hope of owning a car, so why bother? Now I wish I actually knew how to drive.

"Are you sure about this?"

"It's perfectly easy." Kathleen leans over me to point out the letters on the shift. "You know the alphabet, right? *D* is for drive and *R* for reverse. Obvious." She points at my feet. "The gas is the long, skinny pedal on the right; the brake is the fat one on the left." She shrugs. "The rest is blah-blah and practice."

I study the creamy seats — spotless — and wonder guiltily what Mr. Mac would say if he knew we were stealing his prized possession. Nothing good, that's for sure.

"Ready?" she asks.

I turn the key in the ignition and feel the power vibrating beneath me. I turn it back off and lean my head against the wheel.

"He would kill us," I say.

"Only if he finds out." Kathleen turns the ignition back on. "And he won't. He's on for the next two days, remember?"

Mr. Mac has been working extra shifts, and not really by choice. Landlords are torching their buildings for insurance money. Kids are messing around. That, or people are finally so sick of everything that they're burning their shitty lives to the ground. It always makes me worried about Hector and his Zippos, those trances of his when he runs his fingertips through the flame.

Anyway, with Mr. Mac at work and Mrs. MacInerney attending a women's conference meeting, the Impala is ours for the taking.

"I have a bad feeling," I tell her.

"Where's your nerve, Nora?" Kathleen says. "Just stick to the plan. We'll be fine."

I go over the plan in my mind. We'll drive over to Sal's to "pick up my paycheck," which I left behind on purpose. I'll pull into the loading-zone spot. Pablo, a car fan, will be dazzled by the Impala and, by extension, me. We'll offer to give him a ride. And then, who knows? An invitation to get us in at Eléphas? Kathleen did my hair nice just in case.

"Just relax," she says. "It's only a few blocks. What can happen?"

I grip the wheel as I pull out of Kathleen's street. It's a wide, curvy road, so I don't have to worry too much about hitting the parked cars. When I start to drift, Kathleen leans over to guide the steering wheel. Still, every time we start to build some speed, I want to hit the brakes. We're bucking like a horse.

"Quit it! You're giving me whiplash," she says, gripping the dashboard.

"Sorry."

Finally 162nd Street comes into view. "After this turn, drive real slow so he can get a good look at you." She moves my hair over my left shoulder. "Think Cher."

I start the turn but cut too sharply.

"Whoa!" Kathleen lunges for the wheel to straighten us out before we climb the curb. We only narrowly miss Matt from the drugstore as he hauls Mr. Farina's trash. He jumps out of the way just in time and shoots me a dirty look.

Sweat beads up on my forehead. I hadn't counted on how many cars would be double-parked outside the shops. And when did this block get so damn narrow? In a boat as wide as the Impala, it's hard to squeeze through. I crawl up the street, maneuvering as best I can.

"There he is!" Kathleen points at Pablo. He's changing the price signs on the bins. "Slow down!"

I jam on the brake, but Pablo's back is turned and he doesn't see us. Kathleen taps the horn and he turns around. My mouth goes dry as I give him a little wave.

His eyebrows shoot up in surprise, and he smiles wide. "Wow!" he calls out.

"Perfect," Kathleen whispers. "Get to the corner and turn around so you can park."

To get back to the loading spot, I'll have to make a three-point turn near the corner of Station Road and come back from the other direction.

But as I drive farther up the street, something else comes into view, too. Sergio's Monte Carlo is parked outside the Satin Lady, as usual. Hector, of all people, is talking to him outside.

At first, I'm not sure it's my brother. He looks weird. He's wearing a leather jacket I don't recognize, and it makes him look older from a distance. But, sure enough, as we drive closer and he shakes the hair from his eyes, I know it's him. Just this morning, Mima nagged Hector about showering and getting a haircut so he wouldn't look like *"un* hippie."

Unfortunately, the Impala—or really, me driving it—snags Hector's attention immediately. When he spots me behind the wheel, he breaks into a big smile and steps right into the road to block my way.

"What's he doing?" Kathleen asks.

I roll down the window and lean out. "Move, Hector."

"I'll have to ask for your license and registration, miss," he says.

I'm thinking of the times we played Billy Goats Gruff as a kid. I was the bigger one then, so I played the troll. *"I'll gobble you up!"* I'd yell, and Hector would squeal as I ran after him.

"Move," I say again, but Hector just whistles to Sergio, who turns to us, too.

"Nooooora!" Sergio eyeballs Kathleen, too. She's actually reflected in his mirrored shades. "Hey, foxy."

She looks at me and rolls her eyes.

Hector walks over to my window. He doesn't care that traffic is backing up behind me. "Since when do *you* drive?" he asks me.

"Since right now, see? Get out of the way." I look in the rearview mirror nervously. Cars are edging around us, and the passing drivers beep and point frantically to tell me what I already know. We're clogging up the street. One driver even gives me the finger.

Sergio doesn't seem to notice the fuss either as he

surveys the Impala, clearly impressed. "That baby can haul ass," he calls to me. "You better be careful driving, Nora. It's a lot of power you got there." He presses on the gas of his Monte Carlo to make the muffler roar.

"Shouldn't you be fixing something in our building, Sergio?" I snap.

Hector leans half his body inside my window to get a look at the interior. The smell of his oily hair is overpowering.

"Get out of here," I say. I mean the car, but also the Satin Lady, this whole place that features Sergio.

Just then, a truck driver behind me sits on his horn and won't let up. He blares it for so long that Sal finally comes out to see what's the matter.

"All right!" I yell, glaring at the trucker through the rear-view mirror. I shove Hector out of the way and hit the gas so I can make a three-point turn. It actually turns into an eight-point turn in this enormous car. By the time I've finished, I've stopped all the traffic both ways. The shopkeepers are all at their doors to see about the fuss. I'm horrified at what Pablo must be thinking of my driving skills.

I finally start down the block toward Sal's loading zone, but from somewhere behind us, I hear the screech of tires. Sergio has cut everyone off to make a U-turn. He peels out and barrels down the street in our direction.

"He's going to rear-end us!" Kathleen screams.

Flustered, I hit the gas and swerve, just as the Monte Carlo misses us by inches. Hector hangs out of the passenger-side window to his waist, waving and laughing as the car careens down the block.

That's the last thing I really see. The Impala fishtails, and in a flash, we sail over the curb toward the deli. Sal and Pablo dive out of the way as we crash into the produce bins with an enormous *crunch*. Apples and onions roll everywhere. The wooden legs beneath the containers crumple to the pavement.

For a second, silence.

I cut the ignition and sit in a stunned cloud of shame as Sal and Pablo run to the car.

"You okay, girls?" Sal yells as he climbs over the splintered bins to reach us. "Anybody hurt?"

Annemarie stands at the front door, horrified. The phone cord is stretched as far as it can go. "Oh, my God! Do we need an ambulance?"

I look at Kathleen, who is staring straight ahead in shock. No blood.

"No," I call out. "We're fine."

Pablo reaches the driver's side and opens my door. "Are you all right, Nora?" He offers me his hand, but I can't even meet his eye.

Sal yanks open the door on Kathleen's side.

"They tried to run us down," she tells him as he helps her out.

He looks down the road, but Sergio and Hector are already gone. "Punks," he mutters. "I'll deal with them later."

Hobbling on his bad knee, Sal walks around to the front of the car to inspect the damage. After a few minutes, he bangs his open palm against the metal fender. "You're lucky this baby is a tank, sweetheart. Just a couple scratches." He turns to Pablo. "I'll bet your car couldn't stand up to this, Paulie!"

"Scratches?" Kathleen says. *"Scratches?"*

We bolt for the front of the car to see the horror for ourselves. The fender has two long scrapes. Nothing is dented, but we both know Mr. Mac notices every detail on this car. Instantly Kathleen's eyes fill with tears.

Sal might have been brave in war, but he's a coward about crying. He clears his throat and tosses aside some of the broken bins near the tires.

"Gimme a hand here, Paulie. Let's move her off the sidewalk."

Pablo steps out into the middle of the street to stop traffic while Sal backs the Impala into the loading zone.

"When my dad sees this, we're screwed," Kathleen groans.

"Let's park it back in front of your house," I whisper. "Somebody could have hit it on the street. He won't know."

"What if the spot is taken?"

That shuts me up. Kathleen sits on the curb and puts her head in her hands.

Sal comes back and surveys his ruined merchandise. "I'll need an accident report from the police for my insurance guy."

The police?

"Oh, please don't do that," I beg. "We'll pay you for the damage."

"I've got insurance," he says. "That's what it's for."

"But I'll pay you back every last dime. You can dock me a little every week if you want."

He gives me a doubtful look. "Something tells me I don't wanna know why you don't want a report. And something tells me it's not good."

"*Please*, Sal. Kathleen's dad will have a fit."

"Nora . . ." he begins.

"I'll replace the bins, too. In fact, I'll build them tomorrow. We can use all that wood that's cluttering the vault. They'll be beautiful. Better than new!"

Sal heaves a sigh.

"Come on, Sal. I need you to give me a break this one time."

He throws his meaty hands up, his face turning red as he heads inside.

"Thanks, Sal!" I call after him.

But he doesn't reply.

Pablo kicks away an apple. He's looking around at all the work I've just made for him. Cleaning this up will take hours.

"I'm really sorry about this," I say.

He takes a deep breath and heads inside behind Sal. "I'll get the trash bags."

Chapter 11

One does not get a ninety-nine average in wood-shop class for nothing.

I've taken Mr. Stanley Melvin's shop class every semester since tenth grade, mostly because it fits nicely into my schedule, but also because I dig how it feels to smash a hammer down hard. It comes with the added bonus of building yourself a lamp or jewelry box in sixteen short weeks if you are so inclined. Kathleen thinks the guys in shop are hunky, too, but she doesn't know what it's really like on the inside. For starters, I met Angel in here. And good-looking or not, guys in a pack can become goons. Every conversation with them turns to sex when Mr. Melvin isn't around. *Clamp on this, Nora. Tongue and groove sounds nice, right, Nora?* Crap like that, thanks to Angel's rumors about me. Why wouldn't a girl want their attention to her legs, butt, and boobs? Square peg, round hole. The answer just doesn't fit for them.

Anyway, Mr. Melvin claims that I'm his best student. It was his idea that I apply to New York City Community

College in Brooklyn, where they offer a program in construction and carpentry. What would college look like with a bunch of shop guys? More of the same, probably, so no, thanks. And forget asking Mima about it. First of all, the school is in Brooklyn, which she has determined is the center of hell. Besides, on the rare occasions when Mima has talked about my future, she's always said she wants me to have *"una carrera linda"*—a pretty job, which I am very sure does not involve Flexcut carving knives or a lathe.

I show up before the first hour and tap on the door. Mr. Melvin is drinking coffee from his thermos and reading the sports page. He looks up and smiles.

"Nora López." That's how he greets all his students, first and last name, like a walking attendance sheet.

"Mr. Stanley Melvin."

"What can I do for you?"

"I need your help."

"Intriguing." He folds his paper and waits.

"I'm building some bins for a friend who owns a fruit stand. I'd like to make them kind of special."

I leave out the particulars, of course. Poor Mr. Melvin. He looks so happy to know that I'm using skills outside the classroom. It's like shop class has a real purpose other than filler. He draws me a little plan on a napkin.

"It's a simple project, but large or small, the basics of woodwork are always the same, Nora López." He gathers a few tools, a sign of his trust in me. "Mind the details and remember everything I taught you."

I reach for the bucket, but he holds it away from me.

101

"And one more thing." He peers at me over his crooked glasses. "I saw Ms. Friedmor in the lounge. She mentioned that you haven't turned in your college application."

The dreaded teacher gossip network strikes again. What is it with these people? Don't they have their own lives? Besides, not everyone is like nutty Adriana Francesca, who has her whole life—as well as her past ones—all squared away. She told our English class that she's been accepted to *"THE* Cooper Union," where she'll study art and literature, *for free,* with all the other child prodigies in New York.

I smile at Mr. Melvin as I fish for my bus pass. "I haven't gotten to it, but I will."

"We have an agreement that you will apply, Nora López? New York City Community College has a fine technical program."

"A hard bargain, but fine, yes."

He smiles. "Well, remember that my offer still stands." Mr. Melvin wants me to work with him on the Saturday Morning Job Review program after I graduate. It's held on Saturday mornings for kids who need "an alternative to academics" so they can try out jobs in plumbing, auto repair, and carpentry. Does he seriously think I might actually want to be trapped in high school forever with these guys? *Please.*

"I could use a talented carpenter's apprentice like you to whip my charges into shape. Think about it. You can work part-time and study, too. If you want it, the position is yours."

After school, I throw on my Levi's carpenter jeans—for once something more than a fashion item—and lug Mr.

Melvin's tool bucket the four blocks to Sal's. The bruised fruits have been moved inside. They're in big peach baskets marked SALE.

I unlock the sidewalk vault so I can bring up the wood that Sal keeps there. I have to take a deep breath to work up my nerve.

It's dark. The first few steps you take are always blind until you find the cord that's attached to the lightbulb. Who knows what's with you down here? Rats? Roaches? Hector's fire-breathing dragon? A decapitated body?

I click on the light. Thanks to Pablo, the shelves are lined neatly with canned food, cases of beer, and cheeses. Only the wood is still in a messy heap near the old furnace. It takes all my might to pick through it, but I finally find an old door, a few sheets of plywood, and some two-by-fours from the stash. "Use your legs to lift," I tell myself, channeling Mr. Melvin, but those five steep steps back to the sidewalk are still a killer.

I'm setting up when Mr. Farina comes up the block. He's got a head of white hair and mischievous brown eyes.

"I've always admired a girl who can take care of things," he says. "My wife was the same way. She flew planes in the war."

Sal comes out, carrying their coffees. He takes one look at my electric circular saw and frowns.

"Wait a minute, dollface! Maybe I should do the cutting," he says. "A pretty girl like you will need all her fingers to operate a cash register."

I give him a withering look. "'Dollface'? Go inside and

enjoy your coffees. I know how to use the saw," I say. "I've taken shop for three years. I just have to put this door across the cinder blocks so I can make a worktable." I look around. "Where's the closest outlet, anyway?"

"Over here," a voice says.

I turn around and find Pablo pointing with his feather duster.

I'm still feeling bad about the mess I made for him, so I duck my head and toss him the end of the cord. "Thanks."

I follow all the protocols: Set up the orange safety cones. Cover the cords with electrical tape to prevent falls. Earplugs. Then I find my goggles inside the bucket and put them on. I know these babies are ugly, but Mr. Melvin brainwashed us all a long time ago with his horror stories of his glass-eyed carpenter friends.

"Fetching," Pablo says as he helps Sal set up the tabletop.

Sal stands back, but he still doesn't look too confident. "Maybe Paulie should help you," he says.

Safety rule number ten, I think. *Avoid distractions.* Perhaps I can break that one.

Mr. Farina comes to my rescue. "Salerno, have faith in the young lady," he says.

I tape my plan onto the glass door for reference. I don't need Pablo's help, of course. I turn to Sal.

"If you don't like the bins when I'm done, you can file the police report," I tell him. "But for now, you're going to have to trust me."

Sal crosses his arms and sighs. "Let him hand you tools, at least."

"Fine."

Sal heads back inside with Mr. Farina in tow, but not before he leans over and whispers to Pablo. "I'll have the number to the emergency room just in case."

"Thanks for the vote of confidence!" I call.

I turn to Pablo. "Do you even know how to build stuff?"

"It's not my thing, to be honest," he says.

I dig in my bucket for the spare pair of safety glasses. "Well, then, you'll need these. And whatever you do, don't reach over the blade."

We work until almost closing, sawdust flying everywhere. I hardly notice the hours go by, but that's always how it is when I'm working on a wood project. I get lost in the grain of the wood, the squeak of boards against the saw, the smell of hot pine. In no time, I start to think of new things I'd want to do: style better legs, curve the edges into something nice.

I haven't said anything to Pablo about this. He's done a decent job holding the pieces steady while I've cut and nailed. He obviously knows nothing about carpentry, but I haven't mentioned it. He may not think of me as Sexy Nora, but at least now he can see I'm not a total idiot. Not a bad trade-off.

When I'm all done, I pull up my goggles and take in my finished product. Twelve square bins, or at least I *hope* so. I'm soaked in sweat, even though the air out here is brisk. My hair is coated in sawdust, and my hands are blistered. But I feel really good, having accomplished something I can see and touch.

Sal peeks out. It's nearly closing time. "You sure they're sturdy?"

"Bring me the tape measure, please," I tell Pablo. Then I hand him and Sal a couple of pencils.

"Go to each corner of the bins, measure three inches, and make a mark." I demonstrate. "At the opposite side of each corner, like so, measure *four* inches and make another one." I draw another line. "If the distance between the two points is five, they're square. Go check."

They exchange glances and get to work on all twelve bins as I gather Mr. Melvin's tools. *Ta-da!* Every single one is five inches on the nose. Rock solid.

"How does that even work?" Pablo asks, clearly impressed.

"It's that badass Pythagorean theorem," I say. "A squared plus B squared equals C squared in a right triangle. Two right triangles make one perfect square."

"Genius!" Sal says, grinning.

I unplug the saw and turn to Pablo. "Can you help me drag down the scraps?"

Every muscle in my back and arms is aching, but at least I've got my fingers attached and no police report to explain to Mr. Mac. What I most want now is a shower and my bed.

"Those were some pretty impressive skills," Pablo tells me as we stack the last of the two-by-fours.

It feels awkward to hear that compliment. "Thanks. You were a big help."

"Really?" he says.

"Well, no, but it was nice company."

He laughs as I start up the stairs. Suddenly he catches my hand. I turn around slowly and stare.

"I was thinking . . . maybe you might want to go out sometime. I checked the new schedule Annemarie put up. I'm off tomorrow night, and so are you."

I don't move. I stink of BO and cut pine. My ponytail has slid to one side, and I'm pretty sure my breath is foul. But still, my blistered hand is definitely in his.

My mind races. I'll have to sleep at Kathleen's so Mima doesn't find out. He can pick me up there.

"Sure," I say finally, ignoring my next thought, which is the shooter.

He smiles brightly. "Great. I'll pick you up for dinner around seven."

Chapter 12

You can't trust love and happiness.

I once heard Mima say that to Edna on the phone. At the time, I wondered what kind of love she meant. Straight-up romantic? God's love? Parents'? Did they all betray you in the end? Maybe. But Mima has never talked to me about love, exactly, except how to stay away from boys. She's never even told me she loved me, to be honest. She's not mushy that way, like Kathleen's parents.

The sky is still dark as Mima tries to wake Hector for school.

"Vamos, vago. Me vas a demorar." The clock says 6:45. She's got only fifteen minutes before she'll be due at her workstation. She must feel nervous if she's rattling his cage this early. Mr. Small has been cracking down hard, and she can't afford to punch in late. There was a time when things were better there. In fact, Hector and I visited after school a few times to wait for her shift to end. I remember that Mima showed me how to work the whirring machine that sepa-rated the huge spools of tape into smaller ones. She even let

me help her pack the rolls into a teetering stack of boxes that reached almost to the ceiling. Hector couldn't resist knocking them down like a set of blocks, though. That ended our visits. Mima gave me a key to our place on a long shoelace around my neck. "Don't open the door to strangers, and don't ever tell anyone you're alone," she said. "Some things we have to keep secret." I still wear that key to this day.

Anyway, things have changed at her job, that's for sure. Even Edna, who dates Mr. Small on the sly, is careful to get to work on time now.

I'm thinking about all that as I get ready for school in the bathroom. I hold my head upside down and put the hose of our bonnet hair dryer to the brush, trying to drown Mima and Hector out with pleasant thoughts of Pablo. Tonight is the big night. Our first date. I whip up my head and let the locks fall crazily around my shoulders. I pucker my lips in the mirror. I almost look pretty, but do I look like a college girl? Not really, I have to admit.

I come out of the bathroom in search of my jeans just as Mima tries again to pull the blanket from Hector.

"Get off me or I'll break your legs!" he warns.

Those are just words, just expressions, but something in the sound of his voice makes me turn.

Instantly I think back to the day he hid in the clothes racks at Klein's. Mima screamed his name and grabbed at strangers who might help us find her lost boy. She spoke even less English back then, so I had to "be her tongue" and explain everything to the men in uniforms. Turns out, Hector was only a few feet away the whole time. He'd heard Mima's screams, but he didn't move. "I'll break your leg!" he shouted at the shocked security guard who finally found him in the coats. He kicked like a wild animal as they dragged him out.

"Mima . . ." I begin. I can feel something bad coming. He means it, doesn't she know? Or is she walking into the land mine on purpose? But before I can stop her, she reaches out to shake Hector awake again.

Suddenly his foot swings out hard. It catches her in the upper arm with a sickening smack. Mima stumbles back against the wall, where paint flakes off the plaster.

"*¡Animál!*" she hisses, unhinged. "*¡Demónio!*"

"Fuck off."

"Stop," I say.

"Not even a saint could stand you," Mima hisses. "No wonder your father left."

I stand there, trying my best to be deaf and blind. No one moves for a second as her ugly words hang in the air. Usually I hate to hear her gush about Hector, but somehow this unmoors me.

Finally she turns and sees me in the bathroom doorway.

"Get him up," she snaps, moving toward her bedroom. Tiny flecks of plaster are still in her hair. "You're his older sister. Do something."

Cochino. Pig. *Es un loco, un malcriado.* Crazy, spoiled brat. I hear the mumbled insults through her door.

Hector sits up before I have to do a thing. He storms past me and slams the bathroom door closed.

Mima finishes getting ready as I sit on my bed.

How have we gotten here? I think back to Dr. De Los Santos, who looked at us worriedly every time we had to get our polio boosters. It took both of them to force the dose down Hector's throat. When they were done, Hector's eyes were usually puffed and snot was all over his shirt. The office was a wreck. *"Qué fuerte,"* was all Mima would say even when Hector tore the blinds in the waiting room to bits in revenge. It was as though that kind of strength was a thing to admire.

It's a relief when I hear Mima let herself out. She'll have to rush to work, dash across traffic. Maybe Edna will take pity and punch her card in on time, maybe not. The whirring of the machines will start, and Mima can join the ladies in their endless talk as the bowling-ball thunder rumbles over their heads. "My boy hates to wake up in the morning. I don't know what I'm going to do about him," Mima might say.

But will she show them her arm, the bump that's surely rising on her scalp? Will she tell them she called him a lazy pig, a demon?

I can't say.

Kathleen argues with the bus driver to hold the door when she spots me running up the block. I hop in and flash my bus pass before heading to the back.

"Oversleep?" She looks at me knowingly. "Dreaming of the hunk? Tonight's the big night!"

Right now, I hate her for her pretty smile, for that easy way of hers, for her glass half full. No one screams at her house. No one kicks in doors or overturns chairs to make a point. No one is a live grenade. There is no blanket of blame where she lives.

We ride in silence.

"Hey . . . you feel okay?" she finally asks.

"My period," I whisper, a harmless lie.

She gives my hand a squeeze. "Womanhood can really suck," she says.

I close my eyes and lean my head against her shoulder for the ride.

Chapter 13

"You like the Eagles?"

Pablo rummages inside the glove compartment for his cassettes. We finished our dinner at the Villa Bianca, but it's still early, and neither one of us really feels like going home yet. We drove around for a while until he suggested pulling over near the tennis courts at Kissena Park. Kathleen and I sometimes hit balls here, occasionally kicking some boy ass, good enough to make Billie Jean King proud.

But the courts aren't lit, and this isn't about tennis tonight.

I fidget a little, trying not to notice the obvious. This part of the park becomes lovers' lane after dark. Several cars are already here, their windows fogged up, even though the news has been warning people to avoid "secluded places." But where else would you go to make out?

I look around a little. Two of the girls were shot in a car with dates, too, but that was different. They were alone with their boyfriends. I'm here with lots of people around. We're all safe.

"Yeah, I like the Eagles," I say. "I didn't take you for a rocker, though. I thought you liked disco."

He pops in "Hotel California" and shrugs. "I'm into everything, really."

Me? I wonder as the music comes on low. *Are you into me?*

So far, it has been a great first date, maybe the best one I've ever been on, even though my day started like shit. My dates are usually of the pizza-place variety, so it was nice to be in a restaurant with cloth tablecloths. Pablo held open the car door and paid for my meal. I had to watch him carefully for what to do, though. When the waitress asked him what he'd like to drink, he stuck to soda, even though he's obviously old enough to get served. I know from Kathleen, who's up on such things, that they card people at Villa Bianca. Maybe Pablo knows that, too, and didn't want to risk embarrassing me? Class.

Best of all, it hasn't been as awkward as I thought it might be to talk to him. I had to put the morning completely out of my mind, of course, but I managed. I've learned to play my personal game of doctor, carefully cutting away thoughts of Mima and Hector whenever I want to have fun. We laughed about Sal and his crazy Korean War stories. Pablo told me about his family. His parents must have been kind of rich in Colombia. His grandfather was an attorney—and the town mayor on top of that. They had servants, drivers, and a cook. I wonder how they like things here. They live in Hollis, not really a fancy place or anything. Worse, he still shares a room with his little brother, too. Omar is twelve.

"He's a big *Shazam!* fan," Pablo tells me. "Christ, I hate that show."

When Pablo asks about my family, I hesitate. I can feel Mima and Hector banging inside me to get out, so I keep it short.

"I live with my mom and my brother," I say. "My dad and his wife are in the city."

He's quiet for a while, listening to the song. "You know, I've never dated a Latin girl," he tells me.

Dated. We're *dating.* Nice.

"Why not?" I ask.

"Not many at the Hirsch School, I guess. I really didn't think you were Latin when I first saw you."

I wonder if that's good or bad. Sometimes it's easier to let people think I'm Greek or Italian. People have funny ideas about people who speak Spanish, and it doesn't matter where you're from. Once I overheard a lady tell Annemarie that she was sending her kids to private school in the fall. Her zoned school had changed. The problem?

"There's a terrible element now." She lowered her voice. "Everything is *en español.*"

God. It was like listening to grouchy Ed from *Chico and the Man,* except without the laugh track. I gave her the change and told her to have a nice day. I still wonder why Annemarie didn't say anything, and more, why I didn't either.

I smile at Pablo. "So what do you think of Latin girls so far?" Kathleen would be proud of this sass.

Pablo leans back and laughs. "No complaints at all." But then he stares at me for a few seconds.

"What?" Maybe I have food in my teeth? A booger?

"How old are you, again?" he asks. "You've never said."

"Almost eighteen," I say. "In June. Finally."

"Finally what?"

"I don't know. I guess, *finally* done with everything I'm sick of." I hadn't planned on baring my soul, but it's easy to talk to him here in the dark. "I'm tired of school, my mother, just my life right now."

"So, June . . ." he says. "When's the big day?"

"June twenty-third. Kathleen's is the next day, believe it or not. We're going to celebrate big, too. We've had it all planned for years."

"Skydiving?"

"Dancing," I say. "All night long, if possible." I stop myself from inviting him, but something in his smile makes me feel as though he might be thinking the same thing.

He takes my hand as we listen through the rest of the album and talk about everything and nothing. I love that he's so easy and uncomplicated, unlike everything else in my stupid life. His hand feels big and warm over mine, and everything else seems far away. I don't want the night to end, but finally, when the last song plays, Pablo leans over.

"I really like you," he says seriously, "even if you can't drive for shit."

I give him a little punch, but then he pulls me toward him. The gearshift digs into my hip, but I don't care. He isn't awkward like Angel, who always pressed too hard and groped like a brute. Pablo makes no stealth moves. Instead, his lips move gently over mine.

We kiss and kiss until my lips feel chapped and I'm

116

buzzed. When he nuzzles my neck, I feel as though I'm going to come out of my skin. One thing is for sure: my days of dating high-school losers are over. I'm floating as Pablo kisses me when there's a sudden knock on the window. We jump apart. A blinding light flashes into the car.

"Jesus!" Pablo mutters.

A cop is outside, inspecting the dashboard from the driver's side. My heart is still thundering in my chest as I straighten my blouse and scoot back to my seat.

Pablo rolls down the window.

"Nice evening," the cop says, smirking. He looks over Pablo's head at me. "Everything all right in here, miss?"

I nod and drop my gaze into my hands. My cheeks are blazing, wondering how long he was watching us.

He moves his light toward the backseat as he continues. "You need to move out of the park," he tells us. "It's closed after dark, the way the sign says. You can read, right?"

Oh, perfect. A smart-ass.

"We were just hanging out for a while," Pablo says.

The cop flips off his light and shakes his head. "You go to school around here?"

"St. Johns, sir."

"You'd think a big college man like you would know better. How can you read those fat books back there when you don't seem to read the news?" His eyes drift over to mine. He doesn't have to say anything about the shooter for us to know what he's getting at. Finally he gives the roof a hard rap with his palm. "Go find somebody's basement, buddy. Or better yet, take this girl home."

Pablo glances at me as he starts the car. All around us, other cars turn their ignitions, too. Word spreads fast, I guess. The fun is over.

I look back at the cop and the long line of cars that follows us out of the park.

"It was getting late, anyway," I whisper to Pablo. "I told Kathleen I'd be home by midnight."

He keeps the cop in sight in the rearview mirror, and I'm sure I see a little disappointment in his face. Maybe he had more planned. College women don't have curfews, I realize, and they don't have to run their love lives in a park. They have their own dorms and apartments.

"Not a problem," he says.

But as we pick up speed, I can't help but wonder if maybe it is.

Chapter 14

"I don't like it." Stiller's eyes follow a cop car cruising along Sanford Avenue.

She's waiting at the bus stop on Monday morning, on her way to housing court, where she's a witness in a dispute case.

"Don't like what?" Kathleen asks as the squad car disappears. "Cops?"

She nods slowly. "Surveillance."

"What do you think they want?" I ask.

Kathleen and I exchange guilty glances. We don't tell Stiller about our own encounter under the train trestle or mine at the park, but we're both thinking about the killer. Could he be nearby?

"They ought to be looking for whoever broke into Mrs. Murga's."

That idea is no better.

A little jolt goes through me as I think about the radio buried in our closet.

"But for all I know, they've declared our tenant organization dangerous," Stiller continues with a snort. "It wouldn't be the first time. Intimidation tactics. I've seen *those* before."

"You think they'll find who did it?" Kathleen asks.

Stiller gives us a severe look. "Since when does the NYPD care about an old woman like Mrs. Murga! Wake up, honey. There are bigger fish to fry! She's just a complaint number filed in a big box somewhere. Nobody is going to work that case!"

I step out into the road to see if the bus is in sight.

"It's coming," I say.

As much as I hate myself for it, I'm glad that nobody will ever find out who stole Mrs. Murga's things. I flag the driver, relieved.

The racket in Mrs. Pratt's class is deafening, thanks to the thirty students at their IBM Selectrics.

A few of the know-it-alls are way past *The quick brown fox jumps over the lazy dog.* Their fingers fly across the keyboard without even lifting their eyes from the page they're copying. Among them is Ricky, whose current record is on the board. He can apparently coast at sixty-one words per minute.

I, on the other hand, am plodding along, making full use of the correction key and my two index fingers.

"Hunt-and-peck is highly inefficient." Mrs. Pratt has to shout at me over the clacking. "How is it that you didn't take a single typing class in all of your time here, Nora? It's a basic business skill that every young woman needs."

120

Because I have no intention of being a secretary, I want to say.

"I'm almost done, Mrs. Pratt!" I shout back. I backspace and type the correction over my last misspelling. It's almost dismissal time, thank God. It has taken me more than two hours to work on this stupid application, but what could I do? Mr. Melvin reminded me of our deal first thing this morning, and I owe him.

Ms. Friedmor comes through the door just as I'm pulling my application out of the carriage. She holds her ears as she walks toward me and drops a folder down at the desk where I'm working. I stop what I'm doing and flip it open. Financial-aid forms. Will the fun never end?

Suddenly a sharp whistle pierces the noise.

"Time!" Mrs. Pratt announces like a general. The whole place goes still all at once. "Calculate the words per minute and drop your work in my in-box on your way out."

Ms. Friedmor looks relieved as she turns back to me. "I took the liberty of bringing these, too. They're due Monday." She holds up her hand as I start to protest. "Bring your mother's W-9 later this week if you need help."

I grab the folder and stuff it in my bag. I have to admit that typing my application was the only hardship; maybe the rest won't be such a big deal, either. I start to put my application in my bag, too, but Ms. Friedmor plucks it from me.

"I'll hang on to that so it stays safe."

"Where is the trust?" I ask.

She smiles. "Did you pass my message to your mother, Nora? About coming to discuss your brother?"

She looks at me evenly, waiting. Can someone like Ms. Friedmor even imagine what it would take to truly discuss Hector? Mima still has a big bruise on her arm. She's wearing sleeves, even as the weather gets warm.

"She's been busy, but I'll tell her again," I say.

I start up the aisle, but something out the window catches my eye.

There's a cop car at the curb and a police officer standing at the gate. That's new.

Ms. Friedmor follows my gaze and seems to read my mind.

"Safety precautions," she tells me. "That's all."

My ears are still ringing as I open the doors and head for the bus stop. I have to walk right by the cop, and wouldn't you know it? It's the same one who caught Pablo and me at the park. His walkie-talkie sputters as I hurry by.

Safety precaution, huh? Interesting. Then why is it that having the cops everywhere makes me feel so scared?

Chapter 15

The double date is Kathleen's idea, a perfectly logical solution, she says, to the unfortunate dilemma of new love versus a murderer. I don't know why I didn't think of it myself. There will be four of us at the movie, and the .44-Caliber Killer hasn't taken aim at groups. At least not that we know of.

Naturally Eddie jumps at the chance to spend a Friday night with Kathleen, even if it means the late movie so I can get there after work. She asks him at lunchtime, and I swear it looks like he'll faint. He's so into her that it's almost sad. He's our age, and tall like Pablo, but something about Eddie always feels young. Even Kathleen is lukewarm on him, but she's trying on casual dating.

"Your turn," she tells me. "Ask Pablo."

I practice asking on my walk to Sal's. *Be casual,* I tell myself. *Self-assured. Liberated.*

Unfortunately I'm a train wreck.

We're standing outside the john when I ask. I stumble through the particulars, not even making sense. Fresh Meadows, the movies, tonight.

"So, you're asking me on a second date?" Pablo asks.

"What? Well, Kathleen and Eddie are coming, too," I say, muddling the whole thing. "It's hanging out. If you want to. You know, tonight after work."

"So, it's *not* a date?"

My face feels like it's on fire. I tuck the stray hair behind my ear nervously. "No. I mean, it is, sort of." When I look up, he's grinning, so I let out my breath. "Are you enjoying this?"

He looks over his shoulder to check on Sal and Mr. Farina, who are outside. Then he plants a slow kiss on my mouth. My knees nearly buckle.

"Quite a lot, actually," he whispers.

I watch, mesmerized, as he heads down the aisle.

I can't say I love being here with another couple, not that they notice. Eddie just can't hide his painfully horny side when it comes to Kathleen. All night, he's been staring at her legs, her butt, and her mouth until I was sure she might slap him. Really, it's a little pervy.

Anyway, *Annie Hall* was probably a mistake. All that whining and worry from Woody Allen starts to get annoying in no time. I turn to tell Kathleen, but it's too late. Eddie's already locked on.

So I stare at the screen awkwardly. Pablo looks over and makes a face at the two of them. We try not to laugh. Then he reaches for my hand and rests it on his leg. I pretend to watch the movie, but all I can think about are the muscles in his thigh. I wait for each steamy scene. That's when Pablo leans down and kisses me, soft and slow.

It's almost midnight by the time the movie is over. Kathleen has smudged lipstick, and I'm floating. But when we get to the lobby, the magic starts to drain.

The manager is waiting by the glass doors for the last of the stragglers. He unlocks the door and holds it open for us, but none of us moves. It's as if there's an invisible fence that keeps us standing near the concession stand. He frowns and checks his watch.

"We're closing up, folks."

We head to the doors and look outside. The parking lot is empty except for the last of the moviegoers. I wish Pablo's car didn't look so far away under the lamppost. It's lonely out there, especially with all the nearby shops closed and the shadows cast by the awnings. I pull up my hood to cover my hair.

"What if he's out there?" Kathleen says suddenly, which surprises me. Where's her safety-in-numbers theory?

Eddie puffs himself up. "I'll protect you." He puts his arm around Kathleen's shoulder, but she hardly looks comforted.

"Your chest deflects bullets?" I ask him.

Pablo takes my hand. "Look, the city has more than seven million people. It's huge, especially if you count all the boroughs," he says. "Realistically, we'll be okay."

I want to believe him. I want to be able to have fun without looking over my shoulder every second.

So we step outside. As soon as the door latch clicks behind us, we run, our hearts pounding, Kathleen screaming like we're on a roller coaster of some kind. But Pablo is right. We *are* fine, giggling in the car even when Eddie yells, *"Look out,"* just to scare us and make Kathleen jump into his arms. "April fools," he says.

When they drop me off at home, I turn and wave from the lobby. The Camaro looks shiny in the lamplight. Pablo grins in that sexy way of his. Kathleen blows me kisses; Eddie keeps his eyes on her the whole time.

That's how I'll always want to remember them, I think to myself. *Beautiful in the face of fear.*

Chapter 16

"What's this?" Mima asks.

I'm still in a happy daze from my date last night, so I swivel in my chair to look.

She was making Hector's bed and tucked her hands between the mattress and box spring. Now she's holding up a mirror painted with five jet planes side by side, with long indentations like smoke trailing from their engines.

I keep my face as still as possible, even as my heart sinks.

It's a coke mirror. I've seen them in the head shop on Main Street that's conveniently located across the street from the new drug rehab clinic. Kathleen and I buy incense there and gawk at the latest feathered roach clips and bongs. The grooves in the mirror are meant for doing lines of blow, but I am not about to explain that to Mima. If she thinks pot can lead to insanity, I don't even want to imagine what she'll say about cocaine.

Shit. Why can't Hector just keep dirty magazines like any other guy? And why does seeing this make me so mad?

"It's a mirror, Mima. Can't you see?"

She studies it for a minute. If she guesses what it's used for, she doesn't say so, thank God. But then, Mima probably doesn't want any more trouble. She's been trying for days to get the raw egg off the wall but hasn't asked me a single detail of how it got there.

She props the mirror up on our dresser like a decoration and keeps dusting. A nervous giggle bubbles up from my stomach. Maybe she thinks my brother is still interested in playing army, a little boy lining up his GI Joes and plastic bombers. I hope so. It's a sweeter thought than what he's probably doing. Maybe this explains all the changes in Hector, though. That edginess, his all-nighters.

I get dressed for work early and slip on the latest staple of my wardrobe. I wear a hooded sweatshirt to hide my hair. It was either that or Kathleen was going to get her hands on me with some Clairol.

I slide the coke mirror inside my front pouch on my way out. I should be spending my time deciding where Pablo and I might have a next date without getting shot, not figuring out how to dispose of a coke mirror that my mother just shined with Windex.

"I'm on until closing," I call on my way out.

"*Cuidate, niña,*" she says. She's moved on to the egg stain again. "And ask Sal if he can give you daytime hours at the *bodega. ¡Hay un loco!*"

Oh, good, the .44-Caliber Killer has crossed the language barrier. Even the ladies at Small's Adhesives talk about him, trying to figure out who *el loco* might be. Mima

128

is partial to the idea that the killer is one of Fidel's international henchmen.

I look up and down the block when I get outside, but Hector isn't around. I'll have to catch up with him later and see if he'll tell me what's really going on.

Fat chance, but what can I do?

I'm his older sister, as Mima is always reminding me. And if I don't try to stop him, who will? Mima? (Ha!) Smoking—even smoking pot—is one thing, but snorting blow is way over the line, and frankly, it's a little scary. Adriana is one of two people I know who have tried it. She stopped after a couple of times, though. "The hit makes you fly, but it doesn't come cheap," she told me once. "I have my priorities." The other person is a girl named Carla, who snorted a hole right through her septum last year, no lie. She disappeared from school for six months—to where, nobody knows. Maybe rehab? When she came back, she had scabs on her nostrils, and she was so skinny we hardly recognized her. Nobody talks to her now.

I go around the corner and make my planned pit stop. I bang on Sergio's door.

No one answers.

I climb back up the stairs and sit down for a second, trying to decide what to do. Finally I opt to leave a message that even a dimwit like him will understand. Taking aim like a pitcher, I hurl the mirror against his door. It explodes into a hundred shards, just like Hector's egg.

Then, without waiting, I run.

*　　*　　*

129

All afternoon, it's pretty quiet at Sal's. I doodle Pablo's name on the edge of the newspaper I keep at the register to kill time. Sal is sitting on an overturned crate on the sidewalk with Mr. Farina. They take their afternoon coffee outside now that the weather is finally getting nice. Most days, they're like two old ladies, arguing or reminiscing. But today, they're not talking about the Mets or how the block of stores has changed over the years. The .44-Caliber Killer is on their minds, too, same as everyone else's.

I can hear their whole conversation from here.

Sal thinks he's got to be a deranged vet from Vietnam, somebody who could work that powerful gun.

Mr. Farina argues that the killer is just cold-blooded, and he lives somewhere close. For a sweet grandfather type, he's got some pretty grim theories.

"He might be right under our noses," he says. "I've been checking my prescription records just in case."

"Clean your glasses good when you're checking, okay?" Sal says. "You're getting blind as a bat, friend."

I try to block them out, but maybe Mr. Farina isn't too far off. You've got to look fairly normal to dodge the police for months, right? What if I've bagged this psycho's groceries? Cashed out his milk and bread?

Pablo startles me out of nowhere.

"Wait for me after we close," he says, stopping at my register. His eyes drift to my doodles before I can shut the newspaper. "I think about you, too."

I'm melting. *Ave Maria purisima,* he's going to ask me

130

out again. Now what? I am dying to say yes, but the thought of a .44 in my face comes out of nowhere.

"Back to work, Romeo," Sal calls from the sidewalk. "I got my eye on you."

"Just sweeping up, boss." Pablo wiggles his eyebrows at me and pushes his broom along the aisle to the back of the store.

A little while later, the bells on the door jangle.

It's Hector, and he looks pissed. Well, *that* didn't take long. I fold my arms and brace myself as he marches over to my register.

"Where is it?" he says.

"Lower your voice." There are no customers in the shop, but his voice can carry. I lock the register and pull him away toward the last aisle, out of view.

"I want the mirror," he says. "Why were you going through my stuff, anyway?"

"Nobody was going through your stuff. Mima found it while she was cleaning. Excellent hiding skills, by the way."

"Gimme it," he says. "It's Sergio's."

"Figures. Don't worry, I gave it back," I say. "He might even be done gluing it back together by now." I take a step closer and whisper. "That loser is going to mess you up, you know that?"

Hector grabs my wrist and squeezes until I wince.

"Why did you do that, Nora?" he asks.

I stare up at him, trying to see the little kid inside as his nails dig deep into my skin. He's never actually put a hand on me before.

"Let. Go," I say. "We're in public. People will see." But he only squeezes harder, and I feel my knees start to buckle.

Just then, I hear footsteps running toward us. Pablo races in our direction from the top of the aisle.

"Hey!" he shouts.

With all my might, I wrench free from Hector's grip. "Get out of here," I growl.

But Pablo reaches us too soon. Before I can stop him, he shoves Hector hard and sends him flying back into the shelves. Cans topple and roll everywhere. "Hands off her!" He looks at me. "Are you okay?"

I stand there, holding my breath. What can I possibly say? So far, there's been no reason to tell Pablo anything about Mima or Hector. He only knows that I have a brother, that we share a room, nothing else.

"Fuck you," Hector says, getting back on his feet. He lunges for Pablo, but not before Pablo clocks him hard in the jaw.

"Stop! He's my brother!" I shout, getting between them.

Pablo stares at me. "Your *brother*?"

"It's nothing. He's leaving."

Just then, Sal and Mr. Farina run back inside. They've heard the commotion. Sal looks at the three of us and then at the merchandise on the floor. His face is stern, and he suddenly seems the size of a mountain.

"Got a problem here, Mr. Wonderful?" he asks, his eyes boring down on Hector with a hard look.

Hector's cheeks are blotchy, and he's bleeding from the lip. He points at Pablo. "Keep your fucking hands off me, man. And fuck you, too, Nora."

Mr. Farina goes bright red.

"Watch the mouth!" Sal roars.

But Hector doesn't listen. He swings open the door and storms out.

In the long quiet that follows, I pray to be sucked underground. *Trágame tierra,* I say to myself in shame. Anything would be better than standing here with my lousy life suddenly on display. No one—not even Kathleen—knows all the details of Mima and Hector these days, or that it's getting worse. It's too embarrassing to share, for one thing. How can you make people understand about brothers who hit and spit? How do you explain why you listen at your own front door before going in? How do you explain that it's not only parents who beat kids, but sometimes the other way around, too?

You can't. At least not without feeling like the word LOW-LIFE is stuck to your forehead.

I walk back to the register as calmly as I can. I don't dare rub at my wrist, although it stings in the spots where Hector dug in his nails. I'm fighting to keep tears inside. If I make it look like a big deal, then it will be.

"I should get back to the shop," Mr. Farina says quietly. "Matt's probably done cleaning up by now."

Sal signals Pablo to pick up the cans and then gives me a long look over his glasses. "Looks like the kid is having some bad days, Nora." He waits for me to answer. "I see him up the street a lot, you know."

For a second, I want to crumble inside a bear hug, let someone else, someone grown, take the load. But I keep my eyes on the ground instead. Sal hates tears, I tell myself. And who wants to wade into a gross family hell like mine?

"He's just being a jerk," I finally say. "It passes."

Pablo picks up the cans from the floor and stacks a few of the dented ones on the counter. He's probably wondering about what sort of trashy girl he might be dating.

"He grabbed you pretty hard, Nora," he mumbles.

Suddenly I'm angry. Can't he see he's making me feel worse?

"He's a *kid*." I reach into the drawer and break open a roll of dimes I don't need. "It didn't even hurt."

I give him a cold look, hoping he'll get the hint and leave me alone, but he stands firm. Finally I realize I'll have to close the door another way.

"It's not really your business, anyway," I say without meeting his eye.

Pablo's face is a stone. He glances at Sal for a second, but finally walks up the aisle, an icy silence in his wake.

I don't wait for him at closing time after all.

Chapter 17

"Is this a joke?" Kathleen asks.

"No."

"But why on earth would you want to end it with Pablo?" Kathleen asks me in desperation. "You're not making sense. You just started dating him, and he's absolutely gorgeous." She folds up another pair of jeans and gives me an exasperated look.

I shake my head. "I don't think we're right for each other, that's all."

"Oh, bull. You've gone on two real dates; how would you even know? Besides, gorgeous is right for everybody. What's wrong with you? Live a little!"

I've been helping Kathleen pack for what she calls her "kidnapping." The MacInerneys own an old bungalow in Breezy Point, out by the Rockaways, and they're spending Easter break there, same as always. It's a one-room box on stilts that used to belong to Mrs. MacInerney's grandmother. To say it's a fixer-upper is generous. There's always something going wrong there. If it's not a leaky faucet or stuck windows, it's missing or broken doors. It sits in the middle of a ridiculously narrow street, too, so if you stick your arm out the window you can graze the bungalow next door. Still, it's a nice place to go, nestled between Jamaica Bay and the Atlantic. At night you can sit barefoot on the deck eating watermelon and watching sunburned guys lug beer coolers to the shore. As "kidnappings" go, it's not bad.

I'm not going this time, though. Sal scheduled me all week, and awkward as it's going to be with Pablo, I can use the cash. Now more than ever, I want to save enough dough to get out.

Kathleen sits on the bed and sighs. "You sure you can't come? *Please?* I'll die of boredom with my parents." Kathleen lobbied hard to stay home, but her parents put the kibosh on the whole idea. First, there's the .44-Caliber Killer, but they also know Eddie is lurking, so no dice.

"You will not. Work on your base tan," I tell her. The long winter has left her roughly the color of Elmer's glue. "Besides, I have to work."

"Some friend." She goes over to her dresser and tosses me her house key. My job is to feed her guinea pig, Gloria, and to water Mrs. MacInerney's houseplants for a week.

Kathleen sits back down on the bed and puts her hands on my shoulders. "Just promise me you *won't* officially break up with Pablo before I get back," she says solemnly. "That gives you a few days to reconsider this *muy stupid-o* idea."

"*Idea estúpida,*" I correct. "And it's not stupid. How can

136

we break up? We've only had two official dates. You said so yourself. Maybe this doesn't even qualify."

"Just don't do it," she snaps.

Cooling things off with Pablo won't be as easy as I tried to make it seem to Kathleen. When I got to work today, the sight of his car made me yearn for him. My only hope is that things will be so busy around here with Easter orders that I can ignore him. So far, so good. Every time he comes to the register, I go to the bathroom or make up some excuse to change the signs on the bins or check expiration dates. Anything so I don't have to talk to him.

To my relief, Pablo is nowhere in sight after lunch. He's down in the dungeon working on inventory and pricing merchandise. If Luck smiles on me, he'll be stuck down there most of the day, and I won't have to face him at all.

I'm finishing up my sandwich when I hear Sal calling.

"Paulie!" he shouts.

No answer.

"Paulie!"

The pricing gun is on the deli counter. Sal juts his chin in its direction. "Take that thing down to Knucklehead before you finish your break, Nora," he says. "How's he gonna price anything without the labeler?"

"Me?" I ask.

He stops slicing the boiled ham and frowns at me over his glasses. "There's somebody else named Nora?"

"Fine." I grab the price gun and walk outside to the open

vault. I stand at the top of the stairs, wondering for a second if I should just toss it down and leave.

"Pablo?" I call. There's still no answer; he must be far in the back. "Hello?"

I climb down the steps carefully. The farther inside I go, the more the vault smells of mold and damp. It's strange how it feels like the dead of night instead of the middle of a pretty day down here. I walk past the old furnace as fast as I can. It may not work, but it still reminds me of that horrible story Hector told me about the roasting head.

I don't see Pablo anywhere, so I maneuver past the mess of remaining lumber and turn the corner.

"Boo!"

I jump back and drop the pricing gun. Pablo is standing by a pile of cartons near the back wall, the box cutter in his hand.

"That's not funny." I let out a nervous sigh. "Sal says you forgot this." I pick up the labeler and hand it to him. Then I turn to go.

"Wait." He tosses down the knife and follows me. "I didn't really forget. It was just the only way I could think of to get you down here alone," he says.

I turn back around. My cheeks get hot, I'm sure of it, but I can't think of a thing to say.

"You've been ignoring me, so I had to think of something." He motions to the cartons. "Can you sit down a minute? Please."

"I hate it down here. It's creepy."

"Two minutes, that's it," he says.

This is going to be trouble, I know it. My stomach flutters as I sit down and feel his warm leg next to mine. I start rehearsing the words: *This isn't going to work out. I have another boyfriend. I like someone else. I think I'm a lesbian. I am dying of incurable cancer.*

"I'm sorry I shoved your brother," he says. "I didn't know it was him. I shouldn't have done that."

I fidget against a crack in the concrete with my sneaker.

"I just reacted," he says, "but I wouldn't have hit him if I'd known who he was. I've seen him on the block with Sergio, but I didn't make the connection." He pauses uncomfortably. "And that night with the dog—"

"Forget it," I say, wishing there really was a way to do just that. Erase the whole thing.

Pablo lowers his voice. "It looked like he was hurting you, though."

It feels as though the vault is closing in on me. I don't want him to pry. Besides, I've been wondering if what Hector did was such a big deal. He only grabbed me hard, after all. When we were little, we'd wrestle until one of us cried. Was that bad, too?

"We were having a fight," I say finally. "You have fights with your little brother, don't you?"

He shrugs, but something in his silence only makes me feel worse. I don't want to imagine what he's thinking.

"Look, Pablo, my brother has a bad temper, and it's kind of complicated." I stand up. "I should go."

"Wait." He laces his fingers in mine and holds me back. "Please don't be mad, Nora."

139

I feel a shot through my arm.

"I'm not mad," I say quietly.

"No?"

I shake my head. "I actually don't know what I am."

"Then *talk* to me."

I shake my head. I'm afraid that if I open my mouth, my voice will crack or I'll cry.

"At least let me take you out again."

Say no, I tell myself. *Be strong.* But when I lift my eyes to look at him, I can't do it.

"You don't want to see me again?" he asks. "If you say so, I'll leave you alone, but I want you to tell me one way or the other."

We wait there in silence until he stands and takes my face in his hands. Then he presses a soft kiss on my lips. Everything inside me melts.

"I've been wanting to do that again," he whispers. "Haven't you?"

Just then, Sal's booming voice interrupts us. "Nora! We've got customers!"

I try to move off, but Pablo won't let go of my hand.

"He's going to come looking," I say. "Let me go."

"Tell me *yes,*" he says. "Please."

"Nora?" Sal's shadow darkens the top of the steps. "You okay down there?"

"He's going to blow his stack," I warn.

Pablo only holds on tighter. "Then say yes and save us."

"There's a shooter . . ." I begin. "It's not even safe—"

"We'll go somewhere that the shooter won't find us," he says.

"*Nora!*"

"*Coming!*" I call up. "We're moving boxes." Then I turn back to Pablo, unable to resist his smile.

"All right," I say.

"Tomorrow night," he whispers. He gives me one more kiss before letting go.

"Fine." Breathless, I run for the steps.

The words *tomorrow night* keep me up late, wondering how I've gotten into this big mess. It's only going to be a matter of time before Pablo finds out everything about my screwed-up family. Dating him again is only going to make it harder and more embarrassing to cut things off later. Still, when I squeeze my eyes shut, all I can think about is how good it felt to have him kiss me again. He tastes like mint, sugar, sexiness all in one. Just thinking about it makes me ache.

The news that night drones on about the manhunt that's now spanning all the boroughs. I rack my brain trying to think of a safe place where Pablo and I might go to be alone. There has to be *someplace* in Queens where a maniac would never think to bother us.

And then I remember the MacInerneys' key.

Chapter 18

Kathleen's street dead-ends at the train tracks, so it can be a lonely stretch sometimes, even in bright daylight. And with a killer on the prowl, everything on this block makes me jumpy tonight. Even the windows on the houses look like eyes. I pull up my hood as Pablo and I hurry to the side door, hoping none of the neighbors will see. He parked at the far end of the street near the concrete barrier that separates the road from the tracks. Though neither one of us mentioned it, we checked the rearview mirrors before we got out, just in case somebody was out there.

I jiggle the key in the sticky lock the way Kathleen always does, my hands shaking a little, and shove hard against the door to open it. The whole house smells of MacInerney as soon as we step inside. It's strange how a family can have its own scent. Theirs is laundry detergent, wood, and ash, a comforting smell.

I flip on the light, and we hang our things on the wall pegs next to Mr. and Mrs. MacInerney's coats. There's no way Kathleen's parents would be okay with this, I think guiltily. But ballsy as it is to use their house for a love shack, it has to be smarter than sitting in a parked car, right?

"When are they coming back?" Pablo asks, studying the family pictures on the wall.

"Friday," I say. "The parlor is that way. I'll be right back."

Mrs. MacInerney keeps the watering can in the kitchen. I stand at the sink to fill it and try to peer into their backyard, but it's too dark. All I can see is my own reflection in the glass. God. Anybody could be out there watching, and I wouldn't know. I lower the blinds, just in case, and put my hand on the Blessed Mother that sits on the windowsill.

I water Mrs. MacInerney's prized Chinese evergreen first. Then I climb the stairs to get the two spider plants that decorate the upstairs hall.

Usually the MacInerneys' house is filled with Kathleen's dirty towels on the floor, with the static of the police scanner, with Mr. Mac's stories from the firehouse, with all those family moments that I watch and study: pecks on the cheek, easy jokes, chores. Their absence makes the house seem strange, as though I'm walking through some sort of Museum of the Ordinary American Family. I step into Kathleen's room. Gloria, a ball of blond fluff, is standing on her hind legs, waiting for me and twitching her nose. We were ten when Kathleen bought her. We named her after Gloria Steinem, our favorite feminist.

"Hey, Glo." I pull her out and place her inside the nightstand drawer where Kathleen keeps her corn nuts. Then I change her water and stroke her head for a while as she munches. A stack of old *Tiger Beats* is tucked near her cage.

We shred them for lining now, but not long ago we used to decorate Kathleen's room with all the pinups that came inside. Our first Freddie-Prinze-in-a-tux came straight from the back cover, in fact. The sight of those relics of our growing up suddenly reminds me of when we used to put Gloria in the Barbie car and give her rides with Ken. It makes me sort of sad.

When I finish upstairs, I go back to the parlor, where I find Pablo sitting in Mr. Mac's favorite chair. There's no rule, really, but nobody ever sits there except Mr. Mac.

"What?" he says. The TV is tuned to *Switch*, that crime show about an ex-cop and an ex–con artist fighting crime.

"Nothing." I sit on the couch.

"It's this or *Jesus of Nazareth*," he says. "Or maybe neither?"

He joins me on the sofa and wraps his arms around me. Then he buries his nose in my hair and takes a deep breath.

"What are you doing?"

"I can't help it. It smells nice, like lemons."

"You've been working produce too long," I say.

"Either that, or you're incredibly hot."

Everything bad between us melts away as soon as we start kissing. He moves slowly and sweetly, until eventually, we're lying down next to each other, our legs intertwined on that narrow couch. He hooks his fingers through the belt loops at the small of my back to stop me from falling off.

"Staring contest," he says. "I warn you: I am undefeated."

His eyelashes brush against mine as he keeps his eyes

steady. I breathe in his spicy smell of aftershave and study the yellow and green in his eyes that I haven't noticed until now.

What's going to happen tonight? We have a whole empty house to ourselves. No cop is going to appear to shine a light into our car. No passerby is going to interrupt us from whatever. But I've only just started to date Pablo. I've been down this road with Angel, haven't I?

Tears fill my eyes as I fight to keep them open for our contest. He, on the other hand, looks completely calm, a smile curling at the edge of his lips.

"Do you surrender?" he whispers.

"Never."

"Be stubborn, then."

He disappears into a blur as the stinging finally forces my lids closed.

"Damn," I whisper. "You're freakish."

I bury my face in his neck. Every part of me feels weak and fluttery, though in the back of my mind I wonder if he'll throw the switch, morph into a groping beast like Angel.

Still, when he kisses me again, I find myself falling away from all those worries. He's pressed against me in a way that makes me shiver, and I can feel him go hard. He bites my lips softly and nuzzles my neck, but unlike Angel, Pablo's hands don't wander where I don't want them yet. Everything about him feels good.

The phone rings.

We freeze mid-kiss, as if caught.

Four rings, then silence.

He smiles at me and we start to kiss again, but again the phone sounds.

Could it be one of the neighbors wondering about the lights on?

"Should I answer it?" I whisper.

He shakes his head, still running his lips along my neck and collarbone. Six rings sound this time before the caller hangs up.

No one is with us, and yet it suddenly feels like someone is right here, tapping me on the shoulder. It's harder to concentrate on Pablo. When the phone rings yet again, I finally sit up.

Pablo sighs heavily. "Maybe Kathleen's messing with you," he says.

"She doesn't know we're here," I say.

Eight, nine times.

I can't stand it anymore, so I pick it up. If it's a curious neighbor, I'll say I'm here watering plants.

"Hello? MacInerney residence."

There's no one on the other end.

"They hung up." I glance at the clock: just past eleven. "We should probably get out of here."

He gives me a disappointed look as I slip out of his arms and head to the bathroom. I splash water on my face to clean the smudged mascara from around my eyes and run Kathleen's favorite brush through my hair. Then I gather my hair back up into a ponytail.

When I come back, Pablo has turned off the TV. He

hands me my sweatshirt and follows me through the house, clicking off lights behind us. We walk through the house in pitch-black, groping along the walls and giggling nervously as the old floors creak.

My hands are sweating as we reach the side door. Somehow I can't bring myself to step outside. The driveway patch where Kathleen and I once drew hopscotch suddenly seems eerie.

Pablo must see my fear.

"It's okay. Wait here." He steps outside and peers into the yard before jogging to the front of the house. He comes back for me. "We're good."

But when I follow him toward the sidewalk, I hear a rustling in the bushes and freeze. When I look, I see that it's only Tripod. His hackles are up, though, and his teeth are bared. When he sees me, he dashes off in the direction of the buildings.

Pablo slips his hand in mine as we hurry toward the car. I can't shake the feeling that we're like those paper ducks in a carnival shooting range. Maybe he feels the same, because we're practically running.

He opens my door and I climb inside, fast. But when he gets to his side, Pablo doesn't get in.

"No . . ." he says.

"What?" My heart is pounding the longer we're out here in the dark. "Get in!"

But Pablo doesn't listen. He walks around his car, his lips drawn to a hard line. I have no choice but to get out to see what's the matter.

Long key scrapes mark the entire length of his car. The grooves have dug out the blue paint all the way down to the metal. Someone has keyed his car from his door to the rear fender. He pounds the Camaro's roof in frustration and looks up and down the street, his jaw set tight.

"Who the hell did this?" he says.

I get back in the car and stare straight ahead as he starts the engine and pulls out, clearly upset.

Coincidence. I force the word through my mind, but it won't stick. My hands are shaking when I get out at my building. I run up my walkway, but it's not just the shooter I'm worried about. I have a tight feeling in my stomach that I always get when I want to "unsee."

Why was a Zippo lighter lying near the tires?

Chapter 19

"Where were you last night?"

"'Where were you last night?'"

Hector has always been good at mimicking me. He can say the words at the same time I do. Sometimes you can't tell who is doing the talking and who is copying.

I take a deep breath.

"Only creeps stalk people, you know that? Creeps like the shooter."

"'Only creeps stalk people, you know that? Creeps like the shooter.'"

He grins.

"Did you follow me last night, Hector?"

"'Did you follow me last night, Hector?'"

"Did you keep calling the MacInerneys?"

"'Did you keep calling the MacInerneys?'"

"Stop."

"'Stop.'"

"It was you, wasn't it?"

"'It was you, wasn't it?'"

"You can't mess up someone's car."

"'You can't mess up someone's car.'"

"Did you key Pablo's car?"

"'Did you key Pablo's car?'"

"*Answer* me."

"'*Answer* me.'"

"Asshole."

A snort, the finger. Conversation over.

Chapter 20

Sal closed early today for Good Friday, and I'm waiting for Kathleen to get home, if for nothing else than to get out of here. Hector is clicking through questions about rock formations on the Cyclo-Teacher. We've been giving each other plenty of icy space. He hadn't hassled me about the mirror again, and I haven't tried to force a confession about Pablo's car. I know he's behind it. I feel bad for Pablo, though. There's nothing I can do about it except give him the name and number of a good body-shop guy. He's the one Mr. Mac used to fix the mysterious scrapes on the Impala.

I glance at the clock. It's almost four in the afternoon, so Hector will be out of here soon. He's been leaving the house every day around this time and doesn't come home until I'm already in bed. I'm doing my best to pretend the little stalker doesn't exist, but his stench makes it impossible. Mima says boys this age always stink, but this is a lot worse than rank sneakers. His jacket smells like some sort of dying animal.

Anyway, the sound of keys in our lock makes me look up. Mima.

Maybe she has an Easter surprise? When we were little, she'd buy a Paas egg-coloring kit and let us loose in the kitchen with vinegar and those fizzy tablets.

She sets a twelve-pack box of transparent tape and two foil-wrapped chocolate bunnies on the end table in the living room. Then she looks at us for a few seconds, blinking back tears. Her skirt is turned slightly, and the crooked seam makes it look like her hip is broken.

"Mima?" I say.

"Me botáron," she finally blurts out.

Hector looks up from the Cyclo-Teacher. "You got fired?"

The *lay-uff* she's always worried about has finally happened. Mima's voice is flat. Mr. Small gave her the free tape, she says, along with her final paycheck in cash, when he laid her off this afternoon.

I feel the same queasiness I get when I ride elevators in tall buildings, that feeling of the floor dropping away. I can practically hear Mrs. MacInerney mentioning the latest unemployment figures over dinner: three hundred thousand people have no jobs.

"You need to come with me to the unemployment office to fill out forms, *oíste?"* Mima tells me. "Edna told me what I have to do, but those people talk too fast."

Already my mind is whirling like one of Mima's old tape spoolers. How will I fix this? What can I say to Papi to get some cash? How do I grovel to Manny so he won't call in the painters and try to whitewash the memory of us right out of the building? How will I fit in more hours at Sal's?

152

I put my head down, suddenly tired. I know I should say something to make Mima feel better, but I can't manage it. In fact, I'm angry at her. Shouldn't she be able to take better care of us? Isn't that what adults are supposed to do? Take care of their kids? Shield them from stuff? Pay bills? Why is everything the wrong way around for us?

Mima steps close to me and runs her fingers through my hair absently, the way she used to when I was little. I can barely breathe; her touch revolts me.

"Stop, Mima," I say.

She pulls away, and her hurt look drains every last bit of my energy. A chilly shame goes through me. I try to imagine Mima back when she was young and maybe happy. I think of that picture of her in a short veil on her wedding day, her shiny hair past her shoulders like mine. I've always wondered if she had to wear old shoes that day, too, if the dress was borrowed.

As if reading my mind, she takes a step closer.

"I was pretty and young once, too, Nora. I was carefree. I wanted things." It's an accusation, a disappointment in me somehow.

Hector tosses away the Cyclo-Teacher and grabs his jacket. He doesn't even look at her as she reaches for him.

"*Mijo*," she calls. "Don't be upset."

The door slams behind him on his way out.

And then Mima finally starts to sob.

I can't sleep that night or the next. I try to cheer myself up watching Brick sing "Dazz" on *Saturday Night Live*. It's the mother of all funk songs. Kathleen and I love to dance to it when it plays on the radio. I lie awake in bed, imagining myself dancing to "Dazz" with Pablo and then with Freddie Prinze until eventually the TV screen in my mind goes to electronic snow. A fantasy about dancing is better, I suppose, than thinking of Freddie dazed on ludes the way the magazines say he was before he shot himself, or imagining him boxed up in a marble drawer somewhere in Hollywood Cemetery, all that promise just turning to dust.

Hector's bed is still empty. Part of me is relieved and part of me is wondering what he's doing out so late. Every so often I hear the loud squeak of Mima's bedsprings and her slippers as she shuffles to the window to watch for him. She hates that he's roaming, but as usual, she's powerless to do anything about it. At least she's not nagging me to look for him.

I doze for a while, but finally, when I can't take it anymore, I get out of bed and bring our bedroom phone into the closet with me.

I know I shouldn't do it, but I dial Pablo's line. I want to hear his voice, have him talk to me so I can sleep.

"Hello?" It's a woman, groggy. "Hello? ¿Quién habla?"

I hang up.

It's his mother, I'll bet, and I know what she'd say. Probably what Mima would say. *What kind of girl calls a boy in the middle of the night?*

I dial again, this time to Kathleen. I never did go over to see her this afternoon. She keeps her Princess phone right by her bed, though, and I know she'll pick up. All the MacInerneys are light sleepers, thanks to a lifetime of calls about fires, emergencies.

She answers on the first ring, but her voice is groggy. "Hello?"

"It's me."

"Nora?"

"How was the beach?"

"Dull."

"You see Brick on TV?"

She lets out a big yawn. "Daaazzzzzz!" she says. Then she sings in a copy of his falsetto.

"It made me dream about Freddie."

"Nice." She yawns again. "What time is it, anyway?" I hear a rustle as she reaches for her clock. Then she groans. "You can't sleep?"

My throat gets so tight that I can't answer.

"Nora?" she says. "Are you okay?"

I never talk about my family to Kathleen. There's just no way she would understand how Mima, Hector, and I work. And I wonder, too, if she'd still want to be my friend if she really knew how ugly things can be here. Still, the quiet inside the closet gives me some courage to tell her a piece of it at least. "Mima lost her job yesterday."

There's a long silence, and I think maybe I imagined saying it. Or maybe Kathleen has drifted back to sleep.

"Crap," she says. "I'm sorry. What's she going to do?"

I have no answer, and that's the real trouble. Maybe

155

Mima will do nothing, which is the scariest idea of all. If she doesn't save us, who will?

"Hey. Come over for Easter tomorrow," Kathleen says. "Mom's baking a big ham. Uncle Tommy's coming."

"The chauvinist?."

"Yep. Promise you'll come. We can give him dirty looks while we eat Wilbur together."

"Go back to sleep, crazy."

"Going—but see you tomorrow, right?"

"Yeah."

I hang up and sit for a few minutes, cradled inside the musty coats. Then I pick my way to the back wall and grope for my old boots. I pull out my roll of money; it's as thick as one of those cigars Mima must have rolled as a kid. I hold it for a long while, thinking about what Mima said. What did she dream about when she was young? Did she try to squirrel away her pennies to get it? Or did her life just sweep her along until all those dreams had to be forgotten?

Mima's purse hangs on the doorknob in the hall. I tiptoe in my bare feet and unzip the inside pocket. The sound is loud against the silence of the apartment.

"Hector?" I didn't see Mima staring out the kitchen window again.

"No. It's just me."

She watches as I slip the money inside her purse, but she doesn't say anything. She just holds my gaze a moment and then turns back to the darkness outside.

In bed again, I stare at the ceiling, penniless, until I hear the keys in the lock. Soon enough, Hector's jacket fouls the air in our room.

A little while later, I watch as the sky turns pearl gray.

When Papi calls on Sunday morning, he informs me that our talk has to be quick. Fine with me; I've had no sleep.

"Linda and I hid one hundred and fifty Easter eggs all over the building for Pierre and his little pals," he tells me. "It's bedlam over here right now!"

I sit on the windowsill in my panties and gouge out my bunny's candy eyes, imagining Pierre's friends scavenging for plastic eggs, still believing a surprise is always a good thing.

Papi blathers on, but I can't find the energy to interrupt him. And what would I say? I'm too tired to think up a way to convince him to send us a little extra money or maybe, more important, to make him actually give a shit about what's happening here when it's not a holiday.

When we hang up, I pull on my jeans and a T-shirt. Mima is still curled in bed, exhausted. Hector is out cold.

I don't want to face breakfast with them, so I let myself out the front door and head to the roof to clear my head.

The church bells peal for the ten o'clock Mass. I can see the steeple with the crucifixion scene from here. No stores are open today, and the holiday bus schedule is slow, so there's a strange quiet on the street below. Kathleen will be home from church by noon. Maybe it will be okay to eat Easter ham and listen to Mrs. MacInerney rail against the Pope's refusal to allow women priests. Maybe thinking about the world's problems will be easier than trying to figure out my own.

Families are on their way up the hill to St. Andrew's, but all I want to do is throw rocks at them, spit on their heads. I can't bear the sight of all those pink-ribboned hats and white-patent-leather shoes, all those obedient little girls who believe.

"Sheep," I mutter, hating them all.

I picture myself a burning bird swooping down to frighten them.

Chapter 21

I gave too much change back to the lady who bought the Italian loaves.

That has to be it, because no matter how many times I total up the register, I come up about six bucks short, which never happens to me. I've been distracted, I guess.

"Sorry, Sal." I dig in my pocket for a few singles. "Here's the difference."

He turns to me from the front door and frowns. "Put that away. Mistakes happen."

I hope it's not pity that's making him so generous, but it might be. I had to tell him about Mima's job troubles so I could get time off. Turns out, it takes hours to wait in line at the unemployment office.

It's closing time, and the store is empty. Sal has the front door locked for the night, and he's waiting for Pablo to finish padlocking the back door and set the alarm.

"Thanks." I untie my apron and step out from behind the register. Pablo's Camaro is right out front, still sporting the scrapes. I hate looking at it now. Bodywork is going to set him back five hundred dollars, and he doesn't have all the money. He hasn't said a word about who could have done it, but I can't help but wonder if he suspects it was Hector. He's not stupid.

I've stopped walking home after work because of the murders. But the truth is that getting a ride is the only way I get a few minutes alone with Pablo. He drives like a turtle on purpose, sometimes going around my block a few times before letting me out. It would be nice if we could linger at the curb to say good-bye, but we're careful. The shooter could be lurking, or worse, Mima could see us from the window.

Sal taps his shoe nervously with his golf club, like he's waiting for trouble. Something is definitely on his mind.

"You got plans for that thing?" I ask.

He looks up and clears his throat. "I got something to say to you."

"Okay . . ."

He's actually blushing. "Don't go kissing Paulie too long in that muscle car."

Wow. A prickly feeling spreads across my cheeks. Did he see Pablo steal a kiss when I was fixing the busted door-knob in the john? I glance uncomfortably at the security mirrors he's got bolted at every corner of the store, but I decide to play dumb anyway. "What are you talking about, Sal?"

"Save it," he says. "I lost some of my hearing in the war, but not my eyeballs. I know when two kids are mooning over each other."

160

"Mooning?" I laugh nervously.

"I call it the way I see it, toots." He takes a step closer and sighs. "Look: Annemarie says it's none of my business what you two do after work. But you gotta watch yourselves, hear me? Check around the car before you get in. Don't be stupid and go parking where no one is around. There's a real sicko out there, and I don't want to end up reading about you in the paper."

As if he needs to remind me.

I try to make light of it and point at his club. "So you're going to do a security sweep with that thing before we get in the car?"

He looks at the club and shrugs. It's sad to see such a big guy look helpless. "That's the thing, sweetcakes. I'm no match for a bullet. And neither are you."

Sal sees us off, but we don't go more than a block before bright lights and sirens fill the street. We let the fire truck go by, but as we come up to my block, I see that it has pulled up on the curb in front of my building. My neighbors are outside watching smoke billow out of the basement windows.

I jump out of the car before Pablo has even stopped completely and race toward the crowd.

"Stay behind the tape, please," a fireman orders.

"But I live here!" I point at several other firemen who are on the roof right above my apartment. A few others are armed with axes and are circling behind the building, checking for any spreading flames. "Is there fire up there, too?"

"Standard protocol to check the roof. I'm pretty sure the

fire's only in the basement, but we're checking. Probably one of the dryers."

I look around for Mima and Hector, but it's hard to see in the smoky darkness. Unfortunately I do see Sergio, leaning against his Monte Carlo. We haven't run into each other since I broke his mirror.

Then I spot Stiller and run over. Her apartment is right above the basement. "What happened?" I ask.

"A big mess is what happened," she says. "I saw smoke coming up around the steam pipes. I rang all the bells to get people out, just in case." She frowns. "And were our smoke alarms working? *No.*"

"Nora!"

Mima's near the chain-link fence at the far end of the property, looking as if things are as bad as *The Towering Inferno.* She'd been sleeping when the lobby buzzer sounded, she says. That's when she ran downstairs.

Someone grabs my arm. "You okay?" It's Kathleen and her mom. "We heard it on the scanner."

"Fine—I was just getting home from work," I say.

"Well, it's pretty small, thank goodness," Mrs. MacInerney says. "They'll have it controlled in a few minutes." She looks at Mima and digs in her brain for her high-school Spanish. "*No ser preocupado.* Everything is *bon,*" she says, trying to cobble together some words to soothe her. Her Spanish stinks worse than Kathleen's.

Just then, Pablo joins us, too. "Everybody in your family okay?"

Mima stares at him blankly. This is not the way I would

162

have ever planned on Mima meeting Pablo, so I stand there stupidly for a second, trying to decide what to do. Finally Pablo extends his hand.

"Mima, this is Pablo," I say. "We work together."

Pablo's eyes linger on mine for just a second, but I don't add anything more.

"*Mucho gusto,*" he says. Then he shakes hands with Mrs. MacInerney, too.

Meanwhile, Manny is pacing and coming undone as he talks with some of the tenants, "I don't understand it. There has never been a single frayed wire in the cellar! No paint thinners or kerosene. No loose trash, ever! And look at the mess they made of the door. I just painted it last week!"

"It could have been set by some thug," someone says. "The whole city is burning."

"I keep the basement locked," Manny says firmly.

Stiller crosses her arms. "Well, who's to say the thug isn't our landlord, then? We've got no-questions-asked insurance policies all over this city. What's easier than burning people right out of their neighborhoods?"

Manny stops in his tracks and glares. "What kind of crazy accusation are you making now?"

Stiller shrugs. "It's not crazy and you know it. In fact, I hear that some building supers arrange for a cut of the insurance money if they offer a helping hand."

"How dare you! Watch it with that mouth, Stiller," Manny warns.

She narrows her eyes and seems to grow to her full size. "Watch it or what?"

"Stiller, for heaven's sake," Mrs. MacInerney says. "Calm down; you're upset. Mr. Barros has lived here for years."

"I'll calm down when I see the extent of the smoke damage to my place *and* the fire marshal's report." She raises her voice even louder so that every fireman can hear. "And there better be a thorough inspection!"

"Mr. Barros?" Thankfully two firemen call Manny over before things between him and Stiller can get any uglier.

But is Stiller right? Would Manny help burn our homes to the ground for insurance money? I'm not one of his fans, but it's a stretch, even for me. Sergio, that's another story. Who knows? Maybe that's why his uncle sent him this way: because he's perfect for the job. You'd have to have absolutely no conscience to do something like that.

That, or be a pyro.

I look around. "Where's Hector?" I whisper to Mima. Could one of the flame balls have hit something? Was he screwing around with his stupid lighter again?

She shakes her head. *"¿Crees que está en el techo?"* she whispers, knowing the roof is one of Hector's favorite hangouts. *"¡Ay, Dios mio!"*

I look up at the firemen leaning over the roof ledge. "They would have seen him by now."

It takes another thirty minutes for the firemen to finish, but Hector never shows up. The firemen start to detach their hose lines and replace the caps on the hydrants. They're leaving behind a big mess. The basement door is in splinters, and there is broken glass everywhere.

"Why don't you stay at our place, Stiller?" says Mrs.

MacInerney softly. "The stink lasts for a while." She lowers her voice. "I have some Baileys that might make us feel better. And we can ask Pat to get the inspectors over here for you."

Stiller's eyes are glued to two firemen talking to Manny, though. "I want to hear what they have to say first," she says. "I'll come by in a little while."

Mrs. MacInerney sighs. "Come on, then, Kathleen. Let's get the guest room ready."

Kathleen gives me a hug and whispers in my ear. "Save me. It'll be like being trapped in a twenty-four-hour civics class with these two."

"I'll call you later," I say.

"I should head out, too," Pablo says.

His voice startles me. In all the commotion, I'd almost forgotten he was here.

"I'll tell you what happens at work tomorrow."

We stand there awkwardly with Mima looking on. What I'd really like to do is hug him good-bye, but I keep my arms crossed, hoping he'll get the message. Luckily he does.

"Good night, then," he says, sticking out his hand like a goof. He gives me a crazy grin and walks away.

It's still a while longer before Manny gets the all clear to let us back inside. Finally he gathers us tenants on the stoop for a meeting. He's wrung out, but on the flip side, he looks a little puffed up with his man-in-charge role.

"By order of the fire department, the basement is off-limits completely until further notice." He points at the yellow caution tape blocking the steps. "The good news is that the rest of the building looks structurally sound except, of course, for 1E, which has sustained smoke damage only."

"Which will be repaired promptly," Stiller grumbles. That's her apartment.

Manny crosses his arms and stares right at her. "Now, to be clear: according to the firemen in charge, nothing points to negligence on the part of building management."

"Then what happened?" Stiller asks. "Spontaneous combustion?"

There's a murmur among the neighbors, but before Manny can answer, one of the firemen steps forward. "It is too soon to tell, ma'am. Unfortunately we do see alligator charring near the beams over the trash cans, but we'll have to wait for a report. Could take thirty to sixty days for the lab to tell us for sure. There's a backlog."

Stiller frowns. "Alligator charring? What does that mean?"

"It's the way wood burns when a fire accelerant is used to ignite it."

It takes a second for the information to sink in. She turns slowly toward Manny and arches her brow.

"Oh, you mean like *arson*?" she says pointedly.

Manny holds up his hand. "Stop right there, Stiller." He looks around at all the tenants, who suddenly don't look so sure about him. "I don't know who set this fire, but I *will* find out. I promise you: whoever started this little blaze isn't going to get away with it."

I shift on my feet, thinking about Hector and about all that Mr. Mac has told me over the years. It's not always money at the bottom of fires. Sometimes, it's just the power of watching things destroyed.

"*¿Qué dijo el hombre?*" Mima whispers.

"They're investigating," I say.

Mima crosses herself.

Manny wraps up the meeting. "If you find smoke damage, see me in the morning," he calls after us as we file inside. "There will be paperwork."

The smell is overpowering on the lower floors, but at least it gets better at each higher landing.

Mima left the door unlocked when she ran out, but everything looks fine in our apartment. The only damage I can see is a tiny soot mark by the heat pipes where the smoke probably billowed up. I can touch it up myself and not wait for Manny to get around to it. God knows how many forms it will take for him to show up with a can of paint and a roller.

Mima rubs her temples. "This smell is going to give me a headache," she says. She walks to the bedrooms, trying to throw open our old windows to let in some fresh air. I hear her grunting. "Nora, come help me," she calls. "This one is stuck."

But I don't answer.

I'm still standing near the door, where we always hang our keys.

Our basement key is gone.

Chapter 22

"Nooooora! You didn't get roasted in the bonfire!"

I squeeze my eyes shut in prayer. *Lord, I beg you: all I ask is that he falls and breaks his leg.*

Sergio is busy nailing sheets of plywood against Stiller's window, a cigarette dangling from his lips as he works.

I try to hurry inside, but the front stoop is a cluttered maze. Everybody's junk has been hauled out of the storage units. Manny's sign is taped to the glass doors.

BASEMENT UNDER REPAIR!!!

CLAIM YOUR ITEMS TODAY!!!

UNCLAIMED ITEMS WILL BE DONATED!!!!

Next to it is a sheet of looseleaf with Stiller's writing: *If any of your personal belongings are illegally confiscated, call me.*

The MacInerneys' number is listed next to her name.

I pick my way through ash-covered boxes of Christmas ornaments, rusted bed frames, and old cribs. There's even a couple of Mattel Big Wheels that belonged to the kids from 3C. The plastic wheels have melted down like crayons. It's practically modern art.

My own bike is propped against the building among the junk. It's covered in soot, spiderwebs cling to the spokes, and the chain hangs off the gears. Other than that, though, it's in miraculously good shape. It's been so long since I've ridden it that I almost forgot I even owned a bike.

I pull it free to take it upstairs, but Sergio hops down from his stepladder and saunters over to me just as I'm struggling with the door.

"You'll never be able to haul it up three flights of stairs all by yourself, babe."

"We'll see." I kneel down and crank the pedals so I can hook up the chain. "And I'm not your babe."

"You know, if you weren't so bitchy, I might offer to help you bring it upstairs."

"And if you weren't such a dreg, I might want you to." I stand up and wedge the door open with my butt. Then I spot Hector's bike. It wasn't so long ago that he'd race down the block on that thing. I go back and drag it out of the pile, too.

Sergio leans against the mailboxes, watching as I struggle. "By the way, you owe me some money for a certain mirror. Didn't anybody ever teach you to respect people's property?"

I stop what I'm doing and face him square on.

"I don't owe you a dime," I say. "And I've already asked you to leave Hector alone. He's got enough problems without adding in you."

Sergio pretends to rub his eyes as if he's crying.

"A troubled kid. *Waaaaah . . .*"

I wobble up five steps to the first landing and drop my bike. The fender scrapes my leg. I look up the next set of stairs, a much longer climb. As much as I hate to admit it, Sergio is right. It's going to be a bitch to get up to the fourth floor.

"Have fun doing it the hard way." Sergio blows a kiss at me. Then he takes off, whistling.

That night we're eating dinner, side by side on our portable TV tables as usual, when the doorbell rings. No one buzzed from the lobby. Mima puts the chain on the door and peers through the peephole, just in case it's Stiller.

"*¿Quién es?*"

"Fire Department."

She looks over at me and opens the door with the chain still on.

"Ma'am, I'm James Costa with the Bureau of Fire Investigation." The man in the hall holds up his badge. "We're investigating yesterday's incident. We'd like to ask you a few questions. We're interviewing all the tenants regarding a suspicious fire."

For once in my life, I'm pissed that Mr. Mac has so many friends willing to do him favors. There are dozens of other fires they could be investigating, entire boroughs that they could be digging out of rubble, but no, here they are, investigating a blaze that took out a few garbage cans.

Mima holds up her finger to tell him to wait and closes

170

the door. She turns to me. *"Nora, mira a ver lo que me dice este señor . . ."*

I never like translating for Mima, but this really puts me on edge. I didn't say a word to her about the missing key, deciding I'd ask Hector myself. Unfortunately I've tried to get him alone all afternoon, but Mima has been in the way.

I glance at him, but he doesn't even seem to notice that we've been interrupted. He keeps eating his *congri*, eyes glued to the TV screen.

I go to the door to slide off the chain.

"Hi," I say. "My mother doesn't speak English, so—"

"This will be brief," the fire marshal says without looking up from his pad. He writes down the number of our apartment and our surname from the handwritten tab over the doorbell. He has a holstered gun, I notice, and a set of handcuffs.

Mima stands next to me as I repeat each question he reads from his list.

Does she know if anyone kept a grill downstairs? Did she notice paints or paint thinners? At what time did she first become aware of the fire? Had she seen anyone unfamiliar in or around the building yesterday? Who was home with her at the time?

"Mi hijo," she says. *My son.*

I blink.

"She says my brother was home."

"How about you? Were you home, too?"

"I was at work," I say. "I got back just as the fire trucks were arriving."

He looks past me. "Is this your brother over there?"

I nod, uneasy. "Yes."

"Do you mind?"

"*¿Qué dice?*" Mima asks as he steps into our living room. "*Estamos comiendo, por Dios.*"

"We're eating," I repeat.

But the fire marshal is already standing near Hector. He looks back at me and smiles. "I'll be out of your way in a moment. All right?"

My heart is pounding, wondering if Hector's yellow sheet is about to get longer. Cops and firemen are pals, after all. Mima and I stand by helplessly as the marshal asks him the same questions. My brother answers with precision, but they are all lies. He'd seen the smoke around the pipes. He'd run down the stairs in the first rush of tenants. No, he'd seen no one "suspicious" in the cellar or around the building.

The fire marshal flips his notebook shut and glances at the full ashtray. One of Hector's lighters is sitting beside it.

"Were you down there at all yesterday?" he asks.

The pressure in my ears makes me feel as though my head is going to explode.

"In the basement?" Hector says.

The officer smiles. He reminds me of Mr. Mac somehow. Calm, unassuming.

"Just taking out the trash," Hector says with a shrug. "That's it."

"Was the door locked when you went down there?"

Hector leans back, thinking. "No. I don't think it was."

"No?"

"No." He shrugs. "Weird, right?"

"Is it usually locked?" the marshal asks.

"I don't know." He turns to me. "Nora is the one who's in charge of taking out the trash. I did it because she was working. Ask her."

My mouth goes dry as the officer turns. Hector grins at me from behind his back. My eyes flit to our bedroom, where the closet door is slightly open.

"It's usually locked . . ." I let my voice trail off as I look back at him. "People forget sometimes."

I want to scream in the quiet that follows as he writes my words down.

"Are you a friend of Mr. Mac?" I blurt out. "His daughter, Kathleen, is my best friend."

He looks up and smiles pleasantly. "Mac's the very best."

Hinges squeak behind us. Mima holds open the door.

"Dale las gracias."

"She says 'Thank you,'" I say, although I'm sure what she really means is *Get out.* "I'm sorry we couldn't help."

He hands me his card. "Sorry to have disturbed your dinner." He nods at Mima. *"Gracias,"* he says.

I close the door and sit back down to stare at my cold dinner. The doorbell rings at Miss Burne's apartment across the hall, and a moment later, I hear the murmur of voices.

Hector leans back and lights up.

He's lying, and there has to be a reason. I turn to him, ready to ask, but one look at Mima's face and the words turn to ash on my tongue.

No one says a word.

Chapter 23

The basement is off-limits. Manny was very clear on that point.

I step over the caution tape anyway, grinding broken glass under my shoes as I climb down the stairs in the dark. I waited until Hector and Mima were asleep before I came down.

The lamp must have been smashed when the firemen hacked down the door, so I have to sweep the flashlight beam on the steps as I go, but it doesn't help much.

As soon as I push the door open with my foot, the stench of a cold fire greets me. I move my flashlight along the sooty walls. The washers and dryers are ruined, their metal warped and black. Same for the garbage cans.

Maybe this is just my stupid imagination. We've mislaid that key plenty of times before. It's possible that one·of us just forgot to put it back when we took out the trash.

I step inside.

Water drips down from the overhead beams, and the ash on the floor is like shoe-sucking silt. I'm not even sure what I'm looking for, except for some reason to believe that

Hector didn't set this. My eyes scan the mud for any sign of him, his lighters, a can of fluid, anything.

But just then, a shadow flickers outside the window. I switch off my light and hold my breath, waiting. A few seconds later, I hear scratchy footsteps coming down the stairs. Panicking, I dash for cover and wedge myself behind the door just as it swings open.

Soon Tripod's wet snout is poking at me. His fur is matted and his three paws are completely covered in muddy ash.

"Get out of here," I tell him.

"Who's there?" a voice calls out.

I hold my breath, but a second later, I'm blinded by a flashlight.

Manny stands there in a dirty undershirt and pajama pants, looking like he's going to explode.

"Nora? What are you doing down here? I told you to keep out!"

I point suddenly to the dog.

"I saw him slip in here and tried to get him out."

"At three in the morning?"

I swallow hard. "I couldn't sleep with all the commotion. I saw Tripod from my window. He was sniffing around the cellar steps. I didn't want him to get hurt. There's glass everywhere."

He crosses his arms, and I can tell he doesn't believe me.

"Let's go, Tripod," I say, whistling to him.

Manny stands in my way. "Are you sure this is about the dog?"

"What do you mean?"

"I mean that it's strange to find a kid wandering around here in the middle of the night, especially since we've been having some trouble lately. A break-in . . . A fire . . ."

Can he smell a rat? I channel the spirit of Stiller and stand my ground.

Tripod watches us, growling and circling.

"First of all, I'm not a kid. I came for Tripod. That's all. Somebody ought to care about a disabled stray, for God's sake."

Manny gives in and shakes his head. "Stay out of here. You could get hurt," he says. "And stop feeding this mutt, will you, please? This is a no-pets-allowed building, remember?"

I edge past him.

"Come on, boy," I call out. "Let's clean you up."

Chapter 24

I WILL DO IT AGAIN.

I wander the deli, trying to look busy instead of thinking about the newest murders or the message left behind.

Pablo and I don't talk about Valentina Suriani and Alexander Esau as we work, but it feels like they are around every corner. They were eighteen and twenty years old, more or less like us. They went to the movies and found out that the city isn't huge at all. In fact, it can shrink down to the size of a gun barrel, just like that.

Customers are crowded around the deli case, but nobody is clamoring for coffee or orange juice. Mr. Farina, on his afternoon break, isn't arguing with Sal about Joe Frazier. It's Wednesday afternoon, and despite the big crowd in the store, it's so quiet that I can hear my own footfalls against the grit on the floor.

A special news report of Valentina's funeral airs on the TV set that's bolted near the ceiling. Reporters are crawling all over St. Theresa's in the Bronx, holding up microphones to kids dressed up in their Sunday clothes. Cops photograph the crowd in case the killer is hiding in plain sight and has come back to see his handiwork.

I glance at the screen in time to see Mrs. Suriani being helped up the church steps.

And then I wonder: Does the shooter have a mother, too? Does she know he's a monster? Is she afraid to say so and turn him in?

I WILL DO IT AGAIN.

The threat is at everyone's throat. The shooter left a note to the city in the laps of the victims as they lay dying.

The question now is: Who's next?

I tuck a loose bobby pin back inside my bun and reach for the next row of cans as Pablo and I check expiration dates. I move down each section like a machine, growing more irritable as the news report goes on and on.

Cream of celery soup, 1978, fine. Chicken and stars, 1979, good.

I stop at a can marked for this month.

"Does April 1977 count as expired or what?" My voice is too loud, annoyed. I show Pablo the suspicious green pea soup. "What do you think? Can it kill you or not?" Tears spring to my eyes.

He stands so close to me that I can see a tiny shaving nick near his jaw. He takes the can and tosses it into a box marked PERISHED.

"Why don't you take a break?" He glances at the mesmerized crowd. "It's stuffy in here."

*   *   *

I let my feet dangle off the concrete ledge and drink a Coke to clear my head. There isn't much fresh air out here on the loading dock, just smelly puddles and rusted fencing. The lots behind all the stores are stacked with odds and ends: buckets, broken broom handles, old signs. Still, it's better than being trapped inside with the funeral coverage.

But the truth is that it's not just the funeral that has me in a funk. It's everything. It's wondering why Mima lied about Hector being home when the fire broke out. It's the fact that she hasn't found a full-time job. It's about how Manny will start breathing down our necks again any day now. And it's about people knowing we're not making it.

In desperation, Mima made up some flyers and advertised herself for cleaning jobs. They're in every shop on the block, except Sal's. GOOD HOUSECLEANING. GOOD PRICE. CALL ALBA, followed by our phone number. I know I should have put one up on the bulletin board out front, but I couldn't bring myself to do it, not with Pablo around. His family had servants back in Colombia, *mujeres* like Mima to wash their dirty underwear and wipe the crumbs from their tables.

I close my eyes and let the sunshine warm my cheeks. *Please, God, let the summer come soon.* I make a mental list of all the things I love about summer. High school will be over forever. I'll hang out at Jones Beach and swim past the breaking waves to the deep. My skin will clear up, and I'll be tan. I'll flash my ID and dance where and when I feel like it. And, if I'm lucky, I'll save up again and move out, far away from Mima and Hector.

I'm just starting to relax a little when a loud metal bang

makes me jump. Through the fence slats, I can see into the lot next door where we all dump our trash. Matt wrestles two garbage bags toward the Dumpster. He hasn't said much to me since I almost ran him over with Mr. Mac's Impala.

The stink of rotting trash wafts in my direction, and I wish he'd hurry up and close the lid.

Matt tosses the first bag over his head, and it lands with a thud. But he doesn't toss the second one right away. Instead, he pulls out a marker and makes a large X on the side of the bag before pitching it in. The lid slams down with a head-splitting bang, and he walks off.

What the hell is *that* about?

"Gross."

Pablo stands behind me, fanning off the stink in the air.

"Tell me about it," I say. "I don't know how you can stand dumping the trash back here."

"The smell isn't even the worst part," he says. "There was a rat the size of a beaver in there two nights ago."

Pablo sits down beside me and nudges my ribs with his elbow. When he's sure we aren't being watched, he puts his arm around my shoulder. "You okay?" he asks. "You seem a little freaked out."

I shrug. "You don't look so relaxed yourself, you know." And it's true. His eyes are bloodshot and he's got a day-old beard.

"Tax Accounting is kicking my ass, and finals are coming up. I'm working a D right now. I have to talk to Sal about time off to do some studying."

The thought depresses me. Seeing Pablo every day at work is one of the few things that keeps me sane.

"You wouldn't miss this cushy job?" I wave my Coke over the expanse of the loading dock.

"Just for a couple of weeks — if Sal goes for it."

"I can help cover you, I guess," I say. "I'll be here any way." I don't add a word about needing some extra cash. He doesn't need to know.

"Yeah?"

"And then you'll owe me a favor." I arch my brow. "That will be fun to hang over your head."

"It's pretty physical," he says. "And not in a good way." He smiles wickedly and gives me a quick peck. "You have to tackle *that* rancid heap, for one thing." He points at the Dumpster. "You sure you want to deal with that?"

"It'll be better than being trapped at home, believe me."

He stares at his feet, thinking. "I won't be here to give you a ride home after work," he says quietly.

I know what he's getting at. I'll have to wait for the bus or else walk home alone in the dark. But who says that it's any safer with him at my side? Look at Val and Alex.

I drain my soda and crush the can against the ledge.

"It's four blocks," I say, trying to brush it off. "Nothing is going to happen."

Chapter 25

Stiller moved into Mrs. Murga's old apartment while her place gets completely repainted. I have no idea how she talked Manny into it, but Stiller obviously doesn't see it as a favor.

"It's the least that man can do for an inconvenienced and displaced tenant," she says.

She pushes a chair to the center of the room and looks around at the studio. She looks out of place here, if you ask me. Mrs. Murga was tiny and shriveled, the perfect size for a studio. But Stiller is different. Everything about her is big. Her height, her hair, her personality—all jumbo size.

"It's kind of tight, isn't it?"

"I've lived with less," she says simply. "Besides, this is the perfect way to keep my eye on the repairs. Who knows how that chump will try to take his time or cut corners?"

"So, are they still trying to find out how the fire started?" I ask casually.

"*Hmpf,*" she says. "It'll be months before we get that report, and it'll be inconclusive. It's a racket, I tell you. You'll see." She turns to me. "Why? You have any theories?"

"No," I say quickly.

It's been two weeks since the blaze, but the whole building still smells faintly of a cold hearth. Worse, we're all crowded with our junk from the storage units. Manny won't let us keep anything in the hall, either. I've been trying to make the best of it, but it's a pain to use my bike as a drying rack for bras.

This is why I'm here to see Stiller.

"So, I need a favor," I say.

She turns around from taping up her posters. This one is a big ink drawing of Flo Kennedy wearing big peace earrings. DON'T AGONIZE. ORGANIZE.

"Manny's hassling you." Her eyes practically glimmer at the prospect of a good fight.

"Not any more than usual."

"Oh."

"I was wondering if I could park my bike in here for a couple weeks."

"Why?"

"I want to ride to work. The shooter is after girls in cars. Nobody's been shot on a bike, right?"

She holds my gaze a moment too long. "Your mom still looking for work?"

I nod. She must have seen the flyer on the lobby bulletin board and put things together.

"That thing's pretty big," she says, checking out my bike. I've got it leaned against the wall in the hallway.

"It'll be at work most of the time."

"I don't know."

"It's hard to climb the stairs with it," I say. "You'd really be helping me out."

Stiller sighs and points to the wall. "Over there."

It's actually nice to ride again the way I used to when I was little. I pump my legs and lean into the turns as I go around the block for a trial run. The tires feel low. Mr. Mac is washing the Impala in his driveway, so I stop.

"Borrowing supplies, Mr. Mac," I tell him. I grab the tire pump and the oilcan off his work shelf in the garage and get to work. "Is Kathleen around?" I ask.

"She's inside studying with Eddie," he says.

"Oh, good."

He gives me a knowing look and then bends down to suds up the Impala's tires.

Studying. Yes, I'm sure. Kathleen and I talked about Eddie last night, in fact.

"I'm going to lose you again," I told her on the phone. "You always forget me when you're in love." Only last weekend, she canceled our plans because Eddie wanted to go dancing with her.

"I'm not in love. I'm in boredom. And how about *you*? Pablo is all you think about."

"Touché."

"I promise. We won't let that happen again," she said. "Men won't crowd out our friendship. We agreed, remember?"

We'll see.

When I'm done filling the tires, I put everything back on the shelf and get on my bike.

"So, what do you think of my wheels?" I ask Mr. Mac.

"Sharp. Getting exercise?"

"Getting to work." I pedal to the end of the driveway and ring my dorky bell. "Tell Kathleen I'll call her later," I call to Mr. Mac. Then I take the long way, just to have a few more minutes before I have to get to Sal's.

•   •   •

SON OF SAM—

WE KNOW YOU ARE NOT A WOMAN HATER—AND KNOW HOW YOU HAVE SUFFERED. WE WISH TO HELP YOU AND IT IS NOT TOO LATE. CALL CAPTAIN BORELLI OR INSPECTOR DOWD AT 844-0999 OR WRITE TO THEM AT THE 109TH PRECINCT, FLUSHING, NEW YORK.

"Some pen pals," Annemarie mutters as she closes the *Daily News*. "*He's* suffered? What about those families who aren't going to see their kids anymore? *That's* suffering."

She puts one copy of the paper aside and ties a string around the rest of the unsold newspapers that I'm supposed to put in the trash. The copy she keeps out is for her creepy scrapbook of disasters. She has cutouts from Pearl Harbor, Nixon's impeachment, and (strangely) Woodstock. Today's paper is going in, too, as part of history.

So far, no paper has run the whole letter left by the

shooter at the murder scene last week—and that's driving Annemarie crazy. She reads the *Daily News* and the *Post* every day to get the gory details. Today's tidbit: he calls himself by a strange new name: Son of Sam.

Who the hell is Sam?

I toss the bundle of newspapers out on the curb near my bike.

The sun sets around eight o'clock now—closing time— but thanks to having to cover Pablo duties, I'm at Sal's much later. I cash out and write up the deposit slip, as usual. But then I sweep the aisles, lock up the vault, pull the grates, and (my least favorite) dump the trash, too. It's tough to get it all done before nine, and by then it's pitch-dark, like now. I never knew the five minutes that it takes to pedal home could feel so long.

Sal cuts off the lights and locks the front door. He watches as I unchain my bike. "I don't know how you can steer a bike with no hands."

"It's in the hips, Sal," I tell him. "Besides, it's faster than going back and forth to the alley on foot." I make a muscle. "And look at these biceps I'm getting."

Up the street, the neon sign on the Satin Lady Lounge is blinking brightly, and a few men are already gathering outside. Naturally Sergio is one of them. I see the dome light shining inside his Monte Carlo.

Sal frowns at the sight of him. "The good-for-nothin' is starting early tonight, I see." He yanks down the grate and clicks the padlock in place.

186

"Good night," I say.

"Take care, then, sweetcakes," he says.

The walkway that leads back to the shared Dumpster is right behind the pharmacy. If you don't know it's there, you can miss it: just a narrow stretch of brick that sits between Mr. Farina's place and the candy store. Twice a week, one of the store owners opens the back fence at the other end of the alley for the dump truck to clear it all out.

I lean my bike against the candy store's stoop, grab up the bags, and head toward the dim lights.

The smell makes me gag, even before I get close. Soon enough, I see why. Someone left the top open by mistake. The late spring sun during the day is hot enough to cook the trash into a rank heap.

I've already discovered that the Dumpster is crawling with roaches, but rodents in there all night would be a nightmare, especially the rats that Pablo mentioned. Without the lid down, they'll drag everybody's trash all over the place. It'll get strewn everywhere, and guess who will have to clean it all up?

Just as I'm about to toss in my bag and slam the lid, I hear something moving inside that metal box. I take a step back and look around for something to scare away the rats. A chunk of broken cement will have to do.

I step back a few paces and send it sailing, praying that whatever animal is rummaging inside will take off instead of charging at me.

The clang is enormous.

But to my shock, it isn't a rat or a raccoon that pops its head out and snarls at me.

It's Hector.

He stands up waist deep in that smelly pile and stares over the side.

For a second, neither one of us moves. But then he recognizes me, and his eyes narrow to angry slits.

I walk toward him slowly, the smell catching at the back of my throat.

"What are you doing?" I ask as I reach the side of the Dumpster. The thought of vermin crawling all around him makes me shudder. Is he hungry? I wonder. Is he Dumpster diving? Has it come to this? "It's filthy in there. Get out of there before you get the plague!"

"Get out of here, Nora," he says. He turns from me and grabs something out of an open bag near his leg. When I look, I see that it's marked with a large X on its side.

I remember Matt right away. Something's up.

"Why are you going through Mr. Farina's trash?"

But Hector ignores me. He shoves what he's taken into his pocket and lifts himself over the side. Bits of trash cling to his clothes. Suddenly I understand the rancid smell that always hangs on his leather jacket. He's been doing this for a while.

He starts to walk off, but I reach for his arm. "Hector, I asked you a question. Answer me."

He twists violently and gets out of my grip, but I'm not about to let him off without some answers. Just as he turns, I stuff my hand inside that grimy pocket to pull free what he's hiding.

It's a plastic sandwich bag filled with about a dozen yellow pills.

My heart sinks. I know what they are. There was a time when Mima had to take them for her nerves, but everybody knows that Lemmons are good for a buzz, too.

And everybody around here also knows where to find them.

Sergio.

"What are you doing with quaaludes?" I ask. "Are you taking *this* shit now, too?"

Hector doesn't answer. Instead, he shoves me with all his might. I hold tight to the plastic bag as he presses me against the brick wall.

"Give it!" His spittle flies in my face.

"No."

We're too far in the alley for anyone to see what's happening. Suddenly my brother's expression goes as dark as I've ever seen it. Before I can scramble away, he leans his forearm against my windpipe and presses hard.

"I could kill you," he growls. "I could just fucking kill you."

The last shred of my little brother disappears. I tug on his arm, but he leans in harder until I can't get air. My eyes water and bulge as I claw at his jacket, trying to break free, but the only sound I can manage is a series of little gasps. I kick and squirm, but his eyes fix on mine, and I feel my tongue grow fat, and a ringing sound starts in my ears. The smell of rot rises between us. Silver pinpricks dance in front of my eyes as a cold wave starts at the base of my skull. Finally my hands go limp, and I slump to the ground, gagging.

He snatches the bag from where I've dropped it and shoves it back in his pocket. He's breathing hard, as though he's run a marathon.

I hug my knees, waiting for him to kick me the way he did Tripod, but in the end, he doesn't. He adjusts his jacket collar and wipes some filth off the sleeve. Then he stalks off and leaves me alone.

I drop my bike outside Stiller's door. I don't give a shit if it gets stolen or if Manny complains. I'm halfway up the stairs when I hear her door open.

"Hey." She takes one look at me and frowns. "What's the matter, Nora?"

I don't answer.

Instead, I run all the way up to the fourth floor and go straight to the bathroom.

"Nora?" Mima calls. "*¿Llegaste?*"

I let the water get as hot as I can take it. Steam clouds the mirror as I strip down. Only when the scalding water hits my skin do I finally let myself cry.

Chapter 26

Hours later, and the skin on my neck still feels raw.

I lie perfectly still and listen to him pee in the bathroom. I cover my mouth and nose with my sheets and pretend to sleep; the stench from the jacket he's dropped in the hall makes me more nauseous than usual.

Click! The only light is the orange ember from his cigarette.

"Stay out of my business," he says.

Silence.

"Why do you care, anyway?" he asks.

I don't answer. Why *do* I care? Because he's my brother? What does that mean beyond DNA?

He takes a few more drags and then comes to my bed. I clench my fist, ready to punch him hard in the face if I have to, scream like I'm being killed. But instead of hitting me, he stands there until I finally open my eyes. Then he reaches into his pocket and pulls out a wad of bills.

"See this? Sergio pays nice for Lemmons, Nora. Five bucks for Matt, who skims them, and five bucks for me, a finder's fee."

"You're stealing from an old man," I say. "Not to mention helping a sleazoid like Sergio."

"That blind bastard probably drops more of these than I'm stealing, idiot. Besides, they go to people who *want* them, Nora, so what the fuck do you care?"

I'm shaking now. "The question is why *don't* you care, Hector? Why can't you think about how you're hurting other people with this shit?"

He rains a fistful of bills on my head as though they're rose petals. "Sorry to disappoint you, Mother Superior," he says. "I guess I'm just a disciple of hell."

Chapter 27

The bruise on my neck is compact and the color of liver. It's right at my voice box, too, so when I stand at the mirror, it looks like a bullet hole to the throat.

Mima pretends she doesn't see it.

We're in a secret club together. All those times I never asked about *her* wrists, about the fleshy part of her thigh, even the faint circle of teeth at her cheek all those years ago after one of Hector's tantrums. More recently, the days she uses my CoverGirl without my permission.

Her eyes flit across my throat, but she looks away and goes back to the dishes in the sink.

"I need you to read a letter that came yesterday," she tells me. "It's from the school."

There's a small stack of mail propped up against the bowl of plastic fruit. There's a fat one addressed to me from the City University system, which I slide into my back pocket.

Then I find the one she means. It's from the guidance office at school, and it's addressed to PARENTS OF HECTOR LÓPEZ.

Mima scrubs the black bottom of her frying pan as I translate each sentence. He's flunked English and math, and he's racked up so many absences he'll have to attend summer school if he's going to graduate next year at all.

"*Ese niño es la candela,*" she mumbles. "He's brilliant, but that school has never known what to do with him."

I lay the letter on the table, my stomach suddenly queasy at the smell of Ajax in the humid air. I don't want to spend one more second thinking about Hector and his problems.

"It says you have to request his summer-school site by next week," I say.

Mima stops scrubbing and stares at me.

"Summer school? How do they think I'm going to get him to summer school if he won't go to regular school during the year? Are they stupid over there at the Board of Education?"

I shrug. "What can I tell you, Mima? He has to go."

"You'll have to talk to him," she says.

There's a long pause, my finger traveling to my throat. "No," I finally say.

Mima puts down her sponge and turns to me slowly. The truth about my brother hangs in the air between us, electric.

"No?" she says. "You're his older sister, and you know he listens to you better."

"That's not true," I say. "He doesn't listen to me anymore, Mima, and you know it," I say. "He doesn't listen to anybody. He's totally out of control."

Mima turns back to the sink and starts scrubbing harder.

Tell her, a voice inside my head screams. *Say it.*

Mima is in a cloud of steam as she talks. "You're too young to understand, Nora. Boys go through these things," she says. "It's hormones. Then they become good men, believe it or not. He'll meet a good woman one day who will straighten him out."

I think about my bullet-hole neck, about how my head bounced against the brick wall.

"Good men don't hit their mothers and sisters, Mima."

Mima stops what she's doing and glares at me, and just like that, the rest of my words shrivel on my lips. I've broken the unspoken rule: Don't name it. Don't see it.

She points at some bills folded under the napkins. "See that? He told me to buy food with it this morning. He's starting to think, Nora. It's not hopeless."

I stand up and count it. Fifty dollars. It's what I earn in a whole week at Sal's. And this isn't "help." He's demanding something to eat and he's showing off. Mima won't see the difference, though.

I ball the money in my fist.

Mima's eyes get wide. "¡*Cuidadito!* That's good money! We need that!" She snatches it out of my hand.

"Don't you wonder where he got that from, Mima?" I whisper. "Where does a kid who doesn't work come up with fifty dollars?"

But Mima just turns back to the sink. "He's helping, Nora," she says. "He has a part-time."

"Part-time? He works about as much as he goes to school!"

"*¡No seas una fresca!*" she hisses. "You're making me crazy. I'm going to end up in the loony bin from you two."

"And *he's* going to end up in jail. He's doing bad things — and you know it, or at least you've thought about it."

"*Cállate ya con las mentiras, Nora.*"

I lower my voice and step even closer. "I'm not telling lies, but maybe you are. Why did you tell the fire investigator that Hector was home when he wasn't?"

She doesn't answer.

"*¿Por qué, Mima?*"

She throws down her sponge and turns to me. "What do you want, Nora? You want us to get thrown out of here? You want your fancy friends to point at us and say 'Those are the lowlifes with a troubled kid'? I hope you never have to raise kids alone, *niña*, especially not ungrateful ones. You don't know how good you have it! This part of Queens is nice. This apartment you hate so much is actually a lot better than what you could have, *oíste?* You could be living like an animal in the Bronx."

She's out of breath and red in the face.

There's a long silence between us. I think of the biting and kicking that's already going on. We've already stopped being human. Mima just doesn't know.

"*Soy una buena madre*, Nora, even if you don't think so. All I'm asking is for you to stand up for your flesh and blood, to have patience as he grows up. What kind of daughter won't help her own mother at her time of need?" Her eyes fill up with tears.

"Mima —" I say.

"A good sister doesn't abandon her brother, either," she tells me. "She helps him. She protects him and guides him. If you don't do that, it's *you* who's the disgrace."

That afternoon, I tie on a cameo choker with a black velvet ribbon. Then I head to Kathleen's.

"Fancy," she says when she opens the door. "But isn't it kind of hot for velvet?"

I touch the cameo to make sure it's in place. "I'm celebrating my college acceptance." I hold out the envelope and paste on a shaky smile.

"Cool!" She takes the letter and gives me a puzzled look as we step inside. "Why the gloomy face, then?"

My throat gets bottled up with all that I can't tell her. I take a deep breath of their house, hoping my borrowed family can ease me.

"I'm going to miss you in the fall," I say.

Before I can stop myself, I start to cry, so Kathleen hugs me tight.

"Come on, Hormone Queen," she whispers. "We have all summer to dance." Then she pulls me up the stairs to her room.

Chapter 28

You don't have to watch many cop shows to know there's always a weak link in a crime chain. In this case, it's Matt. All those years attending Catholic school have to mean some kind of conscience, or at least a fear of pissed-off priests and their paddles.

I've been on the lookout for him for over a week, and finally I spot him dragging trash bags to the Dumpster.

"Where you off to?" Sal calls as I storm out the door.

"Back in a flash," I tell him. "I need some Band-Aids."

I jog down the street and slip into the alley. Matt has already tossed in the first bag.

I walk up behind him and snatch the marker out of his back pocket before he can reach for it.

"Hey—" he says, whipping around.

At most, he's a freshman, all freckles and gangly limbs. I just know he's an altar boy, too, though probably the kind who sneaks sips of wine.

"Shut up," I say, stabbing his puny shoulder with the marker.

"What the hell are you doing?" he asks.

"Me? Nothing. But I know what you're doing."

He stands there, unsure.

"What do you think your mommy and daddy will say when they find out you're stealing ludes from Mr. Farina to make a quick buck?" I ask him.

Matt's face turns bright red.

"I'm sure the priests at McClancy would love it, too. Not to mention Sal, who'll be only too happy to use his golf iron on your skull."

He tries to sidestep me, but I block him.

"If I see you screwing around with the trash again, Matt, you're done."

I swear, it looks as if he's going to cry as he hurries out of the alley.

The next day, Mr. Farina announces a sudden personnel change.

"Matt called to say he's quitting—can you believe it? Now I have to train a whole new kid. What's the matter with young guys today?"

I should have expected it.

"I need to talk to you." Sergio pulls his car over and turns on his dome light. Sal is already gone, and the shops are all closed. I straddle my bike but don't budge.

"I'm not going to do anything to you," Sergio says, reading my mind. "Get in." He flips the power locks.

"What do you want?" I ask.

"I want to talk to you about Hector."

Five minutes, I tell myself.

His ashtray is crammed with butts, and the car reeks of smoke. I glance around, imagining the crevices where he might keep his supplies. For all I know, I could be sitting on a huge stash of drugs right now. I keep my hand on the door handle, just in case.

"Make it quick," I say. "You might have heard, there's a shooter who likes couples in cars. I'd really hate to die with you."

"Still bitchy," he says, sighing.

"Your point?"

"Why are you butting into what's none of your business?"

"My brother is my business, even if he's a jerk. And he doesn't need to be stealing Lemmons for you."

He puts his arm over the back of my seat. "Lemmons?" he says innocently. "What are those?"

I glare at him and move a little closer to the door. "Very funny. I found out about your setup. And if *I* found out, somebody else is going to find out eventually. Then what? Prison?"

"Such a pessimist, Nora. That's never going to get you anywhere."

"Bottom line: fire Hector."

"Who says he works for me?"

"Look, I get it. You want to make a buck, and people want your stuff. You're not scared of jail? Fine. Go. It's none of my business. All I ask is that you leave Mr. Farina alone, and that you cut Hector out of it. Why is that so hard?"

Sergio reaches over my legs into his glove compartment

200

where he keeps a carton of Camels and, disturbingly, a handgun. My heart pounds, but I pretend I don't see it. If this is supposed to scare me, though, it's working. What the hell is he doing with one of those, anyway? And more important, is it a .44?

He pulls out a pack of smokes and taps it against his knuckles before pulling one free.

"I'm not the one who needs money, Nora. He is. And by the way, Farina isn't the only pharmacy in town, babe."

I take a breath to calm myself.

"Come on, Sergio," I plead. "Use somebody else to build your empire. Why not one of those fine specimens at the Satin Lady?"

"Drunks," he says, lighting up. "Very unreliable." He takes a long drag and blows a long stream of smoke.

"Okay, fine, think about yourself, then: the cops aren't going to go easy on you when they find out you lured two minors into stealing pills. I hear life sucks in prison, Sergio. Maybe you should consider what I did a favor."

He picks some tobacco off his tongue and smiles pleasantly. "Wow, Nora. I didn't know you cared so much about me," he says. "I'm touched."

"Glad to hear it. And I'm touched that you care about Hector's money troubles. The thing is, I can't let you screw him up any more than he is."

Sergio throws his head back and snorts. "News flash: your bro is already screwed up, Nora."

"Are we finished here?" I ask.

He strikes a new match and leans toward me, holding it

to my face until it burns to his dirty fingers. His voice goes steely, his lips practically brushing my cheek. "Do us both a favor, Nora. Don't make a problem for yourself. I have some stories I can tell, too. The kind that can get a pyro and his family thrown out of their building for good."

I don't dare say a word, too afraid that he'll tell me what I already suspect about Hector and the fire. Where would we go if we got thrown out?

Sergio holds my gaze as he reaches for my face. His stained fingers linger on my neck.

"Don't," I mumble, but all I can think of is the gun in the glove compartment, how easy it would be for either one of us to reach for it.

I pull away, but not before he bites my lower lip hard enough to break the skin.

"Sweet," he says, laughing when I flinch.

I reach for the door handle and jump out of the car. But just as I slam the door and turn to grab my bike, a tall figure steps out of the dark.

Adrenaline jolts through me until I see who it is.

"Christ," I say. "You scared me."

Pablo looks from me to Sergio's car as it pulls out.

"Having fun, Nora?"

I have to jog to keep pace with Pablo as he storms down the street to reach his car. He's obviously gotten the wrong idea.

"It's not what it looks like."

"It looks like my girlfriend was hanging out in a car and kissing another guy."

"It's not another guy. It's Sergio. Gross. I was talking to him for a minute, that's all, not hanging out." We reach the Camaro, and I slip in front of the driver's-side door before he can unlock it. "What are you doing here, anyway? You're supposed to be off."

He stares straight ahead, fuming. "I finished my last exam tonight. I came to surprise you and see if you needed a ride." He crosses his arms. "I can see you've got that covered, though." He tries to nudge me out of the way, but I have my butt pressed against the door lock. "Move."

I don't budge. "What's that supposed to mean? I wasn't getting a ride. I had to talk to him about something important."

"Like what?"

I hesitate. How would I even begin to explain this mess? "It's private."

"Private," he repeats. "You keep a lot of things private, you know that? Get out of the way, please, Nora."

"I was sitting in a car with someone! What's the big deal?"

"You're too scared to spend any time in a car with me, right? I'm glad to see he helped you get over your fear."

My temper is roiling through my veins now, spilling over from Sergio to Pablo. "Don't make fun of me, and stop having this fit."

His eyes flash in anger. "This. Is. Not. A. Fit. This is me deciding not to get played by some chick acting like a—"

The breath goes out of me as I wait. "Like a what?"

"Move, Nora."

"Like a *what*, Pablo? Some chick acting like a *what*? Say it!" I shout.

He takes a deep breath, like he's counting. But I don't give him the luxury of space.

"What is it you want to call me, Pablo? A *ho*? Is that what's on the tip of your tongue?"

I shove him as hard as I can, and it sends his car keys flying.

"Don't use your hands on me, Nora."

"Believe what you want to believe," I hiss. "But you *don't* get to trash me because I'm sitting in a car with someone. You want to know what I was acting like back there with Sergio? Like a freakin' savior, not that you'd understand one thing about my life."

I get on my bike, but Pablo grabs my handlebars. The muscles in his arms are bulging as he holds the bike still.

"Let go." I wrench my handlebars hard to one side, but he hangs on, staring at me. "I said let go, Pablo."

"I wouldn't call you that," he says quietly. The corners of his mouth are turned down. "I'm sorry. My temper got ahead of me."

"This isn't about your stupid temper. It's about respect. *Move.*"

But he holds firm. "Be fair. How would you feel if you'd seen me with some other girl in my car? You'd let it go? You wouldn't wonder if I was lying to you? What am I supposed to think? You won't even explain except to say 'It's private.'"

I can't help him there, of course. I tell a thousand little

lies about my life every day so I can feel like a normal person.

"Well, you don't have to wonder anymore," I tell him. "I *am* a liar, Pablo. And good people like you don't date liars, right?"

I yank my handlebars free and take off.

"Nora!" he calls.

But I don't look his way. I push with all my might along the dark streets, swerving between cars and running through red lights. I speed along, remembering how Hector and I used to race each other. Then and now, with every push forward, my heart is nearly bursting.

Chapter 29

If ever I have been grateful to get out of Flushing, it's this Memorial Day. Hector must have gotten wind of my chat with Sergio. I found my best lip glosses burned to ashes in the bathroom sink as a thank-you note. From the looks of it, I think he used Mima's Aqua Net as a torch.

Anyway, Kathleen and I are actually enjoying our first-ever taste of freedom: a parent-less beach getaway in Breezy Point. Kathleen calls this a graduation present from God, even though it came our way because of lousy news: my fight with Pablo, and Mr. Mac's friends ending up in the burn unit.

The Everard Baths near the Empire State Building burned to the ground this past week. One of Mr. Mac's firefighter friends got hurt when the walls crumbled on top of him. If that wasn't bad enough, a couple of days later, the Atlantic Lacquer factory exploded when paint thinner ignited and turned everyone inside into human torches. Mr. Mac grew up in Brooklyn and knows some of the people who got hurt.

We were sure that our plans for a beach weekend were gone until Kathleen piped up.

"Why can't Nora and I do an overnight at the bungalow on our own?" she asked her mother.

At first the answer was no, but Kathleen dug in, arguing like an attorney about how safe Breezy Point is, since you have to pass through the guard gate. The she delivered her clincher: "Nora is nursing a broken heart, Mother. She needs this. Besides, we are days away from graduation and a week from legal adulthood. It's time to let us breathe."

And so here we are, lying side by side in the sand. It's sunny and only in the high seventies, perfect weather. Stevie Wonder is singing "Isn't She Lovely" on the radio.

"Am I turning orange?" Kathleen asks.

I lift myself to my elbows on our beach blanket and look over. Even if she were the color of a cantaloupe, no one on this beach would care. Her hair is sandy and bleached, and her legs stretch forever from that yellow bikini. When we brought out our cooler, one of the guys tossing a Frisbee saw her and smashed into the lifeguard stand.

"Just your palms a little," I say. We had to buy her QT quick tanner on the drive over to Breezy. My skin gets deep brown with baby oil, but hers turns the color of boiled ham every time.

"So. Deep question. Do you think I should do it with Eddie?"

I look over. "Do what?"

"Sex, for God's sake. Are you slow?"

I won't lie. I'm shocked. "Like, soon?"

She shields her eyes and looks at me. "Yeah, maybe."

I study the clouds for a second. "You don't like him *that* much, do you?"

She sighs. "He's okay."

I knew it. There aren't many sparks on her side. His biggest perk seems to be his new summer job at Carvel. Still, free cones don't make up for lousy chemistry.

"Has that even come up?" I ask.

"We're talking about Eddie, here, Nora. He's a total horn toad. Something's always 'coming up.'"

We giggle. "Well, that's *his* problem, not yours," I say. "If you're not into him, why bother? He might be an asshole in disguise. Remember Angel."

"Because I sort of hate going off to college as a virgin. I feel too young or something. It's pathetic."

I flick tiny shells in the sand. "It's not pathetic."

"Easy for you to say. You've left the Society of Virgins."

"So trust the Voice of My Shitty Experience. It sucks to do it with somebody you don't care about."

"Why? Guys do it that way all the time," she says. "Maybe we shouldn't care. It would be easier." She leans up on her elbow and lowers her voice. "So, did you and Pablo do it?"

Hearing his name still stings. "No. And I'm glad."

"You didn't *want* to do it with him?" she whispers. "You must be superhuman. He's such a fox."

"I *did* want to. Don't be stupid. But now I'm glad we didn't. It would have been even more complicated to break up with him."

She takes a sip of her beer and shrugs. "So what are you going to do now? You have to see him every day at work."

"There's nothing to do. We broke up. Period. Life goes on."

But Kathleen is right about things feeling awkward. Pablo tried to call a couple of times after our fight, but I wedged a cold space between us with one-word answers until he finally stopped.

"So, it's over?" she asks.

"It's over."

"And you're glad?"

"We're just not right for each other, Kathleen."

She rolls her eyes. "Oh, *that* again."

"Back to Eddie," I say.

She stares up at the sky. "Okay, okay, so *if* you did it, what position would you pick?"

"God, Kathleen."

"*Tell* me."

I glance at her uncomfortably, remembering the times we read *The Joy of Sex* that she sneaked from under her mother's bed.

"Who knows? It all looks kind of tricky."

She giggles again. "Yeah, that's supposed to be the fun."

"You know what's not fun? Babies. Especially babies with Eddie. You need birth control."

"Killjoy."

We stay quiet for a while, listening to one song after another. After my time with Angel, I panicked for a whole month until my period. I know Kathleen will worry about the same. Nobody wants a kid, but nobody wants their mother to find out they went to the Planned Parenthood clinic, either. For all the ways that Kathleen's mom is a women's libber, she's also a strict Catholic. Birth control is touchy, and abortion is absolutely out. Where does that leave us? Going to our regular doctors for the pill? Oh, sure. Dr. De Los Santos still has teddy bears and balloons on his office wallpaper. The thought of him writing me a prescription for birth control nearly makes my head explode.

We turn over on our stomachs and lie there looking at each other the way we used to when we were little. Back then we'd tell each other secrets during sleepovers. Who we liked. If we'd cheated on the spelling quiz. *Cross my heart and hope to die. Stick a needle in my eye.*

"Friedmor found me in the hall. She wants to know why you aren't coming to graduation," she says.

"She's so nosy."

There's a long silence. "So, why aren't you?"

"What's the big deal about walking across the stage in a hot auditorium to get a piece of paper?" I say. "I can't believe they even make us rehearse that."

Kathleen stares at me, waiting.

"Besides, I tossed the tickets already."

"You threw them out? Very cold."

"Don't be mad," I say.

"I'm not," she says, "but I don't know why my best friend won't tell me why she's really skipping graduation." She pulls up on her elbows. "You've been kind of sad for a while, Nora. What's up?"

I wonder—if a liar like me can be a true friend? I pinch the sand between my fingers, thinking about how lies and secrets disguise themselves as each other, how they cost you things that matter. I've known Kathleen since kindergarten, and she deserves better.

"It's just a stupid ceremony with a silly gown so you can get your picture taken with your family. And my family isn't like yours, Kathleen," I say at last. All those things she takes for granted: sweet nicknames, rules, chores, harmless arguments, everything beautifully predictable.

"So?"

"So they'd suck the joy out of graduation, and I don't want to deal with it."

"How could anyone possibly suck the joy out of this? We're finally getting out of school after twelve years of hard labor."

"We fight all the time."

"Whose family doesn't fight?"

I hold my breath for a second, trying not to imagine Hector's elbow compressing my throat. "Not like this. It's not like fighting with people you love. It's different. Meaner."

This is the closest I can come to the truth.

She waits for me to add something, but I can't think of what to say that won't make me feel dirtier than I do.

We lie there for a long while, seagulls shrieking overhead. Kids laugh somewhere in the distance, making me think suddenly of us when we were little. Kathleen with her blond braids, and me, a faster runner, the more serious of the two, older than her by a day.

We'll be eighteen and legal next month. For years we've waited to be grown, but now that it's time to cross the chasm, I don't want to let go of the things we shared. When Kathleen leaves for school, there won't be any more dance moves in her bedroom or Gloria to feed or guys to consider. There won't be any more MacInerney dinner discussions and forced volunteer gigs that we pretend to hate. I won't tail Mr. Mac to learn how to make repairs or help set the table like I belong to them. The only family I've ever really wanted will be gone.

I manage a smile, even though thinking of all those good times makes me want to sob. "Hey," I tell her. "I'm going inside to see about fixing that screen door for your dad."

Kathleen pulls down her sunglasses and nestles into the sand with a sigh. "You know where he keeps the tools," she says. "Have at it."

Chapter 30

Adiós, high school.

Graduation day is tomorrow, so it's time to turn in the last of my textbooks and all my final projects. The whole school looks summer-bald. Nothing is tacked to the bulletin boards. Wobbly desks and chairs are stacked in the hall and tagged for repair.

The only thing I'll miss around here will be Mr. Melvin. He actually got emotional when he said good-bye to me, at least by his standards. He put all the senior projects on the worktable and gave us a long speech about how you have to mess up a lot in life and in wood shop to get the product you're really proud of.

"Onward, Nora López," he told me, saluting.

I turn the corner and step into the library. Book carts surround Ms. Friedmor. Her Student Council minions are helping check everything back into the storage room.

"I've been looking for you, Nora," she says when she spots me.

Thanks to Kathleen, I'm ready when she starts in about skipping graduation.

"Are you sure you don't want to join your friends and celebrate this accomplishment? You can still change your mind."

I hand her back my battered English book. I don't have the heart to tell her that showing up for school and passing tests isn't an accomplishment. Living inside Mima and Hector's drama: now, that's the real trial.

"I'm sure," I tell her. "Besides, my mom is working. She'd have to miss it anyway." Not true, but a good touch.

She purses her lips. "I haven't heard from your parents regarding summer options for your brother."

I ignore the comment. "Big news, though. I got into New York City Community."

Ricky pipes up from the pile of science books. "Where you study hammering and welding?" He gives a little snort. "Who doesn't get into tech school?"

I give him a dirty look. He's sporting a Fordham T-shirt to show off, but how smart can he be? He can't even figure out why the books he's stacking won't stay on the cart.

"The wheel's swivel plate is shot, genius," I say as a few more books tumble to the floor. "Maybe you should take some courses at NYCCC."

Ms. Friedmor tries to stifle a smile. "It's a fine construction program," she says. "Don't undervalue what it offers. And I for one think it's fantastic to have women entering nontraditional fields."

She flips through the textbook to make sure I haven't written in it or torn out pages.

"Promise me that you won't forget to pick up the course description guide over the summer. You'll need it to plan for registration in August. I've gotten you this far, but the rest is up to you."

I smile as she hands me the book receipt. GOOD CONDITION.

"Take care, Nora," she tells me. "Remember to reach. You'll surprise yourself."

What does that even mean?

"Bye, Ms. Friedmor. And thanks."

There is a merciful God after all.

Graduation day, and I have the whole apartment to myself.

Mima must be at the Laundromat, which means she'll be gone for at least a couple of hours, even longer if she's got a cleaning gig after, as I suspect. Her bucket of supplies is missing, so I'm hopeful.

I take my cereal bowl to the living room and sift through my records for a while. I'm finally about to drop the Trammps on my turntable when the phone rings. I won't lie. There's a part of me that hopes it's Pablo, even if I'd never admit it to Kathleen. I have to keep reminding myself that Hector fulfills the jerk quotient in my life for now.

More likely, it's Papi making a bonus call. What's he going to tell me? That he's in the Hamptons? That he's bought Pierre a new plastic pail and shovel for the beach? I suddenly think of Mr. Melvin's heartfelt speech this morning about practice and mistakes, and I realize something new. Maybe Hector and I are Papi's practice kids, where he made all his mistakes. The only difference is that he can't totally throw us away. Still, we won't ever measure up. It's Pierre that's Papi's accomplishment, not us.

I let the phone ring until it dies. Then I yank the cord out of the jack of our Western Electric 500. Phone trouble. Sorry, Papi.

I place the needle on the LP.

The trumpets blare down the scale to start the song. I turn it up and close my eyes, imagining a rooftop party. I start to move until soon Freddie Prinze appears in my mind. He's alive and gorgeous. He twirls me to all the corners of our apartment, whispering in my ear, "Looking good, Nora!"

I shake my body, feel his love in my bones for exactly who I am. I don't have to tell Freddie lies. I don't have to know if I'm going to work or going to college. I don't have to worry he'll think I'm shit because of my family. He knows how hard it is to keep up a show, how tough it is some days to hang on.

I grab our broom the way I did when I was five and dance and dance until my heart is pounding. When the music's done, I flop on the couch, out of breath, dizzy. All I can think of is the time Mima found me dancing with a broom. I was only seven and already in love with Peter Tork of *The Monkees*. She didn't laugh. Instead, she cleaned the dust off my teeth with the edge of her dress and told me to find something else to play. *El amor,* she said, would only make me suffer.

Of all the crazy advice Mima has given me over the years, it figures that this time she was right. I close my eyes as the needle skips on the dead wax, missing Pablo all over again.

Chapter 31

HELLO FROM THE CRACKS IN THE SIDE-
WALKS OF NYC AND FROM THE ANTS
THAT DWELL IN THESE CRACKS AND
FEED IN THE DRIED BLOOD OF THE DEAD
THAT HAS SETTLED INTO THE CRACKS.

Son of Sam has found his inner poet, I guess. Jimmy Breslin at the *New York Daily News* got this one from him yesterday. That's why we've sold out of every copy of the paper before noon, except for the one that Annemarie swiped for her collection. Normally people would be yapping about Joe Frazier getting canned as the Mets' manager, but not today. People have been streaming in all morning, still dressed in their Sunday clothes. They toss change at me, not even waiting to step outside the deli door before opening the paper wide to see what the serial killer has to say.

HELLO FROM THE GUTTERS OF NYC,
WHICH IS FILLED WITH DOG MANURE,

VOMIT, STALE WINE, URINE, AND BLOOD. HELLO FROM THE SEWERS OF NYC WHICH SWALLOW UP THESE DELICACIES WHEN THEY ARE WASHED AWAY BY THE SWEEPER TRUCKS. DON'T THINK BECAUSE YOU HAVEN'T HEARD [FROM ME] FOR A WHILE THAT I WENT TO SLEEP. NO, RATHER, I AM STILL HERE. LIKE A SPIRIT ROAMING THE NIGHT. THIRSTY, HUNGRY, SELDOM STOPPING TO REST; ANXIOUS TO PLEASE SAM . . .

I stand at the cash register, trying to concentrate on the rambling poem again. Pablo pushes a broom along each aisle. When I look up, he's staring at me like he wants to say something. I turn the page and force myself to keep reading.

The next night, I sit up, terrified, slapping at imaginary ants that march across my bloody arms. My nightgown is soaked with my sweat as I catch my breath, waiting for the fan to turn in my direction and offer a few seconds of breeze. Is it the heat or the nightmare that finally wakes me?

No. Someone is knocking at the door.

Mima hears it, too. She comes to my bedroom in her thin nightgown, her eyes wide with worry. It's almost four a.m. When I look across the room, I realize that Hector isn't in his bed yet. He wouldn't knock, though. He would have let himself in with his key.

"*Cuidado*," Mima says as we tiptoe to the door. She slides on the chain and then looks through the peephole. Her face darkens.

"*La comunista*," she whispers.

Stiller, she means.

There's a louder knock that makes us jump. Mima tries to still my hand as I start to unlatch the chain.

"Stop," I say, and open up.

Stiller is in slippers and a nightshirt. Her head is wrapped in a silk kerchief.

"You better get down here," she whispers.

"*¿Qué dice?*"

Stiller looks from Mima to me. "Your brother is in the stairwell. And he's out of it."

I'm still barefoot as we run downstairs. Mima can't help pulling in her breath when she sees him. Hector is crawling on all fours on the first landing. Even from here, the smell of vomit is overpowering. His eyes are glassy and unfocused. He's flying as high as I've ever seen anyone.

"*¡Ay, Dios mio!*" Mima says, dropping to her knees. "*¿Hijo, qué te pasa?*"

"He was trying to put his key in my lock," Stiller whispers. "The noise woke me up."

Hector struggles to his feet and leans against the wall. He pulls out his cigarette and lighter, flipping his wrist uselessly until his Zippo flies out of his hand and goes clattering across the hallway floor. His face is soft and dreamy, and you could almost like him, until he raises his middle finger in a dazed salute.

220

Mima props herself under one of Hector's arms. She motions to me for help, even as he tries to shake her away. "Get off me," he says, slurring. "Get off."

Stiller reaches for my arm to stop me. "Get him to the hospital. I can take you." She turns to Mima. "*¿Hospitál?*"

But Mima only looks at Stiller with pure venom in her eyes, as if finding Hector at her door is the most insulting thing she could have done to us.

"*Es una borrachera, na'mas,*" Mima insists, although I don't smell any alcohol on him at all. Then she turns to me. "Nora!" Her voice is sharp. "*Tu hermano.*"

There's not going to be any hospital, of course. A hospital means questions. It means that others will think we're not good people. It means that our neighbors will whisper about us when we go by.

I can't read Stiller's expression as I sling my brother's arm over my shoulder. Mima and I lead him to the stairs, his dead weight between us. He stinks of cigarettes and puke and sweat, and the smell seems to grow worse as we climb higher into the heat of the building.

When we finally get him to our floor, I realize that Stiller has climbed the stairs from a distance behind us. She holds our door open with her foot and watches from the threshold as we drag Hector into the kitchen and drop him into a chair.

"Don't you lock this door," she tells me. "I'm waiting out here in case you need me."

I'm out of breath, and I can smell my brother's body odor on my shoulders. Mima pops ice cubes from a tray and wraps them in a dish towel to hold to his head.

221

"Why are you just standing there?" she snaps. She unbuttons his shirt and yanks it off him. "¡Ayúdame!"

Stiller is right. Without a hospital, he might die. I know that, and yet I help her hold up his head as she sticks her fingers down his throat to force a vomit.

Hector heaves and drools over and over again until I finally don't see his head lolling or the dreamy gaze of his high. I don't see the boy who played Clue or even the one who pressed against my throat in an alley. He's somebody I don't know.

Mima and I sit up all night, making sure he's breathing and cleaning up as he vomits all he has inside. Son of Sam's poem goes round and round in my mind as I doze in the chair.

HELLO FROM THE GUTTERS OF NYC, WHICH IS FILLED WITH DOG MANURE, VOMIT, STALE WINE, URINE, AND BLOOD. HELLO FROM THE SEWERS OF NYC WHICH SWALLOW UP THESE DELICACIES WHEN THEY ARE WASHED AWAY BY THE SWEEPER TRUCKS.

When it's time for work, I get dressed and tie up my hair, ignoring the faint scent of pine disinfectant in my skin, the feel of Stiller's eyes on me as I go by her door without a word.

"Good morning, sunshine," Sal calls to me when I step behind the register. "How you feeling today?"

Pablo stops what he's doing and turns.

I don't know what to say to either of them. For the life of me, I just don't feel anything at all.

Chapter 32

I hitch up my tube top, an early birthday present to myself from Janice Shop on Roosevelt. Even with the sun going down, it feels like I'm wearing a lot of clothes, though. It's a freaking broiler out here.

The little kids on the block are still out playing tag, but the lightning bugs are starting to blink, so they're almost out of time. Once the streetlights click on, we'll have a ghost town. Around here we always used to hang out on the stoop until midnight to keep cool. But not this summer. We're all on house arrest thanks to Son of Sam.

"God, why won't it cool down?" Kathleen says, leaning back against the windshield of Stiller's Malibu. We're currently using it as a chaise lounge. Kathleen's hair is piled high on her head, little blond curls by her temples.

Before I can answer, the lobby doors open.

Manny. He points in our direction.

"Off the car, girls! You know the rules."

Kathleen gives him her lawyer look. "I'm not aware of any such rule, sir," she says.

"There's a rule against loitering and disrespecting property," Manny says. "And *I* made it."

"Disrespecting property?" I study Stiller's car. It's got a plastic sheet for a side window, and one of its doors is a totally different color from the rest. The seat springs are poking through. Stiller herself calls it a heap.

"I don't know, Manny," I say. "I think we might actually make this car look better. Kathleen's a model, you know."

She poses coyly.

"Beautiful. Now, *off,*" he says.

"Leave them alone," Stiller calls from the stoop. She has her shorts rolled up high on her skinny legs like denim underwear. She's been working all day moving back into her apartment. "Who are they hurting?"

"You making the rules here, Stiller?" he asks. "It's an eyesore. Next thing you know, we'll have people playing dice out here."

"So what? A little cee-lo never hurt anybody."

Manny turns bright red and looks back at us, glaring.

Sighing, Kathleen grabs her radio and slides to the ground. The backs of her track shorts are streaked with hood grime.

"And lower the radio, too," he says. "This isn't a disco."

"Yes, warden," Kathleen mumbles as we head to the stoop.

Satisfied, Manny turns back to what he came out to do in the first place: tape the latest sketch of Son of Sam to the lobby doors.

"Oh, good," Stiller says, fanning herself. "New artwork for the lobby."

The new police sketch is everywhere now. It's the fourth version so far, and none of them look the same. This one is on the Q12's fare box. At the library. Inside Sal's meat case next to the weekly specials. At the candy-store register, where some clown has drawn a mustache on the face.

He's a pale guy with dark, curly hair and thick eyebrows. He's nobody, anybody, everybody. And that's the trouble. You can imagine him everywhere. Was he pressing his face against the glass at Thom McAn Shoes? Or did I give him change at Sal's? Was he straphanging next to me on the bus? If I squint he even looks a little like Pablo, but then, these days, much as I hate to admit it, I sort of see Pablo everywhere, too.

Kathleen wipes the sweat from her forehead and checks her watch. We've been waiting for the ice-cream truck, but it hasn't come down the street. Just then, we hear Mr. Mac's loud whistle, surprisingly powerful for just using two fingers. It's Kathleen's signal to get home soon. He does that every night now if he isn't working.

"Does he think I'm a dog?" she grumbles. "I need something cold or I'm going to die." She looks over at Stiller pleadingly. "How about a ride to Carvel?" That's the ice-cream shop where Eddie works. He always gives us free cones, but it's too far to reach walking.

"I'll lose my parking spot," Stiller says.

"There's a chocolate soft-serve in it for you," Kathleen counters.

"I'll get my keys."

I'm riding in the backseat as Stiller's car creaks and groans its way along. Even with the windows rolled down, I'm dying against the hot vinyl. If I'm not mistaken, there's a smell of dead squirrel in here, too. I don't say so, though. I've been trying to keep my distance from Stiller since Hector's puke-fest at her door. To her credit, she hasn't hassled me about it once.

The floor is littered with old flyers and petitions, broken pens, and a stack of magazines. One catches my eye. It's that back issue of *Ms.* magazine that everyone buzzed about last summer. A woman's face is on the cover, and she has a black eye.

BATTERED WIVES: THE SECRET VICTIM NEXT DOOR.

I close my eyes tight and try to concentrate on the hot breeze. Finally Stiller pulls into the lot and throws the car into park. Some Bayside girls gawk at us until Stiller says, "Problem?" I jump out as fast as I can.

"With sprinkles," she tells me.

"Be right back."

There's a line, but we wait patiently until it's our turn.

"Who's next?" Eddie calls out. His paper hat is still crisp in all that refrigerated glory.

Kathleen steps forward and puts a hand on her hip. "Hi."

Eddie takes one look at her in shorts and Dr. Scholl's,

and he starts to melt faster than one of his cones. He pulls off his silly paper hat. "Hi."

I hang back, trying not to be alive right now. They're flirting and laughing, and the whole thing makes me sick. What's worse than feeling like a third wheel, especially when your own love life is in ruins?

Kathleen waves me over after a few minutes. She hands me my cone and the one for Stiller.

"I was telling Eddie that we want to go dancing for our birthdays this weekend."

"I can probably get us passes to Eléphas," he says.

I give Kathleen a look. She knows Pablo hangs out there. "No, thanks," I say.

"Or the Arena," she says quickly. "It's got a bigger dance floor anyway."

"Sure," Eddie adds. "No problem." He'd probably say he could get us passes to Studio 54 if Kathleen said she wanted them, but whatever.

"Maybe," I say. A whole night as a tagalong isn't my idea of fun.

Kathleen gives me a look. "Not maybe. We've been planning an all-night dance party for our eighteenth birthdays since junior high. It's happening."

I start to argue, but she cuts me off. "Don't worry about a date, either. We can ask Ricky."

I give her a withering stare. "Ricky? Student Council Tight-Ass Ricky? No, thanks."

"He's a great dancer," she says. "You don't have to talk. Just move."

"I have to get this to Stiller." I escape just as a rivulet of chocolate slides along my arm.

I walk back to the car and hand the cone through the window. She's been watching us, amused.

"So," she says, chuckling, "what's she jivin' about?" She bites straight into her scoop.

"Going dancing. We're turning eighteen this weekend, remember?"

I take a bite of my ice cream, too, but a brain freeze grabs hold.

"Eighteen, huh?" Stiller chuckles. "It's going to be a long-ass summer for your parents."

The mention of parents makes me cringe. The last thing I want to talk about is Mima or the night Stiller came knocking.

No luck, though.

"Oh, I've been meaning to give you this," she says.

She bangs hard on her glove compartment until it falls open. Then she hands me Hector's Zippo lighter from inside. I'd forgotten that he dropped it that night.

"He doesn't need that back," I tell her. "He's got plenty. Probably too many."

She takes another bite. "Yeah. You're probably right."

What does she mean? I wonder as I pretend to concentrate on my ice cream. "I'm sorry he bothered you, by the way," I say. "Puberty has him by the balls these days, I guess."

"That's not puberty, Nora." She says it quietly, never taking her eyes from Kathleen and Eddie. "Not what I'm hearing through the heating pipes, anyway."

It's as if my brain freeze has extended all the way to my toes. This is absolutely not the conversation I want to have with Stiller or anybody else. Where the hell is Kathleen? I wave at her, annoyed.

"Well, I'm moving out soon. Whatever it is, I'm out of here."

Stiller turns to me at last. "Yeah, you can go, Miss Eighteen-and-Legal. But you can also take a stand, even when you're scared. If you *think* you're powerless, you are."

Kathleen runs back and jumps in the front seat. "Sorry. We were working out the details." She gives us a weird look. Something is in the air, and she can tell. "What are *you* guys talking about?"

Stiller turns the ignition and glances at me as she backs up the car.

"The damn heat on all of us, child. What else?" she says.

Chapter 33

Naturally Papi forgets my birthday.

Mima bakes me a yellow cake, and even though it's frosted with cement-like merengue, I slice a piece for breakfast.

Sal is still grumpy over Tom Seaver getting traded to the Reds, but he tries to be festive anyway. He sticks a candle in half a ham-and-provolone hero for my lunch and croons "Happy Birthday" with Annemarie.

But it isn't until closing time that I find a little box inside the cash register.

When I open it, I find a tiny disco ball on a silver chain. There's a folded note.

Happy Birthday, Nora — P

It takes us hours to beautify at Kathleen's. I brought my sleepover stuff in a bag, and now it's spread all over her bed. My hair is gathered up high, and big hoop earrings graze my neck. Our lips glisten with the same shade, Cherry Bomb.

At eleven o'clock, we finally head downstairs. Mr. Mac glances up from the TV. He takes one look at Kathleen's metallic halter top and high heels, and he shoots to his feet.

"You're going out like that?" he asks.

"I am." She touches up her lipstick in the mirror over the mantle.

"Mary!"

I smooth down my wraparound skirt and close the dip in my bodysuit a bit. Pablo's necklace sparkles at the V.

Mrs. MacInerney comes out from the kitchen and stops in her tracks. "Oh." Her eyes travel to the deep neckline in Kathleen's top. I warned Kathleen that the shirt might be a problem, but she said turning eighteen made it fine. "Well. You look so grown."

Mr. and Mrs. Mac exchange uncomfortable looks. "Are you sure you don't want Dad to give you all a ride?"

"What a perfect way to welcome adulthood," Kathleen quips. "Letting your daddy drive you."

Just then, the doorbell rings. It's Eddie and Ricky, looking like disco-perfect bookends in the doorway.

"Hello, sir." Eddie sticks out his hand. He's in white flare pants and a wide-collar shirt. He takes one look at Kathleen and beams, but for once he has the sense not to drool for too long.

"Hello," I say to Ricky. His platforms are almost as high as mine. It makes me wish for Pablo even more.

"I want you girls home by three," Mr. Mac tells Kathleen.

"There are no *girls* here, Dad. Just women." Kathleen grabs her clutch purse and gives him a face. "And, no-can-do on three a.m. Sorry. Nobody even starts dancing until midnight, and we're going to have breakfast at the Blue Fountain Diner after." She starts to head for the door.

232

"Three or nothing at all, Kathleen Elizabeth. And no hanging out in the car." Mr. Mac looks at Eddie. "Not at all."

Kathleen's cheeks go red. She turns to her mother with a determined look. "Mother, this is ridiculous. I'm of age. Talk to him."

Mrs. MacInerney frowns at Kathleen. "You are, but three is fair, Kathleen. Especially when you consider everything that's been going on."

Kathleen looks about to explode, but suddenly Ricky turns up the charm. "My dad is a police officer, ma'am," he says reasonably. "I understand your concerns. We checked this afternoon. The Arena has put extra security guards outside the club."

God, all those years on Student Council have had an upside for Ricky after all. He can now bullshit like a pro. Ricky's dad, I happen to know, is a mason. He always brags about how his dad once ate lunch on the gargoyle ledge of the Chrysler Building.

Mr. Mac is no fool, though. He holds up three fingers. "Three thirty a.m. Best offer and nonnegotiable."

Kathleen glares at him, but Mrs. MacInerney just steps forward and gives us each a kiss.

"Happy birthday, ladies," she calls from the door as we head to Eddie's car. "Have fun!"

It's drizzling when we get to the Arena. As it turns out, it's true that there are extra security guards outside. But as soon as we flash our IDs and step inside, all worries are forgotten.

The club pulses with strobe lights, and the walls seem

to shake with the heavy bass of "Car Wash." Lounges and couches are arranged at different levels around the dance floor, so people can drink and watch the action. The light show is amazing. Every hustle breaks into silver-plated moves as DJ Vic melts one song into the next without skipping a beat. His head bobs into his headphones as he works the turntables, turning "Boogie Nights" into "Do What You Wanna Do" by T-Connection.

We don't even stop at the bar. Instead, the four of us elbow our way to the dance floor right away and start moving to the bongos and singing to the chorus.

In no time, I'm lost in the beat. The air is thick with Charlie perfume, cigarettes, and sweat as we spin and bump. The light show pulses in time, brightening the smoky haze suspended above us. At this point, I don't even mind Ricky. Just as Kathleen promised, he is a great dancer, completely uninhibited. All around, people watch as we move, and I notice that one guy in particular is locked on me. No matter where I go, he's watching from his spot on one of the couches. Part of me likes his gaze, but a little voice inside me wonders if he's a creep.

It doesn't take long to find out.

"I need the john," Ricky shouts over the music.

We walk off the dance floor, and he drops me off at the bar to get us something to drink. I'm sweating, and strands of my hair have fallen loose around my face.

"You look hot." Mystery Guy is at my elbow.

He's cute, but his eyes are glassy, and his voice is slow

and dumb. What a turnoff. "It's from the dancing." I wave at the bartender, but he completely ignores me.

"It's noisy in here," Mystery Guy says, leaning close to me. "You want to come outside?"

I look for Kathleen, but she and Eddie are still on the dance floor.

"I'm getting a drink," I say. "And waiting for my friend. So, no."

"Is he your old man?"

I don't answer and wave at the bartender again.

I wonder suddenly if Pablo is at Eléphas tonight, if he ever uses pickup lines like this or if girls giggle and hang on him, stoned, like the pack across the bar.

Mystery Guy leans over and fixes his eyes on my necklace and then, of course, my boobs. "I've got some good shit with me," he says, smiling. "And I'm willing to share with the right chick." He opens his palm to reveal a fat joint.

"You need somebody else," I say just as the bartender arrives. "Two rum and cokes."

As soon as I spot Ricky, I bolt in his direction like he's the love of my life.

The porch light is on when we pull in, right at three thirty. There's movement in the front curtain and a shadow.

"How long you think he's been standing there?"

Kathleen rolls her eyes. "All night, probably."

Ricky and I sit there awkwardly as Kathleen kisses Eddie good night. Thankfully, it's quick.

"I know you waited up, Dad," Kathleen calls as we step through the side door. "Stop hiding and come have breakfast."

The wood floors creak, and Mr. Mac comes out, scratching his head, shamefaced. "How are the two dancing queens?"

Our lipstick is worn off. Our hair is down, and we're barefoot. "Absolutely great," I say.

Kathleen pulls out a pan while I grab eggs, bacon, and bread from the refrigerator.

"Fried or scrambled?" she asks her dad, melting down butter.

"Shhh. Don't wake your mother," he says.

We cook up a feast in no time. But as soon as we sit down to eat, the police scanner lights up. The sputtering chatter on one of the channels gets insistent. Mr. Mac starts to turn it down, but then the dispatcher's flat voice comes through the static.

It's not the firehouse. It's the police station in Bayside.

There's been a shooting at the Eléphas discotheque.

"Code 10-34S. Victim, female, seventeen. Victim, male, twenty. Shot at close range. Coupe de Ville, maroon, 1972. Suspect, white male, seen fleeing on foot toward Forty-Fifth Drive. All units, all units respond."

Chapter 34

It has taken me forever to get here, sleepless, on two buses. Forty-five minutes plus a five-block walk. I feel like the disco walking dead.

But here is the proof I need so that I can exhale.

Pablo's Camaro is parked in his driveway.

He's not hurt. Maybe he wasn't even there tonight. Mr. Mac told me as much, but I didn't dare believe him, even after he drove to Eléphas earlier to find out everything he could. Lupo and Placido, he told me. No one named Pablo Ruiz.

I have only a few details. A couple outside Eléphas in a parked Coupe de Ville. A stranger shooting through the passenger side and running away. I'm already imagining it was Ralph's car, the one Pablo says he loans out, the ones the girls like. I think of the Mystery Guy from the Arena and name him Lupo. He's flirting, leaning in close to a girl at a bar. "Come out and take a look."

All that, but still I had to see this with my own eyes.

His house is a tiny brick Tudor with a cat sitting in the window, washing itself. I keep hoping to see someone move around inside or to get a glimpse of Pablo himself, but everything is quiet.

Maybe this is crazy. Who am I to need this information? The whole bus ride I fought with myself, wondering whether I should get off and head back home.

I am not Pablo's girlfriend anymore.

I am not a girl whose life he will understand.

Get out of here, Nora, I tell myself. *You're stalking.*

The mist in the air becomes a light drizzle. I can't stay out here for much longer, but I don't dare ring the doorbell. It's too early, not even eight in the morning on a Sunday. I haven't slept; I'm still wearing my disco clothes, and my makeup is surely smeared. His mother would take one look at me and think what?

So I reach into my purse and pull out the only things I have to write with: a Kleenex and my Cherry Bomb lipstick.

Had to know you were okay. —N

I stick the note inside the driver's window, which never quite rolls up, and hope he sees it.

Hobbling, I turn back for home.

The heat is already rising off the pavement on Monday morning as I roll open Sal's awning and drag in the bound stack of newspapers from the sidewalk. The awful headline and photos are a reminder all over again.

.44 KILLER STRIKES AGAIN: WOUNDS 2

My eyes linger on the caption beneath Judy Placido's picture on the front page. She had been celebrating her high-school graduation, it says. She's barely alive at Flushing Hospital.

I crawl under my register counter to find the utility knife to cut the stack open. Everyone will want a paper today, hungry for every ghoulish detail. They will share theories that will make my skin prickle and make me look over my shoulder wherever I go.

The bells sound, even though the lights are still off.

"Just a minute." I brace myself for customer number one and stand up.

But when I straighten, I find Pablo standing there, work apron in his hand. He's got dark circles under his eyes as he regards me. I know that kind of tired, I want to tell him. It's the deep kind from seeing what you don't want to. It's the one that makes you afraid to sleep.

"I got your note," he says.

I put down the cutter and walk over to where he's standing. The corners of his lips pull down as I put my hands gently on either side of his face. I kiss him as softly as I can on the cheek.

"She was trying to run back inside," he whispers. "There was glass in her hair."

He leans his forehead against mine and closes his eyes. It's a hot morning, and still his hands feel icy when I take them.

I don't say anything more. Why would I? I know there aren't always words when we need them.

Sal's footsteps sound along the aisle toward us, but we don't move apart.

I feel Sal near us, but then he turns on his heels and his footsteps fade.

For once in his life, he just lets us be.

Chapter 35

"The world is ending! Sinners, repent!"

That's what the religious wingnut told Kathleen and me last year when we went to see the tall ships in the Harbor for the Fourth of July. We laughed at his tie and his crazy eyes. But now I think, holy shit, maybe he was right.

Kathleen and I are sitting in her yard, cooling our feet off in the baby pool. Her family didn't go to Breezy Point this year for the holiday weekend. The sink leaked and flooded the place, so Mr. Mac is fixing it and is then stuck doing one of his workdays with no pay.

I close my eyes, trying to pretend I'm at a beach and not closed in on all sides by other houses. Unfortunately the train rumbles by every hour or so, and we can still hear the MacInerneys' police scanner from here, too. It's crackling inside the house, with all the normal garbage: a purse snatching near Bowne Park, a burglary, a loud altercation between two homeless guys, a car break-in. But it's also been spilling the dirt on today's big news. A Panamanian guy hijacked a bus at lunchtime. He's still at JFK right now, shooting people and dumping bodies on the tarmac. He says he wants six million bucks plus a plane to Cuba, which Mima told me only proves he's nuts.

But here's what's really weird. We're all too hot and tired to even care. In fact, no one acts surprised because, face it, what disaster hasn't happened this year? We're burning. We're broke. We're laid off. We're ripping each other off or being murdered or pulling the trigger.

Maybe it's finally all too much to care about. It's like the color wheel in art. You spin the colors fast enough and everything eventually looks blank and white all over again.

Kathleen flicks water in my direction with her toes. "What's up with him?"

"Have a heart," I say. "Who can think in this heat?"

Pablo is across the yard, waiting for Mrs. MacInerney to flip our burgers off the grill. I don't tell Kathleen the rest. That he's been quiet this week. That the slam of Sal's back screen door made him jump yesterday, that we walk to the Dumpster at night together, each of us cautious for different reasons.

"You think he's okay, though?" Kathleen asks.

"I think the world is ending—*that's* what I think." I open my eyes and imitate the wingnut. "Repent!"

"Repent for what?" Stiller grabs a folding chair near Kathleen. Her face is shiny with sweat.

"Nora thinks the world might be ending," Kathleen says. "Thoughts?"

Stiller takes a swig of beer. "Nothing ends," she says. "There is only transformation, ugly as it may be."

242

She could be right. I just hope the end point isn't this. What if a whole city can transform into a hot shithole and then stays that way?

Pablo comes back to us, his plate loaded with food to share. He hands us each a cold soda before he straddles the aluminum chaise and sits down. He puts the bottoms of his bare feet against me like a backrest. It could be a thousand degrees outside, and I would still love how it feels.

Just then firecrackers explode somewhere down the street. Pablo's plate ends up in the grass.

"I'll get us more," I say, trying not to make a big deal.

"IIIIIIIII love New Yooork!"

The Broadway stars sing and dance on the TV screen above Sal's counter. Twirling their top hats, they urge us to get to the city, to our nightlife, to the shows.

Please.

Maybe they can still sing that la-di-da tune in Manhattan, but not out here in the boroughs.

In fact, I'm starting to hate New York.

First of all, Son of Sam's one-year anniversary is just around the corner. Who wants to be in on *that* party? Nobody's hanging out; every disco I know has become a ghost town.

But worse, the temperature has ticked up to the inferno range. It'll be nearly one hundred degrees for a few days at least. Nobody in our building has air-conditioning.

Sal has the ceiling fans going full blast, but they just move the sawdust around. Each time someone walks in, a new wave of heat smacks me in the face at the register. I've been glaring at customers, trying to ward them off before they pull open the door and heave their stinking bodies in my direction.

Right now, the only relief is the refrigerator case. Pablo and I stand there, trying to let the cold air soothe us. His T-shirt is soaked at the neck and armpits.

"If we don't find a way to cool off, I'm going to lose it," he says.

"We could hose off the loading dock again," I say. We've done that twice today already.

Pablo gives me a sidelong glance. "Or we could go to the movies tonight. There's air-conditioning."

I close my eyes and lean into the cold, thinking. We've been speaking again, but not about us. "As friends?" I ask.

"If that's what you want." He waits for me to say something in the long pause that follows. "Is it?" he asks.

I give him a careful look. "How about you?"

"No. But I'm not going to beg you," he says. "You either want to date me or not."

I take a deep breath of cold air. "It's more complicated than that. Look, I really care about you, Pablo. You know that. But there's a lot of sad crap in my life right now that I'm trying to figure out."

He shrugs. "So what? There's always crap to figure out, Nora. You can't exactly wait for everything to be perfect before you date somebody."

"This is really, really far from perfect," I say. "But that's

244

not all. How about what I saw that night in you. Those accusations. Your jealous side is—"

"Not going to ever happen again. It was stupid of me, and I know that."

I look at him a long time, trying not to focus on his mouth or how much I'd love to feel his arms around me again, even in this heat. He draws a heart for me in the steamy door.

"I miss you," Pablo says, taking my hand. "And you miss me, too."

"Shut that door already," Sal barks at us from the back. "You're melting the ice cream."

The bells on the doors sound, and another wall of hot air hits my back again.

"What's playing?" I ask.

Star Wars is at the Prospect. For two blessed hours, we shiver happily in the air-conditioning, our eyes filling with the wonder of Luke Skywalker and Princess Leia kicking intergalactic ass. For the first time in two weeks, I'm not thinking of the shootings or my brother or Mima or how to get away from them. Instead, I'm holding hands with Pablo in the cool darkness, transported to a time and place where good guys band together and there is still hope.

Fantasy, but who cares?

The credits roll and the house lights come up, but neither one of us moves, even as people have to climb over us to get out. Finally the only ones left in the theater with us are the ushers sweeping up popcorn kernels and candy boxes.

"Let's watch it again," he says. "Or at least, let's sit here in the dark again." He reaches for my face and pulls me into a deep kiss that sends a jolt right to the very center of me. "You don't want to go out in the heat, do you?" I answer with a deep kiss of my own.

"Sorry, pal, you gotta buy another ticket," the head usher warns from a couple of rows behind us. "We're selling out."

Pablo pulls away from me and gives the guy a sharp look. "Wait here," he says, and heads out to the ticket booth.

We're settling in for the opening scene again—spaceships engaged in battle and, more important, Pablo's hand on my thigh—when the projector suddenly goes black and stutters to a stop.

I twist in my seat and look upstairs, thinking that the projectionist has had a brain warp or something. It happened when I saw *The Blob* a couple of years ago. The guy burned a hole right through what we saw on the screen.

But this is different. The cyclops eye of the projector is dark, too, and the air conditioner has stopped humming. There's expectant stillness that feels strange.

"Hang on, everyone!" the projectionist calls out. Footsteps sound, but when he opens the door, there are no lights shining in the outside hall, either.

I reach for Pablo's hand. "It's just the power," I say, not adding to the crazy thought tapping at the back of his mind, too. *Did someone cut it on purpose?*

The theater door opens a few minutes later, and someone shines a flashlight on us. "The whole block is out. Good old Con Ed, huh?" the voice says about our power company. "Management says to wait."

We all sit in silence for a while, but with the sold-out crowd and the heat wave, the theater grows stifling in no time. In this heat, it doesn't take long for people to lose it. The muttering becomes soft cursing, and finally a guy gets so fed up, he tosses his bucket of popcorn right at the screen. Another guy kicks a chair near me so hard, it dislodges from the bolts.

"Hey, pal," Pablo says, getting up. "Watch it."

People around us start climbing out of their seats, pushing one another as they head out.

"Let's go," Pablo says, but it's not so easy in the pitch-black. Strangers' bodies press on us from all around, just like at rush hour on the train, which I despise. We're holding hands, but somebody behind me actually cops a feel on my ass until I give a hard jab with my elbow.

We finally make it to the lobby and step outside, but the heat is a thick blanket here, too. It doesn't take long to see that something really serious has gone wrong.

It's not just the Prospect that's out of power, or even just this block that's dark.

All of downtown Flushing has disappeared. In fact, the blackness stretches as far as we can see in every direction. Not a single streetlight or traffic signal is working. There are no neon signs anywhere. No marquees. No tower clocks. The only lights we have are headlights, crisscrossed in confusion as traffic starts to snarl.

The air feels charged in a way that reminds me of a

Mima and Hector showdown. It's that same sense of something about to shatter. Does Pablo feel it, too? He squeezes my hand tighter than he probably realizes as we hurry to his car. I know he's thinking the same thing I am as we jog along: what's to stop Son of Sam from being out here with us, too?

We're almost to the Camaro when a crash of glass sounds behind us. Pablo grabs me instinctively and pulls me close, his head tucked down. But it's not gunfire. Two guys have tossed a loaded garbage can through the storefront window of a men's clothing shop. We stand there, watching in shock as they pull off their T-shirts and knock the shards of glass still hanging. All you can hear is the crunch of glass under their sneakers as they step inside.

No power means there are no store alarms to sound. There's nothing to stop them.

Or anybody else.

As if on cue, half a dozen people seem to swarm out of nowhere. They push past Pablo and me and step inside the store, too, grabbing shirts off the mannequins and emptying shoeboxes and racks. In seconds, they run back into the darkness.

Soon there's a second sound of breaking glass and then another farther off.

"Let's get out of here," Pablo says. "It's going to get ugly." We duck into his car and lock the doors just as an appliance repair shop and an electronics store get their windows smashed in, too. In the glare of a bus's headlights, I see a woman about Mima's age run off with a vacuum cleaner. A girl takes off with a boxed turntable balanced on her head.

"What the hell is happening?" I twist the radio tuner, trying to find anything that can tell us what's going on. All I get is static.

Pablo drives north along Main Street only to find when we get there that all six lanes of Northern Boulevard are dark, too. He drives slightly crouched in his seat, especially as we pass people on the streets. It's a night made for Son of Sam, isn't it? The cops will be overwhelmed in no time. It's the perfect night for anybody to commit any crime at all.

Maybe it's the movie still fresh in my mind, but the world suddenly looks like a moonscape to me. We go by instinct and memory, our giddy nerves finally making us laugh as we drive. With the windows rolled down and no signals to stop us, we speed along faster and faster.

"Whatever happened, it's big," Pablo says, sailing through another intersection.

I finally hear a voice on the AM dial. It's DJ George Michael on WABC. He's broadcasting, he says, with a generator.

A lightning strike in Westchester has just knocked out a power station, and like a set of dominoes, every borough — including Manhattan — is completely without power. TV stations gone. The airports all closed. Bridges, the World Trade Center, the needle on the Empire State Building, the glare of Times Square, all of it plunged into total blackness.

There's even a bunch of kids stuck mid-ride on the roller coaster at Rye Playland.

"Citizens who may be trapped in subway cars or elevators are urged to remain calm, please. By order of Police Commissioner Michael J. Codd, all off-duty police officers and firemen are requested to report to their stations immediately. I repeat . . ."

Soon sirens begin to wail somewhere up ahead. And then, with a sinking feeling, I think of Hector.

Where is he? I wonder as the sirens grow louder. *And what's he doing in the dark?*

I turn to Pablo. My mind is starting to race. "Sal's at the Cubs game tonight at Shea," I say quietly. "You think the deli's okay?"

Pablo glances at me. He knows what I do: no one would dare start trouble with Sal and his golf iron around.

But what will happen now that he's not there?

It's completely black when we turn the corner onto 162nd Street, and for a moment, I relax. The grates are still pulled down on the deli, exactly as we left them, and the street looks quiet.

But then, as our headlights brighten the road ahead, I see where the real trouble is.

The glass doors and windows of Mr. Farina's pharmacy have been smashed. Half a dozen guys are inside, clearing the shelves into bags and pockets.

Pablo shines his high beams into the mess, and for a moment, I'm reminded of that year we were overrun by roaches. As soon as you'd turn on the bathroom light, hundreds of insects would scatter back to their corners.

The same happens here. The store empties as the figures take off down the street, but not before I see my brother. Hector is at Mr. Farina's counter. He leans down and, with a whoosh, a flame lights. Then he takes off. I recognize his familiar lope and Sergio right alongside him. Moments later, a car engine guns and the screech of tires fills the street as they speed away in the Monte Carlo.

Pablo and I jump out of the car and race toward the drugstore. I recognize the smell of lighter fluid right away as we step inside. Pretty yellow-blue flames rise from Mr. Farina's dispensing counter, following a trail of what's been doused.

"Where does he keep the extinguisher?" Pablo shouts, but everything inside the shop has been overturned, and it's almost impossible to see as we grope around in the dark. I'm afraid, too, of stepping in fluid that will set my clothes aflame.

It doesn't take long for the smell of melting plastic to fill the air. The flames gain intensity and lick all the way to the ceiling. Thick black smoke billows. We have no choice but to turn back. In seconds it feels as though it goes from a small fire to an entire room in blazes.

I run to the corner and pull the fire alarm, the way Mr. Mac taught Kathleen and me years ago. The smoke and flames grow worse as the minutes tick by. Every one of the stores on this block could burn down, one after the other, and it's all my brother's doing.

In the end, all Pablo and I can do is join the crowd that gathers from neighboring blocks who've come out to shake their heads and see the spectacle.

It takes more than thirty minutes for the fire trucks to finally reach us.

By then, Mr. Farina's shop is gone.

Chapter 36

For a second, I don't know where I am. Two pigeons are cooing at me from their perch.

Then I remember that Mima and I slept on the fire escape. What else could we do? The temperature barely dropped under ninety all night. Without fans on the top floor, we couldn't breathe inside. Instead, we curled up against sweaty pillows and waited for Hector, who never came home. It's probably best that he isn't here. All night, I've plotted how to slap him silly, how to scream at him for all he's done.

I sit up and stretch painfully. It's still early, judging from the orange glow between the buildings. I don't wake Mima, though. She mumbled prayers late into the night, crossing herself every time we heard another siren.

"There was a fire at the pharmacy, Mima," I told her last night. I showed her my sooty hands. "He was there; I saw him set it. Hector was stealing and—" But Mima just put her hand on my lips and cried.

I don't know when or how we finally fell asleep.

I'm cautious when I climb back inside my bedroom, but scanning quickly, I see that Hector isn't inside, either. The rooms are stifling, and I'm starving, too, but I'm out of luck. Without power, the freezer has puddled all over the kitchen floor; a foul odor hits me when I crack open the refrigerator door, too. So I toss down a dishrag to soak up the mess, and head downstairs instead.

Stiller is on the stoop, making a strange matched set with Manny, who's asleep in his lawn chair. He's still got a baseball bat across his thighs. Last night, after Pablo finally dropped me off, all of us tenants gathered around Stiller's battery-operated radio. As news of the looting in Queens was broadcast, Manny dug his bat out of the basement. "In case of trouble," he told us, and for once I thought he was brave.

"Have you guys been here all night?" I whisper.

She rubs her eyes and looks over at Manny. "He's the last man I ever thought I'd spend the night with, but yes."

"Any word on the power?"

"Yeah. Con Ed's got it, and we don't."

She clicks on the radio, and we listen to the morning DJ read off the latest announcements and reports. Ace Pontiac over in the Bronx had its windows smashed to gemstones, and people drove off with fifty brand-new cars. On Jamaica Avenue, a mob shouted *Do it, do it, do it* and ripped the security grates right off a record store and emptied it. Hospitals don't want to see you unless you're having a baby or dying. They're on generators, and they're clogged with people who've shown up shot, cut, and mugged overnight.

"Ladies and gentlemen, as of right now, one thousand fires are still burning, and more than three thousand individuals have been placed under arrest."

I close my eyes and sigh, wondering if Hector is one of those *individuals.*

Stiller clicks the radio off again. "No use running the battery down to hear what we already know: the city has finally gone crazy." She glances at me carefully. "No sign of the kid, huh?"

My throat squeezes tight. "No."

Pablo calls the house in the afternoon. Any hope that maybe I dreamed last night's fire at the pharmacy is gone.

"We have to tell them what happened, Nora," he says.

A while later, we stand together at the door. The pharmacy burned down to the studs. In fact, we can see through the crumbling wall to the candy store next door.

Mr. Farina picks through the debris with Sal. He looks lost standing there, as if he can't decide what to do first. His hands are shaking, and when he sees us, his eyes fill up and his shoulders seem to stoop even further.

"Stay out, kids," he says. "It's not safe in here."

The fact that Mr. Farina is worried about us makes me itch with guilt. How will I ever explain not telling him about Matt and Hector, or how my brother is the reason his business is in cinders?

"Gutted," Pablo whispers to me as we step inside anyway. I can't look at him, wondering what he's thinking of me now. He knows my brother was involved; I know he saw

Hector set the blaze. Any minute, he's going to say what he knows.

"We were at the bottom of the sixth when the lights went out at Shea," Sal says, wiping the sweat from his chin. "By the time we rushed back, it was too late. The fire was in free burn. I tell you, if I get my hands on the derelicts that did this . . ." he mutters.

"It was Nora's idea to check on the block," Pablo says, probably trying to soften the blow of what's coming. "She's the one who pulled the alarm."

My stomach clenches when Sal smiles at me. "Thanks, Nora. It could have been a lot worse without you, I guess."

Shame presses in on me. He won't be so pleased for not coming to him sooner with all that Hector has been up to.

I walk to the charred dispensing area. The old picture of Mr. Farina in front of his store is shattered on the ground. The locked drug cabinet has been forced open and emptied. I can't stand to think that Hector, wherever he is, took part in this, that he set fire to everything that Mr. Farina holds dear. If ever I have truly hated my brother, it's now.

Mr. Farina picks through the few remaining glass bottles. Even from here, I can see that he's pale and sweating through his shirt. Already the heat is ticking up near ninety again.

"We'll help you get it fixed up, Mr. Farina," I whisper, trying not to cry. "I can even build you some shelves if you want. Remember? I'm pretty good."

But Mr. Farina only turns away quickly to blow his nose. "I never thought I'd see the day when my own neighborhood would ruin me, Nora," he says. "I'm an old man. I just don't have it in me to start all over again."

"What are you talking about?" I say. "Farina's Drugstore is forever." I pick up the picture of him and shake off the glass. "You've been on this corner for more than thirty years. We'll rebuild it. And besides, it wasn't your neighbors who turned against you . . ."

I trail off and give Sal a pleading look.

"Come on, geezer," Sal says gently. "The heat is making you talk crazy. Let's all get to the deli and get something to eat at least. We can finish this later."

Silence.

"Mr. Farina?" I say.

A bottle falls from his hands as he tries to steady himself. Pablo rushes to grab him before he hits the ground.

"I'll get the car!" Sal shouts.

Chapter 37

Mr. Farina is still in the hospital. The doctors said that heat-stroke is dangerous in old people with heart problems like him. I know better, though. Mr. Farina got his heart broken, plain and simple. I can't forget the look of anguish in his eyes when he saw his shop in ashes yesterday. And I'm ashamed that I let him down, even though he doesn't know it. What if I had told him about Matt and Hector? Maybe he would have figured out how to stop them. Maybe none of this would have happened at all.

I didn't realize until now that Mr. Farina was everyone's grandfather in a way. He's seen everybody in the neighborhood through colds, splinters, and stomach flus, year in and year out. He's been a constant for all of us over the years, and we barely noticed it until he was gone.

We all miss him already. The block doesn't feel the same with the drugstore boarded up or without Mr. Farina strolling up the street to have a coffee or argue about "the bums who traded Tom Seaver."

Sal is a mess over it. He's got his Mets cap on the deli counter, right next to the framed photo of Mr. Farina that we salvaged. He and Annemarie stop by the hospital in the morning, and they leave early to stop in again on their way home.

Pablo and I are left to close up.

It's weird to see Pablo behind the slicer, especially since the case is nearly bare. We stand here looking out the window, an awkward silence now that it's just us. There haven't been many customers, just people rubbernecking at the damage on the rest of the block. The power came back, but the deli still smells like rotten food. We had to toss all the perishables; the delivery trucks won't be here until Monday.

Pablo studies Mr. Farina's photograph for a second. "If they had any sense, they'd be Yankee fans," he says.

There's a long pause.

"There's going to be a fire-marshal inspection eventually," he says, looking over at me. "You know that, right?"

I nod.

"They're going to ask a lot of questions, Nora."

I know what he's getting at. I had my chance to come clean and tell Sal and Mr. Farina what I knew, but I didn't do it.

I swallow hard. "Yep."

"What are you going to do?"

I stare out at the street in misery. Heat rises from the asphalt and warps the air. "Figure something out, I guess. Same as always."

"What do your parents say?"

I give him a look. "Not everybody's family has a working set of parents like yours, Pablo."

He blushes and falls quiet for a minute. "What a mess," he says.

I pick at my cuticle. "You can't say I didn't warn you."

"I know," he says. "But look: I'm still here."

It was 102 degrees again yesterday. The whole city is boiling mad as we all pick through glass and board up windows. Governor Carey declared us a disaster, which Sal says is like declaring the sky blue. Neighborhoods in all the boroughs, especially the poor ones, look like war zones. Here in Queens, we had 134 fires set and eighty stores looted, but that's nothing. Bedford-Stuyvesant, Crown Heights, the Bronx, Amsterdam Avenue, Harlem. Seems like there's not a store left in any of them, and none of the business owners will say if they'll ever reopen. They don't have insurance, they say, or else, like Mr. Farina, they lack the will.

But mostly it has become a game of nasty finger-pointing as to why people looted.

Customers troll Sal's aisles, picking over the slash-priced items and offering opinions all day long about why ordinary people turned into criminals when the lights went out. One thing is for sure: it's a bad time to be brown or have a last name like López or Ruiz, no matter where you live. The only thing worse might be working for Con Edison.

A lady piles her groceries on my counter and glances at the newspaper there. She shakes her head at the picture of two guys hauling a stolen sofa from a furniture shop in Jamaica.

"Animals! I hate to say it, but we should send all the blacks and Puerto Ricans back if they behave like that here."

Pablo and I exchange uncomfortable looks. She's squeezed the problem down to brown people, all of us. A blush rises to my cheeks, thinking of Hector. It would be easy to say he stole because he's a López, but that isn't it at all. Besides, all kinds of people looted when they had the chance. I saw it myself on Main Street.

I'm biting my lip, not wanting to make trouble for Sal. "Send them back to where? We're all from right here, ma'am," I say pointedly.

Sal looks up from arranging the new cheeses and frowns. His face is bright red from the heat — or maybe because of what I said. For a second, I think I'm in trouble.

"Pablo," he says, not *Paulie*, "get the door for this lady, would you?"

I ring her out and she leaves in a huff.

But it's not just cranky customers. Tempers boil over at the MacInerneys', too. Even Stiller and Mr. Mac get into a spat.

Kathleen's dad came home sporting stitches near his eye after the blackout. The threads still poke out awkwardly so that it looks as if a caterpillar is crawling across his face. He got pelted with a rock as he was working a fire in the mayhem.

261

All week, he's seemed kind of quiet, especially as the accusations build against the police, who sometimes stood by and watched, and fire departments for failing to show up for alarms.

He piles some corn on his plate as Stiller and Mrs. MacInerney gab about the Abzug campaign and how the blackout is going to fit in. Then the conversation turns to Stiller's aunt, who lives over on Jerome Avenue.

"They let that whole neighborhood go up in flames," she says.

"Nobody let anything burn, Stiller. There were twenty-three thousand alarms, and most were false. How could we possibly respond to all of them?"

"But they did respond to some, Pat, just not to very many in the poor sides of town."

It's like watching a tennis match across the dinner table.

He sighs. "The city is in a budget crisis. We're under-staffed."

"But it's interesting that they closed fire stations in the poorest neighborhoods. I'll bet the fire station near the chief's house is running just fine," she says.

Mrs. MacInerney reaches for Stiller's hand. "It's horrible what happened to your aunt's neighborhood, but lots of people do care."

Stiller shakes her head and stiffens her spine. "I don't know, Mary. That sounds like lip service to me. Nobody seems to care if the poor burn up. You can see that for your-self."

We sit in awkward silence. The only sound is the faint

clicks and static of the scanner. Mr. Mac grips the side of the table, his lips drawn to a thin, angry line. In all the years I've known him, I've never seen him lose his patience before.

"Those residents set the fires themselves, Stiller," he says a little too loudly. "Jesus, Mary, and Joseph—they threw rocks and bottles at us. We're working long hours— sometimes for free. What the hell does anyone want from us?"

"I want you to stop pretending this city didn't neglect those neighborhoods on purpose," Stiller says. "You can't do that and still be shocked when it collapses."

He gets up from his chair and tosses down his napkin.

"Pat," Mrs. MacInerney calls as he strides away.

But he doesn't turn. Instead, he throws open the door. "I'll be at the station," he calls over his shoulder. "Let me know when our guest leaves."

That night, I'm home watching Mayor Beame on TV. He tells us we'll rebuild, but I'm not so sure. How do you rebuild people? How do you help them trust one another again? It seems so much harder than fixing buildings.

I turn off the TV and go to the window fan for some relief. Hector is slung across the couch nearby, pawing through new albums and listening through a new headset. He's got a nice shirt, pristine shoes, all stolen. Mima knows this, even as she tiptoes around him in the hot apartment.

"Farina's in the hospital," I tell him. Does he even care? Does he know what he really did?

He looks at my lips moving but doesn't take off his headphones.

Rage feels like rocks in my mouth. Pablo's question loops over and over in my brain as I close my eyes and face the hot breeze coming in through the fan.

What are you going to do?

The heat presses on me, and there's no end in sight.

It may not be the real end of the world, but it feels pretty damn close to me.

Chapter 38

You can't miss the next day's headlines:

MONSTER STRIKES AGAIN!
POLICE HELPLESS AS VICTIMS CLING TO LIFE.
PICTURES IN CENTERFOLD. STORIES PAGES
4, 5, 26, 27.

Two more.

A first date for two twenty-year-olds. Stacy Moskowitz and Robert Violante shot under a bridge in Sheepshead Bay over the weekend.

And now this: Stacy is a blonde.

What is it about that detail that suddenly makes me feel as though everything has broken apart? Maybe it's how helpless the police seem despite what they call the biggest manhunt in the city's history.

But it's something else, too.

Son of Sam has broken his own rule.

Every rule I know is gone, and we're in chaos. There are no rules for how a family should work. No rules for how far loyalty should reach. No boundaries on stealing or looting. No limits on how people ruin one another's lives or how we blame one another for our pain.

Now no rules for how we kill each other, either.

He won't just stalk girls with long, dark hair. Everyone is in his sights now. No one is safe in his random game.

Foul! No fair, my brain shouts.

And it's in that strange moment that I finally decide to take a stand. The question is: *how?*

It happens slowly at first. Small moments of revenge taken from a safe distance.

Maybe this is the way a murderer begins, too, with small crimes that no one can see until later.

I've scratched the B sides of all Hector's new records, spat on his new shoes, pulled the hem apart on the bottom of his shirt in the closet. I've kicked his favorite lighter under the oven where the roaches live, too.

But none of it is noticed. And it doesn't fill the hole or solve the problem of what I'll say when the fire marshal finds me. The investigators already scoured what's left of the pharmacy this week. Pablo saw them shovel samples of ash into gallon cans marked for the crime lab. I kept my eye on them from a distance. I recognized the same marshal who came to our door a few months ago.

As Hector sleeps tonight, the sheets balled at his feet, I stare at the ceiling in misery. The mattress and pillow are hot beneath me. Sweat dribbles along my neck, behind my knees.

Pablo's question chases me again in the heat. I can't out-run it, and it leaves me feeling more trapped than I ever have in my whole life.

I tiptoe out to the kitchen to pour myself a cold glass of water. The picture of Stacy Moskowitz strapped to a gurney stares back at me again from Mima's paper.

Stacy died today. Her date, they say, lost an eye, and is now virtually blind in the other.

Every headline has broadcast the details until I can almost feel Son of Sam at my back in a cloud of heat. I stare out at the moon, wondering for a second if the lovers noticed its fullness in the sky this weekend as they strolled under the bridge, if maybe their killer did, too.

I turn the page, only to find Son of Sam's face staring at me. Beneath it is the hotline number, which gives me pause. Someone in this city may have information, the police say. Citizens should help find the murderer. Surely someone knows something. It's our civic duty to help fight crime before someone else is hurt.

What should I do?

What hotline is there for someone like me? How do I turn in my own flesh and blood when it means that every-thing will be blown apart and I'll lose whatever little family I have left?

I've thought about this from every angle. I know that tell-ing what Hector did won't make him better. He'll come home, maybe beat the shit out of Mima and me. Even if they do arrest him and lock him up at Spofford with all the other juvies, he'll sneak out, or else harden into something even worse.

Hector has left his shirt on the chair. I creep over to it. Holding my breath, I tap down the pockets, almost dizzy with fear. Son of Sam is creeping around the city, but I have my own secret monster right here, don't I?

My fingers close around something metal in the breast pocket. Just a lighter, but I know that in Hector's hands it's as deadly as a Bulldog revolver.

I slip inside our closet next and run my hands along all of his pants, his shirts. I dig with my hands inside his stolen shoes.

I find the radio again, another lighter, a crushed pack of cigarettes, and a wad of rolled bills—his own clever stash! But finally I find a bag with a loose joint and Lemmons.

I take it all to the bathroom and sit on the tiles, where it's cool, to study my finds.

Maybe I will flush these things away, try again to vanish the ugliness.

Maybe I'll light up the joint myself and try to calm the hell down.

Or maybe I should just bury them back inside the dark closet where we all can pretend we don't know.

But what erases the shell of Mr. Farina's store, or that terrible look in his eyes when he fell?

"*¿Qué haces?*"

Mima has come barefoot to the bathroom door. She pushes it open with her toe and gives me a worried look. She can't sleep, she says, with a killer on the prowl.

I don't answer.

"You're having nightmares," she says. "Come back to bed. It's this heat."

Finally she glances at the collection of things all around me. Mima's eyes slide cautiously to where my brother still sleeps.

"*Niña,* go to bed," she whispers.

I get up and edge past her. She follows me to the living room, watching as I dig through the stolen albums.

"Don't look for trouble. Leave his things."

"His? None of this is his. He stole it all."

Mima steps closer. "What's done is done," she says. "And he's not the only one. Everyone went crazy in this heat. Lots of people took things."

"It's not about things, Mima. It's about how he's sick and killing all of us around him."

I snap each LP in two, a wishbone breaking.

"*Por Dios y Maria,* Nora," Mima begs in a whisper. "Can't you see you'll make things even worse?"

"Worse than waiting for him to hit us or burn something else down? Worse than waiting for him to OD?"

"Shhhhhh." She grips my hand, but I pull away.

The floorboards creak behind us. "What the fuck are you doing?" Hector is standing at the bedroom door.

We need to get out of here. "Come with me, Mima," I say. But she doesn't move.

Hector crosses the living room to his stack of albums. He's still groggy as his lizard eyes move slowly over my handiwork. Even from here I can feel the pressure in the room changing.

I grab Mima's sweaty hand and pull her toward the door, but she's rooted to the spot. "Please," I tell her.

Suddenly Hector turns to me. I can read his face, burning with rage. With one sweeping motion, he topples the stereo and all our music. He kicks a chair that goes spinning across the room at Mima. Then he starts in my direction.

I don't wait.

I fly down the stairs as Mima tries to block the door.

"¡Niño!" she cries out.

But in no time, he's close behind. I'm taking the steps three at a time, but Hector's legs are longer. He's close enough for me to hear his labored breath at my back. He grabs at my hair at last and drags me back painfully. I'm lifted off the step, and then, with a sudden shove forward, I go sailing through the air. The floors in this building are old marble, cold and hard. I grab frantically for the rail to save myself. My cheek bounces hard against the wood, but I manage to hang on and avoid smashing onto the floor below. I race as hard as I ever have from one landing to the next.

"Stiller!" I shout. My voice echoes in the hallway as I pound on her door. "Help!"

Hector isn't behind me anymore, but I can hear more furniture overturning upstairs and Mima's voice rising.

Stiller throws open the door.

"Call the cops!" I shout.

And then I race out into the darkness for help.

Chapter 39

Is he hurting her? I wonder.

The side of my head pounds as I imagine Mima facing Hector's fists.

The MacInerneys' kitchen is quiet except for the scanner. The dispatcher's flat voice directs car 50 to my address. Kathleen sits across from me at the kitchen table, quiet, her face unreadable. Her mom has propped open the side door to let in the cooler night air, but the air around us still feels thick and hard to breathe.

Mr. Mac hangs up the phone and turns to me. His hair is damp and all points, but his voice is calm.

"There's a car on the way now for the family disturbance. And I've left word for James at the fire marshal's office to come by as soon as he can for the rest."

"Will they take him away tonight?" I ask.

Mr. Mac sighs. "They'll have a crisis team to calm the situation."

My hands tremble despite the thick heat. "There's no calming this."

"It's going to depend on what has gone on — and on what your mother says, Nora," Mr. Mac explains. "We deal with the immediate emergency first. Tomorrow, we'll see what the marshal can do about the rest."

Mrs. MacInerney shakes her head as she fills an ice bag for my face. "This is exactly why we need better laws," she mutters. "Thank God Stiller is over there."

I put my head on the table.

Mima will help Hector lie. I know it. And more, she'll never forgive me. Even if Mima isn't hurt, she'll be humiliated by having all our neighbors gawk at her. With everyone panicked about Son of Sam, the police car will draw a crowd. Our business will be the talk of the neighborhood.

"Hold this to your face," Mrs. MacInerney says.

I close my eyes against the cold.

A few minutes later, I hear a chair scrape back. Kathleen gets up. "I'll get her bed ready," she announces.

A distance in Kathleen's voice makes me open my eyes. I've come to their door like a lunatic and dumped the ugly details of my life in their laps. Maybe I should have kept my mouth shut, handled it quietly after all.

"I'm sorry to get you involved in this, Kathleen. I didn't know where to go."

She looks back at me from the door. There's a hurt expression in her eyes. "Why didn't you tell me before?" she asks. "All this time, you never said anything about what was happening."

"You couldn't have done anything." But even as I say it, I know I've left her out, hidden things.

She shakes her head. "I could have been your friend, Nora," she says.

Then she slips upstairs.

Chapter 40

Fire Marshal Costa takes notes as he sweats through his uniform.

I try to see what he's writing, but he keeps his page close.

He wipes his face with a handkerchief. "Wait here a moment, please." Then he walks to the parlor, where he and the MacInerneys talk in low voices.

Pablo and I exchange looks, wondering if what we've said will be enough.

"I'm telling you right now, if they don't pick your brother up, I'm taking him out myself," Pablo whispers to me, his eyes glued to the bruise on my face.

"It hardly hurts."

"Stop protecting him," he says. "It's time. Stop."

Costa comes back with the MacInerneys in tow. For my own safety, I am to stay here. Hector will get picked up sometime before tonight, he says. They'll search for Sergio at the Satin Lady, too.

"We'll call you when the arrests have been made. For now, please don't call anyone," he says. "We don't want to encourage anyone to run."

All day, I sit in Kathleen's room, feeding pellets to Gloria and worrying about Mima. Kathleen stays scarce the whole time, as if being around me makes her mad.

So, when no one is looking, I use her phone to call Mima. I know I'm not supposed to, but I have to make sure she's okay.

The phone rings and rings, but there's no answer.

At dinnertime, Fire Marshal Costa calls. Hector, he says, went calmly. Sergio was all mouth until they searched his car.

The tension is killing me. Kathleen and I have almost never fought in all the years we've been friends. Wandering around their house in borrowed clothes for two days, I feel like an intruder. She's been keeping to herself, packing for college and talking to me only when I ask her a question.

I keep busy with the only thing that really calms me. I spackle the broken soap dish in the bathroom for Mr. Mac and hammer down the loose planks on the stairs. I even help Mrs. MacInerney stuff envelopes for the women's conference.

"You girls all right?" Mrs. MacInerney looks cautiously from one face to another. Kathleen hasn't said a word as we worked.

"Fine," Kathleen says, sealing another envelope. Then she gets up and goes upstairs.

I can't take it another minute.

I march up after her.

"You're really going to add on to what I'm going

through now?" I demand from the doorway. "I needed privacy, Kathleen!"

"*Privacy* has never been part of our arrangement, Nora, and you know it. We've told each other everything since kindergarten. We've been there for each other. Or at least I thought we had been." She crosses to the doorway. "If you don't mind, I'm going to take a little privacy break myself right now."

Then she shuts the door in my face.

It has taken five days for Mima to finally answer the phone, but it's a disaster. The judge detained Hector instead of letting him come home to wait for his court date. Wisely, he didn't think Mima could keep the community safe from Hector based on the evidence the fire marshal presented. Mima says that's my fault.

"Are you happy now?" she shouted into the phone today. "Are you proud that you've ruined our family?" Then she slammed down the receiver.

I tried to go over to talk sense into her, but it was no use. Stiller buzzed me into the lobby, but that's as far as I got. Mima wouldn't even open the door when I rang.

So, here I am, on the way to the only other person who might help.

It's been so long since I've been here that I almost don't recognize Papi's building. But then I remember the navy-blue awning and the scrolled numbers for the address. The doorman is standing just inside the air-conditioned lobby. He's in a crisp white shirt and bow tie, watching the cabs zoom by on Lexington Avenue.

He holds open the door for me before I even reach for the handle. I haven't seen Gabriel since I was fourteen, but to me, he looks the same.

"Good afternoon, miss. Can I help you?"

My eyes flit to the art-deco mailboxes. I see my last name on the one for apartment 14C.

"I'm Nora, Gabriel," I say, but he only smiles blankly. "Mr. López's daughter."

His eyebrows shoot up, and he blushes.

"Miss! I didn't recognize you!"

We stand there awkwardly for a second. If I were Papi's daughter and I lived here, I might have a key. I might sail past Gabriel with nothing more than a wave on my way to the elevators behind him.

But I'm basically a stranger, and we both know it. I'm to be managed like any other delivery.

"Can you ring my father's apartment, please?" I say.

He shakes his head. "I'm sorry, miss. Did he know you were coming? Mr. López isn't home right now. He's still at work, and Mrs. López is downtown for the day."

My throat feels a little tight, but I swallow it down.

He looks at me thoughtfully for a second, then glances at a tiny picture of two toddlers tucked near the visitor log at his podium. He motions to the velour sofas in the lobby. "Why don't you wait here for your *papi*?" he says. "He might not be too long."

It actually takes two hours. The whole time, I steal

277

glances at Gabriel. What does he think about? Does he go home and tell his wife about the pathetic lives of the tenants he serves?

Anyway, it's almost five thirty when he finally looks out the lobby windows and smiles. "Here they are!"

He holds open the door, and a little boy in a bowl haircut races in. He gives Gabriel a high five but comes to a screeching halt when he sees me.

I suck in my breath, unprepared for how much Pierre looks like Hector did at that age. The sight makes me so sad that it's hard to stand up.

"Hi, Pierre," I say.

He scoots behind Papi, not an ounce of recognition on his face.

"Nora?" Papi says, coming closer. He puts down his briefcase. "What are you doing here?"

"Hi, Papi."

He flashes a smile and tries to draw Pierre out from behind him. "Look who it is! Your sister! She's come to visit!"

It sounds so pleasant. *I'm visiting.* But Pierre won't budge. Maybe he's as smart as Papi always says. I suspect he's got a little radar of his own. He stares at me in accusation the whole ride up on the elevator.

I wait in the living room while Papi gets Pierre's snack from the kitchen.

It's so quiet up here, except for the air-conditioning. The thick carpet swallows all the sound, so that even Pierre's cartoons and Matchbox cars don't make a racket over the hum.

The furniture matches, and there are pictures of Linda and Papi, and school shots of Pierre everywhere. There's not a single image of Hector or me.

"Are you thirsty or hungry?" Papi calls to me. "You want me to make you something?"

"No, thanks."

Finally Papi, changed out of his suit, comes to the living room. He sits on the edge of the sofa across from me. He's wearing a Lacoste alligator shirt, a nice watch. He's even tan.

"Well, this is a big surprise," he says. "What's the occasion?"

The question gives me pause. We only talk on holidays, so I can see why my visit would surprise him.

"Has Mima called you?" I ask. There is so much to say that I hardly know where to begin.

"Your mother? No." His happy expression starts to dim.

I put the fire marshal's business card on the glass coffee table and wait for him to pick it up. "Then that's who you'll want to talk to," I say.

He reads the card and frowns. "What's this about?"

"They've arrested Hector," I say.

I tell what I can about where my brother is detained right now. My lips are moving; I can hear my voice in the quiet apartment, cartoon sound effects in the background, but somehow I'm numb. It feels as though I'm looking down at myself as I list the charges that Fire Marshal Costa explained. I use his words: *arson, larceny,* and *drug possession.* Hector is sixteen, I tell him, and no judge in New York is going easy on people who looted in the blackout. Even

279

if he's sentenced as a youthful offender, Hector will get at least five years.

He sits back on the sofa, folding and unfolding his neatly manicured hands. "I don't know what to say, Nora," he tells me. "This is coming out of the blue. I didn't know."

I give him a long look. It occurs to me that I've watched Mima make excuses for Hector my whole life. I suddenly realize that I've made excuses for Papi, too. Or at least I've let him try to make excuses for himself.

"Maybe you didn't know because you didn't *want* to know."

Papi looks like I've slapped him. "That's not true. I tried, Nora. I send money. I call you regularly."

"Calling on holidays isn't really trying, Papi. And keeping a roof over your kids' heads is just a basic requirement. Besides, you know as well as I do that you don't even do that so well. How many times have I had to call you about money?"

"I can't control the mail!"

I glare at him until he looks shamefaced.

"I'll admit that sometimes I'm late, but I always come through."

I lean forward, thinking of all the ways he's been missing. "What's my favorite color, Papi?"

He stares at me blankly.

"How is Hector doing in school? Where do I work? What college did I get into?"

Silence.

"You don't know those things because you never bothered to find out."

Papi is quiet for a while. "I don't know what to say," he says. "I've done what I could. I'm sorry if that hasn't been enough, Nora."

Something inside of me closes tight. "It doesn't matter if you're sorry or if you aren't," I say. "You left us behind and let Mima do it all. That sucks, if you want to know the truth."

"Hey," he says angrily.

"Hey, *what?*" My own temper starts to boil. "You can't run from the fact that you have three kids, Papi, not just one, the way you pretend."

Papi's cheeks get blotchy. "You don't understand all the pressures, Nora," he begins. "You're too young to understand them. Life's not a straight line, the way you think. I'm spread thin; I have responsibilities that you don't know about."

I look around his well-appointed apartment and sigh.

"I don't have to understand any of your pressures and responsibilities, Papi. You're the one who should have been worried about the pressures on us."

He starts to say something, but thinks better of it. Finally he leans back and stares at the ceiling for a long while. "What do you want from me, Nora?" he says at last.

The question hangs there for a long time. Is it hypothetical, or does he really want to know? I have expected so little from him for so long that I really don't know how to answer.

"I want you to help Mima deal with Hector's mess."

He throws up his hands. "Nora, do you know what you're asking?"

"Get involved for once," I say firmly. "Mima can't do this by herself, especially not now, and she shouldn't have to.

281

You've left her holding the bag for long enough, and I can't fill in for you anymore. I'm eighteen now, Papi. I'm moving out and have to figure out how to survive on my own. College, rent, food—everything. Did it ever occur to you that maybe you should help with any of that?"

I stand up and take one last look around at all his splendor.

"Call Mima," I say. "You owe her at least that." And then I let myself out the door.

Chapter 41

I get back to the MacInerneys' as the sun is starting to go down. I've missed dinner, but there's a sandwich waiting for me on the kitchen table. A message is scrawled on the napkin that covers it.

Keep up your strength. It's Mrs. MacInerney's handwriting. *Make sure the door is locked!*

I bite into the chicken salad, but I'm so completely drained that I barely taste it.

Kathleen is upstairs listening to music and packing. Half her room is already in boxes. Looking around, I can see that she's leaving behind the little-girl things: her ballerina jewelry box, the old posters of Freddie Prinze, faded ribbons from the fifth-grade spelling bee. Maybe she's leaving me behind, too.

She looks up when she sees me in her doorway.

"Hey," I say.

"Hey."

"Where is everybody?"

"Dad's on his rotation. My mom is at some Abzug meeting."

There's a long quiet, so she points to a stack of messages by her phone. "Pablo called you a thousand times. I didn't know where you were," she says. Again, her voice is an accusation.

I glance in the mirror. My skin is shiny with sweat and my clothes are stuck to my skin. I look like I haven't slept in days.

"I went to the city. I decided to tell my father about Hector."

Kathleen stops folding and looks at me. She knows Papi has barely been in my life. "How did *that* go?" she asks.

Normally I might shrug and make light of it, but this time it's different. "I said what I had to. Now it's up to him to decide if he's going to give a shit. I have no idea if he'll really help." I sniff at myself. "God, I need a shower."

She tosses me a pair of shorts and a T-shirt without a sound.

When I'm done, I find Kathleen sitting near her bedroom window. She's got two beers perched on the windowsill, and the sash is thrown wide open, exactly the way her parents have forbidden us. Son of Sam is still roaming tonight, probably enjoying the fact that even though the city is broke, three hundred laid-off cops have just been rehired to find him.

"Daring," I say, swiping away some of the chipped paint from the sill.

She shrugs. "Shit like this calls for a drink," she says, handing me a beer. "Here's to the worst damn summer ever."

We clink our bottles and take a long swig.

I want so much to make up with Kathleen, to have one space in my life that feels secure. I pull up a box and sit next to her.

"It was supposed to be our best one, remember? Turning eighteen, and everything."

"So much for that."

Kathleen looks so sad to me, and I hate it. She's one of those people whose faces always look alive and bright. But now there's so much hanging in the air between us.

"I don't want you to stay mad, Kathleen," I begin. "I'm running out of repairs to make around here, for one thing, and my nerves are shot. But I want you to know that I didn't cut you out because I don't trust you. I just felt ashamed. Maybe you can't understand that. But you're from all of *this*." I wave my hand around the room. "I didn't think you'd really understand."

"I would have tried."

"I know. I'm sorry."

She looks at me sheepishly and takes another long pull from her beer. "Maybe I'm just mad at myself. How could I not notice what was happening with my own best friend?"

I shrug. "Oh, don't be too hard on yourself. I'm a pretty good liar when I have to be, right?"

We're quiet for another little while.

"But now what?" Kathleen says. "You're my best friend, and in two weeks I'm out of here. We've got to figure out what to do for you. I have to be honest, though, Nora. I'm coming up empty."

My eyes fill. The whole ride home from Papi's house, I turned over my situation in my head.

I need a home, a job, a whole adult life plan.

Right now, though, I have exactly nothing.

Chapter 42

It happens so fast that no one can really believe it.

Son of Sam got arrested.

It's all over TV and radio; his face is plastered on every newspaper. But still it doesn't feel real. Maybe it's the ordinary way it went down. The cops traced him to his address in Yonkers through a parking ticket, of all things. They picked him up as he was getting into his car with his .44 tucked inside a paper lunch bag.

"You got me," he said.

Is it crazy to be disappointed by a monster? He's nothing like what we've imagined. Flanked by two detectives, David Berkowitz is just a paunchy mail clerk with frizzy hair and girlish lips.

I wonder if everything we fear is somehow the same as the unmasking of Son of Sam. Maybe the things that scare us seem more powerful than they truly are when we keep them secret.

*   *   *

It's Mr. Mac who spots Mima a couple of days later. He's watering his garden while Kathleen and I sit at the kitchen table eating sunflower seeds and combing the classifieds. I've been here for over ten days with nothing much to do except help Kathleen pack and figure out my next move. Sal insisted I take a leave until things calm down. So Kathleen and I have been searching for cheap rentals and jobs that might make sense for me.

Mr. Mac pokes his head in the screened window.

"You have a visitor out front, Nora," he tells me. "It's your mom."

I walk out the front door and stare at her from the stoop. She's waiting on the sidewalk.

"Mima?" I say. "Are you all right?"

She looks tired and unsure. "Your father says you went to see him," she says.

I shift on my feet, trying to read her. "He called you?"

She nods, her mouth in a tight line.

I walk over to her. "He should help, Mima," I say quietly. "Now more than ever. I thought he should know."

Mima shrugs. "He's calling a lawyer friend," she says. "And a doctor he knows."

Her eyes get watery, but she doesn't continue. Instead, she looks beyond me to the MacInerneys' house.

"When are you coming home? You can't stay here imposing on strangers forever."

"They're not strangers," I say quietly. But that's how Mima sees things, of course. There is blood family; everyone else is outside of our bubble. I take a deep breath. "I don't think I am coming home, Mima."

She studies me for a long time. *"Que libertinaje,"* she mutters.

"It's not debauchery, Mima. It's getting a fresh start on my own."

"A fresh start?" she says. "Running away from your responsibilities isn't a fresh start."

"That's just it, Mima. I've helped for a long time, but this is for you and Papi. You're Hector's parents."

"And you're his sister."

"I need to figure out how to take care of myself right now, Mima. You don't want me to cashier at Sal's forever, do you?"

Mima bites her lip. Then she holds out a large yellow envelope. "This came for you. He told me he was sending it."

I take it from her. It's addressed to me in Papi's handwriting. "What is it?" I ask, but when I look up, she's already walking away. "Mima?"

She doesn't turn.

I tear open the envelope and pull out what's inside. At first, I don't know what it is, but then I realize that the small plastic billfold is a Chase Manhattan checkbook. Papi has attached a note.

Study hard, it says.

I flip open the cover and stare at my name printed on the corner of the pristine stack of checks.

The opening balance scribbled on the top line is $1,000.

My mind starts to race. This is enough for a whole year of school if I decide to go. Tuition, books, everything.

Mima has disappeared around the corner. My heart is pounding with excitement that I can't keep inside.

"Kathleen!" My acceptance letter is still tucked in the frame of her bureau mirror.

Ms. Friedmor's nagging voice echoes in my ears as I run back inside the house to show Kathleen.

Reach, Nora. You'll surprise yourself.

Chapter 43

People say that bad things happen in threes, but I say good things happen that way, too.

Son of Sam got arrested.

Papi came through.

And now I have a place to live that I can afford.

"You'll be helping us," Mr. Mac says when he suggests the plan. He's waited until dinnertime to spring it on us. I should have known something was fishy. Mrs. MacInerney has been strangely quiet, even though Bella Abzug's campaign is tanking. Normally we'd be having a long "discussion dinner." Instead, she sets a bottle of champagne on the table.

"I don't have the time to keep up with the repairs on the bungalow, and the place sits empty all winter. You can house-sit for us and do repairs as a trade. All we have to do is winterize it a bit."

Kathleen beams a smile at me from across the table.

"I'll have you know, he had help with this amazing idea." She kisses Mr. Mac on his freckled forehead.

Mrs. MacInerney pops the cork, narrowly missing the window, and pours us each a glass.

The Impala is packed to the gills.

We have a shopping bag wedged between us filled with groceries and a bottle of chardonnay Kathleen scored to celebrate later. We've even brought Gloria with us for the adventure, since I'll be her official caretaker for a while. Gloria's cage is on the backseat. Her cheeks are overstuffed with pellets. She's a nervous eater, I guess.

"Adjust the mirrors," Mr. Mac tells Kathleen, setting a big toolbox on the floor next to Gloria. "Move up the seat."

"I know how to drive, Dad," she says, rolling her eyes. "Your precious car will be in good hands."

He ignores her. "And don't leave the top down, in case it rains."

Mrs. MacInerney comes out of the house to save us.

"Call when you get there," she says. "Then I promise we'll leave you alone." She gives Mr. Mac a pointed look.

"Sure you will," Kathleen says, climbing in. Then she looks at me. "Ready?"

I stand on the curb, looking at Mr. and Mrs. MacInerney. How do you thank people for being your family when they didn't have to be? In the end, I give them a big, long hug and say nothing, hoping they will understand.

"The insulation comes next week," Mr. Mac says, clearing his throat. "After we drop Kathleen at school, we'll get busy."

"Sure thing."

They wave at us from the curb as Kathleen drives us around the block to our first stop. We park outside my building and beep the horn at Stiller. She's taping up a flyer for the next tenant meeting right over Son of Sam's face.

"Leaving already, huh?" she asks me.

"In a little bit." I glance at the agenda. Safety improvements in the building. New storage bins.

"Keep giving it to them, Stiller," I say.

"You know it, sugar."

I look up and spot Mima watching for me from the kitchen window. "I won't take long," I call to Kathleen.

I climb the steps to our apartment.

Mima opens the door and motions me inside. The things I asked for are in a neat stack. My turntable—its lid cracked, thanks to Hector—and speakers. A box filled with my clothes, even my coat and boots for when the weather gets cold. It's just like her: neat as a pin to the end. She's even packed me some cleaning supplies of my own.

"I put extra sweaters in there," she says quietly.

"Thanks."

She slips my apartment key back around my neck, too.

"Why are you giving me this?"

She looks at that key for a long time. Maybe she remembers the day she gave it to me all those years ago. Then she stiffens a bit. "I could have a heart attack here by myself. Who would be able to get in to help me? The Communist?"

"You'd be lucky. Stiller would have your back," I say. "But you're not going to have a heart attack, Mima."

"How do you know? I got hired for one of the blackout

cleanup jobs the city is offering," she says. "I start next week. Who knows what I'll have to lift and carry?"

"Mima . . ." I say softly as I start to drag my boxes to the door.

She peers out the window, thinking. When I'm done, I stand next to her to see what she's watching. Down below, Kathleen leans against the Impala, talking with Stiller.

"Your friend is waiting," she says. "You should go."

"Yeah."

But I don't move from her side. I keep my eyes outside on the car, my escape, surprised at how hard it suddenly feels to go.

"There are so many sad things that happen to us in life, Nora," she says after a while. "Sometimes it's almost impossible to know what to do to fix them."

I shrug. "We do the best we can, I guess."

"Maybe. And then maybe forgive the people who have disappointed us."

I can't look at Mima. I think about all the ways Mima, Papi, Hector, and I have hurt one another over the years, all the ways we've fallen short. Is forgiveness really possible?

But when I turn to my mother, she looks so lost that I don't ask. Without thinking, I reach out and hug her.

"*Cuídate,*" she whispers to me. Take care of yourself.

"Don't worry, Mima. You'll see; this is going to be a good thing." When I pull away, her lips start to quiver through her frown, so I hug her again, this time a bit longer.

"I am losing everything. Again," she whispers. "First my country, then my husband, and now my children."

"But you haven't lost me. And maybe Hector is lost just for now. I don't know, Mima. Nobody does. We have to see what happens."

I take in my mother's scent of bleach and sweat. Until right now, I never considered that maybe Mima couldn't talk about the sad things in her life any more than I could talk about the sad things in mine. Maybe all those glowing reports about Cuba and my brother were just the best she could do in the face of things that hurt.

We pull apart, and I walk back to the door to pick up my boxes.

"I'll call you soon," I say before I go.

Mima is still watching from the window when Kathleen and I pull away.

Sal is crammed in his little office when I get there. He's wrestling with a mountain of receipts and paperwork from the blackout. I stand in the doorway for a second, but he's lost in his mess. We talked on the phone, but it isn't making seeing him in person any easier.

"You know, Pablo could probably do that better than he can stack lettuces. He is studying accounting."

My voice startles him. "Nora." He moves folders off a chair and motions me to sit.

"I'll stand, thanks. I can't stay long. Kathleen's waiting."

He looks at me over his smudged glasses. "First, are you all right?"

I shrug and look around the walls at his old business license, his favorite photos at Shea. "Better now that Son of

Sam is done, right?" Sal still has the police sketch pinned to the corkboard, so I yank it down and toss it into the trash can. "How's Mr. Farina?" I ask quietly.

"Still not great, but home at least," he says. "It's a lot on an old guy."

I stare at my shoes. "I know I said it already, but I'm so sorry, Sal, for everything. I should have told you—"

"It's done. And I know it wasn't easy to come clean."

We stay quiet for a while, and then he leans back and clears his throat. "So you're sure about your decision?"

I nod. "People are going to gossip about what Hector did," I tell him. "You know how this neighborhood is. It's going to be hard to hear it. Plus, you know, it might not be safe."

The last part is especially true. Who knows how Hector and Sergio might want to get back at me, and what kind of goon friends they'll get to do their dirty work?

"Safe? Nobody's going to hurt you. Not with me right here."

"Or me."

That's Pablo's voice. I glance at the security mirrors and spot him sweeping just outside the door and eavesdropping. He waves at me shamelessly.

"Get to work," I tell him. Then I turn back to Sal. "It's what's best for me. Besides, where I'm moving is far. The bus ride would be too long every day."

He takes off his glasses and fishes in his desk drawer for my final paycheck.

"I'm going to miss seeing you here, Nora. If you ever need anything, you send word. You know where to find me."

I walk to his desk and give him a peck on the cheek. "Thanks, Sal."

He blushes deep red. "Save that stuff for Romeo out there," he says.

"Yes, please." Pablo's voice again.

I walk back outside with Pablo.

"You need a hand unpacking your stuff?" Pablo asks when he walks me outside. He waves at Kathleen, who's listening to the radio in the Impala. "I'll be off in a couple of hours."

I shake my head. "No, thanks. It's not that much. Come tomorrow, the way we planned."

He pulls me close and gives me a kiss. "I'll be there."

Chapter 44

Our drive out to Breezy Point is gorgeous. We have the top down, and Orleans is blaring on the radio. Kathleen sings at the top of her voice as we cross the Marine Parkway Bridge.

All around, the blue water sparkles as if diamonds are just under the surface, waiting for us to grab them. Over the years, we've come to the beach hundreds of times, but not like today. I look over at her, missing her already, but feeling hopeful for the first time in a long while.

Finally she pulls us into the parking area near the bungalow and cuts off the engine. Then she hands me the house keys.

"Hey, put the lock on your repair list. The top lock is always a bitch," she says.

"There's a list?"

"Dad left it on the refrigerator. It'll take you a million years. Welcome to your life project."

I take the keys from her and smile.

It will be strange to live here. The beach is totally different in the winter after all the houses close and the families go home. But Mr. Mac has friends at the volunteer fire department who'll check on me, and then—who knows?—maybe I'll learn to like the quiet. Anyway, the bungalow has enough dings and little repairs needed that I'll be more than busy, just the way Kathleen says. And on cold nights when I'm lonely, Pablo promised to drive over and join me. I already made an appointment at a women's health center that I found in the phone book.

Anyway, I'll be busy with school. The bus runs along Flatbush Avenue and it will leave me off at the Marine Parkway Bridge, but it takes a while. And then, because I'm crazy, I agreed to the Saturday gig with Mr. Melvin and his bruisers, too. I need some extra cash. I left him a note taped to his lathe, and he called me back right away. "Nora López," he said. "You will make an excellent second-in-command."

I pop open the trunk, and we start to cart out my stuff. I settle Gloria on the coffee table and throw open some windows to let in the breeze.

First thing, Kathleen pins up an old Freddie Prinze poster over my bed. "To keep you company," she says.

"Very funny. But I have Pablo now, remember?"

She closes her eyes in longing. "God, you're so lucky."

When we're done, we grab our picnic bag and head to the sand. Eddie and Pablo both wanted to come today, but I'm glad they're not here. This is our afternoon, just ours, Kathleen's and mine.

It's been a summer from hell, just like she said, and now it's time to breathe easy and say our good-byes.

We walk along the ocean up to our ankles. Little kids

build sand castles all around us, just the way we used to. They dodge washed-up jellyfish and broken shells as they work on moats, drawbridges, and turrets. By tomorrow, maybe all their hard work will be gone, but they don't seem to mind. They'll do it all again if they have to.

Kathleen gives me a smile.

"Remember how we used to do that?"

"Why just *used to*?"

We sit in the wet sand and start digging to make our creations. This time, they're not turtles.

Instead, we make enormous disco-queen mermaids with shell bras and sea-grass hair. It takes us so long that our shoulders burn and our hair gets briny.

BURN BABY BURN, we finally write with an old straw when we're through.

And then, holding hands, we go charging into the deep.

AUTHOR'S NOTE

No one who lived in New York in 1977 will ever forget it. This is a work of historical fiction, but it is set against a time that is legendary as one of New York City's most difficult periods.

I was thirteen that year, just waking up to feminism with the help of my older sister. *Ms.* magazine celebrated its fifth year of publication, although everyone had predicted that a magazine about hard-core women's issues would fail. But the feminists were up for a fight, and women continued to take to the streets to march for equality. Congresswoman Bella Abzug—legendary for her hats and her caustic zingers—launched a mayoral campaign on the heels of her failed Senate bid and presided over the first National Women's Conference, which was held later that year in Houston. The early women's movement provided the basis for so many of the rights and opportunities that girls and women enjoy today, However, it was by no means completely cohesive in its early days. As Stiller implies in this novel, many women of color wondered if the movement truly represented them at all, or if it was mostly a movement for white women of privilege. And of course, then and now, the nuances of reproductive rights created intense debate and divisions.

As this novel suggests, New York was in an enormous downward spiral at the time. The city was on the brink of bankruptcy, race relations were tense, and crime had ballooned. There were 1,919 murders in New York that year, compared to only 684 as recently as 2012. Arson became the signature crime.

The year also included a serial killer who took the name Son of Sam and prowled the streets, shooting young women and their dates. Women all over the city panicked about being his next victim. Even as disco and punk music pumped, and TV ads implored us to love New York, there was enormous fear for personal safety.

All these things converged in July when the city experienced a total blackout. On July 13, a lightning strike plunged the city and all its boroughs into total darkness. The looting and fires that followed are legendary. In those twenty-five hours, the whole city lay in complete darkness and a stifling heat that reached to 102 degrees in the daytime. With tensions, crime, and fear already high, the darkness and heat unleashed a massive crime wave that, forty years later, we are still struggling to understand. More than 1,000 fires were reported, 1,700 false alarms pulled, and hundreds of stores looted in every borough except Staten Island. More than 3,700 people were arrested during that night, causing the city to open jails that they had formerly closed. Entire neighborhoods were devastated, especially poor ones. The authorities later estimated that the total cost of the blackout exceeded $300 million.

Although it is featured in the book, I found no historical evidence of looting on 162nd Street in Flushing, Queens. Other neighborhoods in Queens, such as Jamaica and Corona, did see considerable damage. Limited looting also occurred in downtown Flushing. Accounts of the events on Main Street were taken from the *Queens Tribune,* whose editorial staff was witness to the events.

I took liberties with the names of establishments all over Flushing, mixing real ones, such as Gloria Pizza and the Prospect Theatre, with fabricated ones, such as the Satin Lady and Farina's Drugstore. I did, however, try to maintain the feeling of those streets and the sense of community that existed at the time.

The most challenging part of writing Nora's story was the need to include the historical facts as they related to the murder or injury of so many innocent young women and men. Son of Sam murdered six young people. Many family members undoubtedly still think about and miss their loved ones today. Some of the survivors of those shootings are still alive. Their injuries, both physical and emotional, continue to make an impact. Their suffering is not entertainment. There was no way to write this book, however, without including a mention of those who lost their lives or were injured. I hope I did justice to the horror that each of those deaths and injuries represented to all of us.

All the other details of the shootings were taken from newspaper accounts of the day. In the end, we would discover that Son of Sam was David Berkowitz, a twenty-four-year-old postal worker. He did, in fact, write letters to Jimmy Breslin at the *New York Daily News,* and these were published as the killings continued, adding to the public's tabloid-fueled hysteria. The search for him—dubbed Operation Omega—was based at the 109th Precinct, in Flushing, and was the largest manhunt in the city's history. For months, police struggled to keep up with the thousands of tips and calls from frantic people who were convinced that the killer was their uncle, brother, or boyfriend. David Berkowitz was finally arrested in August, traced by a simple parking ticket that an observant witness remembered seeing on his car the night that Stacy Moskowitz was murdered. He is alive today and is serving six life sentences at the Sullivan Correctional Facility in Fallsburg, New York, where he is considered a model prisoner.

In so many ways, this is a novel about people at their worst. It is a story of family pain and of juvenile domestic violence, a chronically underreported issue. It's the story of community pain—and all the ways that people try to cope in the face of fear.

But for me, this novel is a celebration of people who find their strength even in the worst circumstances. I wrote this story because young people everywhere sometimes find that they have to fuel their hope against a bleak backdrop and outpourings of rage.

When I think of New York in 1977, I think of the city imploding. But one thing is sure. It emerged and transformed. New York City and its amazing citizens have always known extremes. But somehow, even terrible events serve to strengthen it. It stubbornly thrives.

ACKNOWLEDGMENTS

Living through an era is never enough research to write about it. I owe huge thanks to the following people who helped me gather the facts that would allow me to re-create New York City in 1977: Chris Dowdell, former detective with the 109th Precinct Detective Squad, who was assigned to the Son of Sam Task Force; Carmen Vivian Rivera for sharing her recollections of her participation in the Women's Day March of 1977; the National Organization for Women for access to their archives held at the Tamiment Library at New York University; and John and Alice Fitzgerald for their friendship and their honest recollections of that awful summer of 1977.

For questions about mental health, juvenile delinquency, and arson, I turned to local friends and experts. Thank you to Susan Osofsky for input on mental disorders/attachment disorders; attorney Mary Langer for general advice on legal issues and youthful offenders; Jonathan Perry, firefighter with Henrico County Fire and Rescue, for teaching me about fire behavior; Lt. Billy Gerritt, Supervisory Assistant

Fire Marshal, Henrico County, Virginia; the members of Firehouse 9 of the Henrico County Fire Department; and Sheri Blume, communications officer for Henrico County Police, for emergency dispatch information.

Any novel needs trusted readers to weigh in as the author struggles with the tale. Thank you to Sharon Flake for our discussion about Stiller and feminism for black women in the mid-1970s, and to Gigi Amateau, Laura Curzi, Kat Spears, Margaret Payne, and A. B. Westrick, dear friends and fellow writers who made room in their lives to read and offer suggestions.

A big debt to my agent, Jen Rofé; to my Candlewick family: Pamela Consolazio for the beautiful book design; Alix Redmond and Hannah Mahoney for their meticulous copyedit; Emily Crehan and Emily Quill for proofreading; Melanie Cordova for double-checking my lousy Spanish; the entire publicity team for their tireless support of all my titles; and most especially to my editor, Kate Fletcher, whose wise comments, tough questions, and faith in me are always appreciated.

And finally, to my family. Without you, nothing.

Piddy doesn't even know who Yaqui Delgado is—
but whoever she is, she has it out for Piddy.

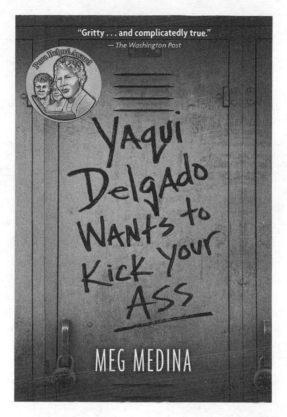

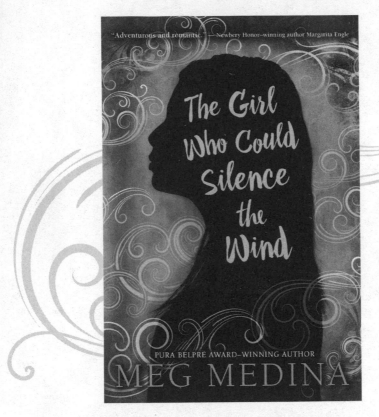